COLD FLASHES

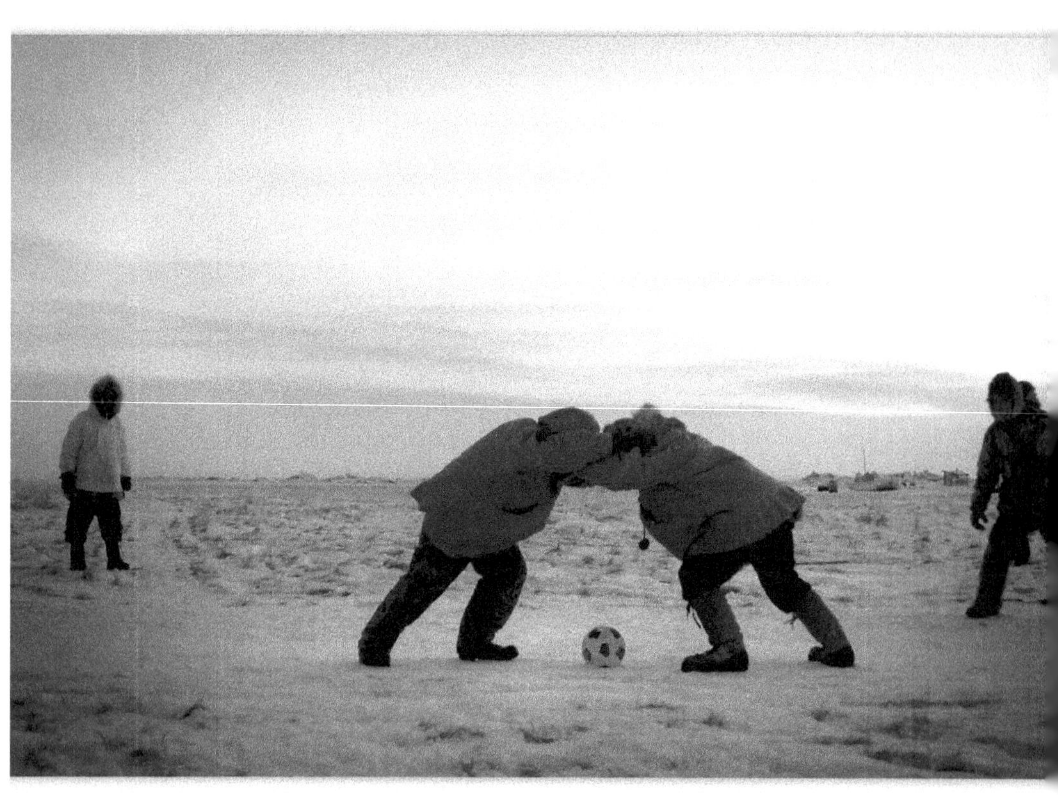

The Match, Brandon Thibodeaux

COLD FLASHES

Literary Snapshots of Alaska

Edited by

Michael Engelhard

University of Alaska Press
Fairbanks

University of Alaska Press
P.O. Box 756240
Fairbanks, AK 99775-6240
ISBN 978-1-60223-093-4

Library of Congress Cataloging-in-Publication Data

Cold flashes : literary snapshots of Alaska / edited by Michael Engelhard.
p. cm.
ISBN 978-1-60223-093-4 (pbk. : alk. paper)
1. American literature—Alaska. 2. Alaska—Literary collections. I. Engelhard, Michael, 1959–
PS571.A4C65 2010
979.8'3—dc22
2010005182

Contents

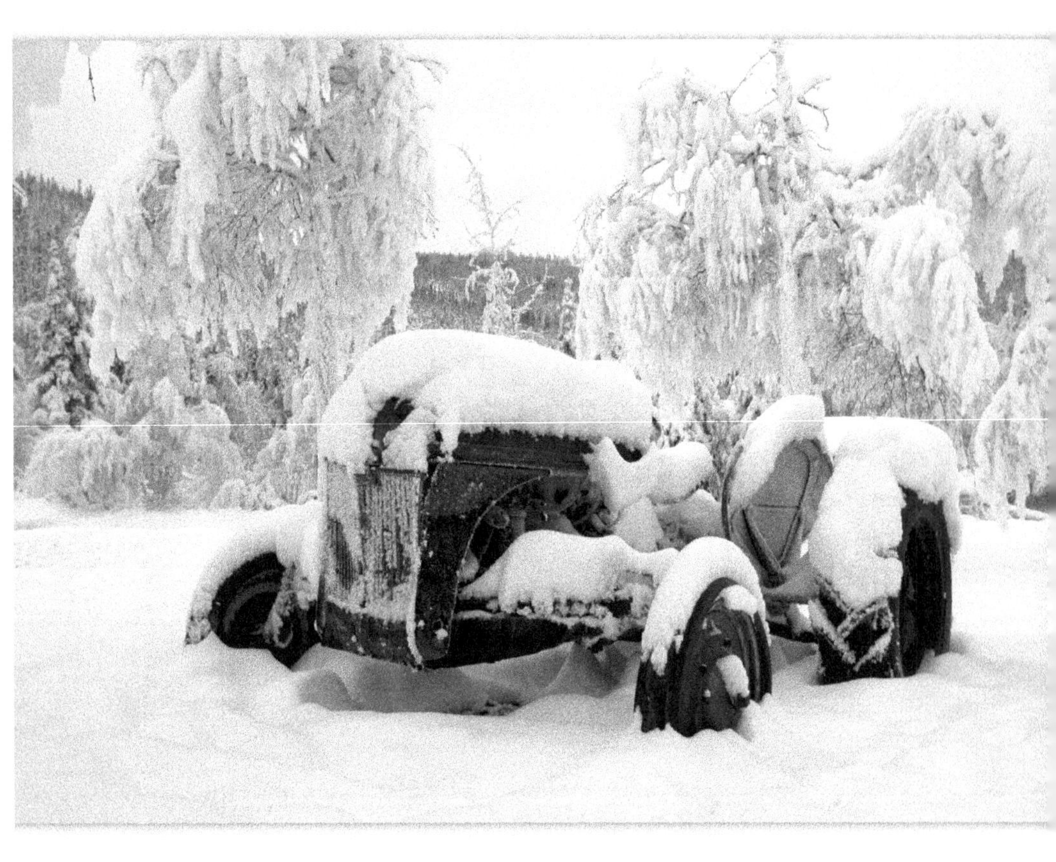

Alaska Antique, Laurent Dick

Photographs

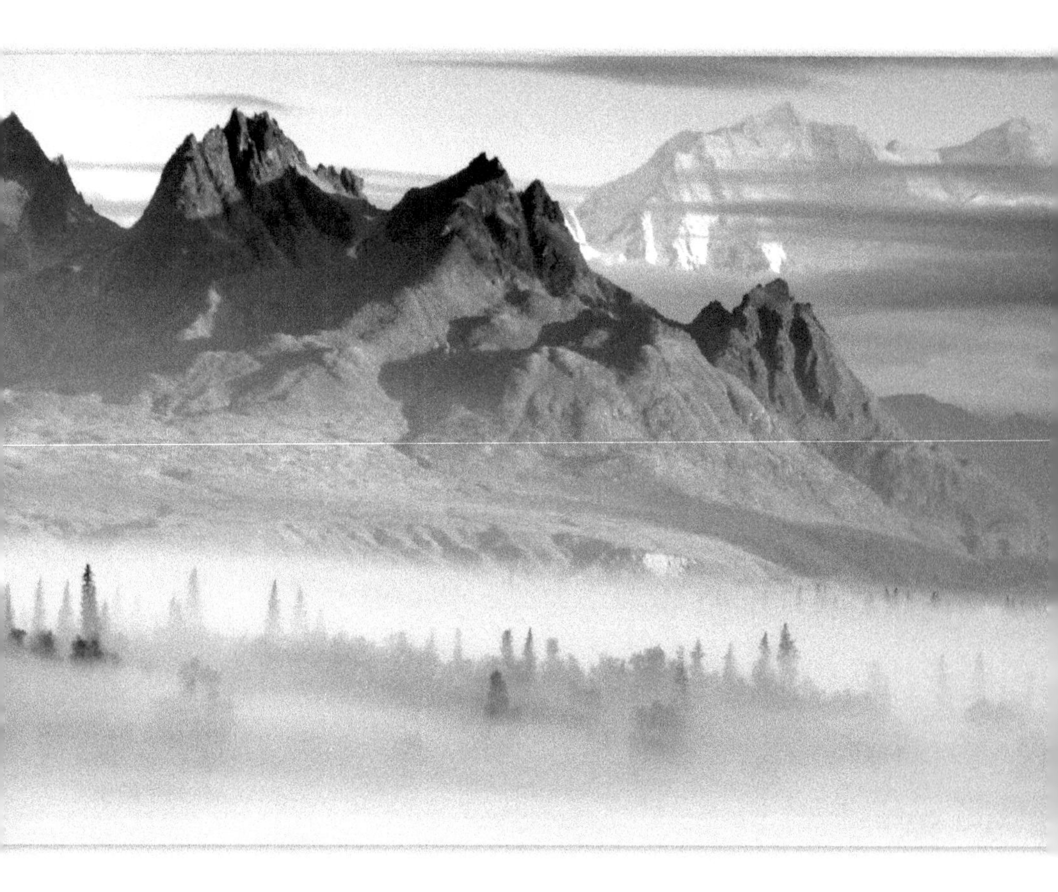

Distant Mt. Hunter, John Frisch

Acknowledgments

Thanks for their support and efforts to turn my idea into this slick little book go to Michael Armstrong, Virginia Berg, Sunny Coulson, Kathy Cummins, Krestia De George, the Flickr community, Melissa Guy, Andrew Johnson, Jim Misko, Sue Mitchell, Jeremy Pataky, Sonja Senkowsky, Scott Slovic, Katie Spielberger, Deb Vanasse, and Emily Wall.

As always, I could not have succeeded without the patience and generosity of all the contributors who entrusted me with their work.

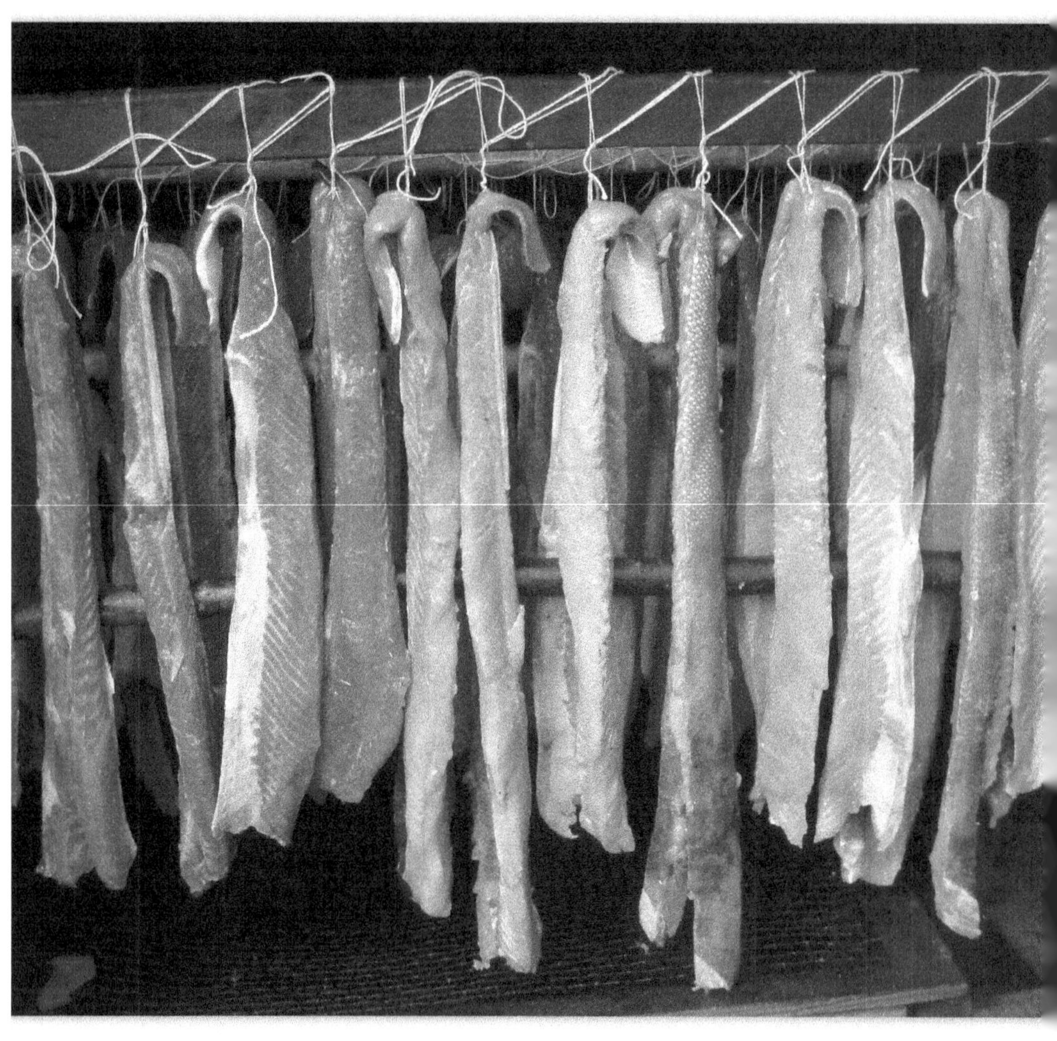

Smoking Strips, Jeremy Pataky

Introduction

Ever heard the old saw "if you can't say it in one page, you won't in a hundred"?

In these times, artists as well have to economize. The book in your hands grew from the idea that less can be more. Its selections—very short prose and black-and-white photographs—embrace the best kinds of nothing: transparency, thrift, and restraint. By minimizing backstory, they stimulate our imagination. I call this "the fishbowl effect," after a long office building with a glass-fronted hallway on the university campus in Fairbanks. The design allows glimpses into cubicles, exposing plots normally hidden and tangential to yours but crucial to each occupant. The insights that can be gleaned in passing provide an idea of the building's "culture," perhaps more enlightening than any one story could ever hope to be. They also leave you wanting more.

This book's prose selections are the literary equivalent of such Peeping Tom stunts—flash-frozen slices of life, highly polished micro-narratives that reveal their protagonists and thereby our state's many facets and lifestyles. Think of them as related to haikus, which leave no room for throat-clearing or verbal calisthenics. They favor the unexpected turn of events, the shortcut to human and nonhuman nature, the sort of episode that could form the heart of a novel. They are fiction or nonfiction, with both genres stalking the same truths. They are dense as Sitka spruce, sweet as smoked salmon, short as summer nights and winter days north of the Arctic Circle. But beware: this is not the Alaska of glossy tourist brochures. There is birth here, and death, and the messiness in between, all with an unmistakable Northern Exposure twist.

Like the writers, the photographers were challenged to squeeze the state and its super-size subjects into a nutshell—the picture that says more than a thousand words, freeze-frames that are eloquent and artistic and resonate with the prose. I chose black-and-white photos over color, for their frugality and because I think them a better fit for Alaska's disjointed moods, for its contrasts and improvisations.

This collection is meant for sophisticated readers with little patience or time and thus, very timely. It can be savored piecemeal, at the coffee shop, on the bus, in the outhouse at thirty below, in a tent on the tundra, waiting in line at the post office, while the children are playing, during break-up, breakdowns, or breaks. I hope these images and words connect with each other and with the reader, fusing into something sublime yet substantial, very much like the big, cold place we call home.

There. I did it. In fewer than four hundred and fifty words.

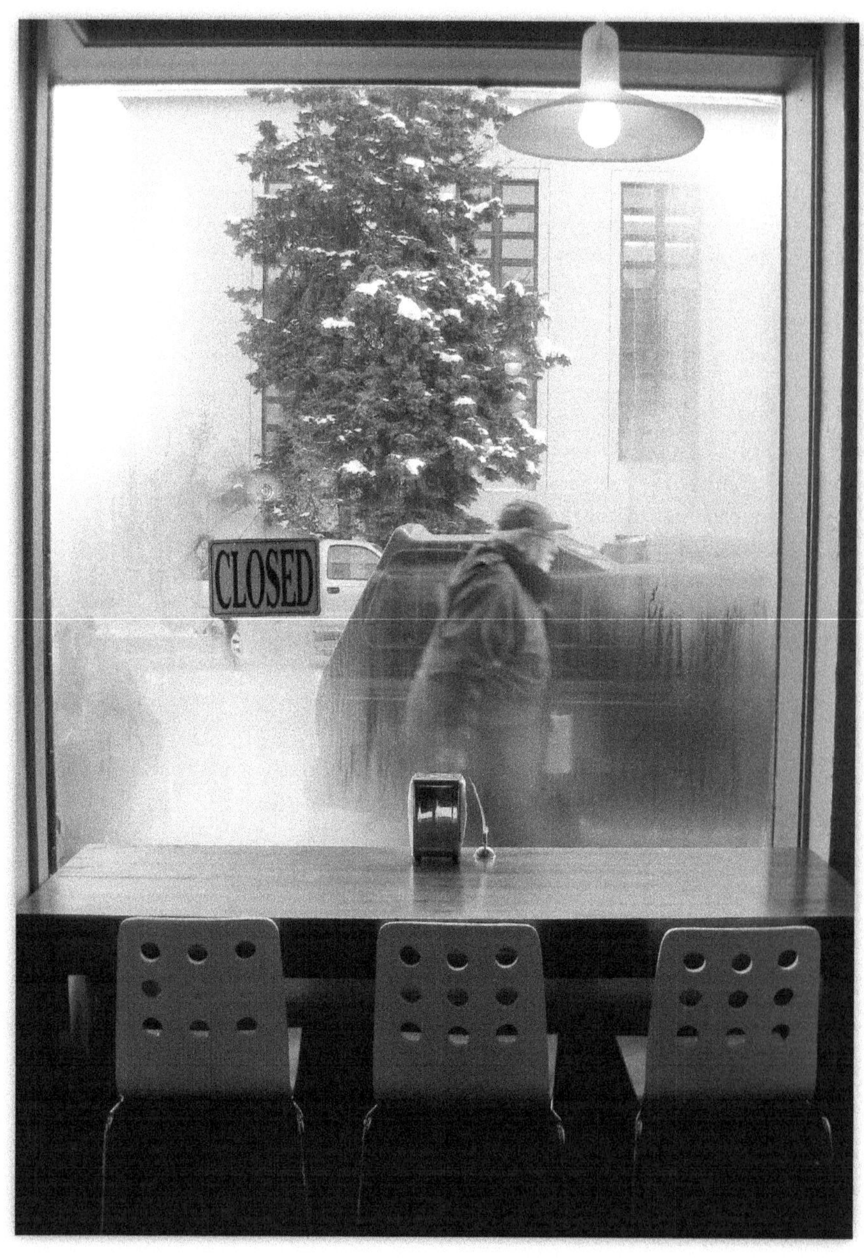

Street-watching, Stephen Nigl

Labrador Tea

EOWYN IVEY

I am resting on the side of a mountain in the Alaska Range, among wild blueberries and summer sun, when I catch the scent. I am confused, as if I'll open my eyes and be somewhere else, but I'm not sure where. I sit up and find it beside me. Labrador Tea.

That old, familiar sickness sinks into my chest, all the more powerful because it has hit unexpectedly, while I lie vulnerable and almost at peace. But there it is—guilt and grief in a knot at the base of my heart.

I break a twig from the bush and put it to my nose. I don't want to inhale the fragrance, but I can't resist.

When my mother was on the tundra, hunting caribou or gathering berries, she would pick these leaves, crush them in her palms and rub them across the backs of her hands. She loved the smell, bitter and strong, musky and floral. Even before she fell out of the sky, the scent haunted me. It reminded me of something I could never name, could never hold on to. Now I know what it is—my mother.

I think of Thoreau. I find myself reading him reluctantly, compulsively, sadly. It is a collection of his essays my mother gave to me as a birthday gift several years before she crashed her Super Cub airplane. As a teenager I was tired of hearing her philosophies on wilderness and life and death, and so I never opened the book, not until recently. Even today, with its inscription "To my daughter, my life," all the more significant, I'm constantly tempted to give it away, discard it, abandon it. I've almost left it at airports and in hotel rooms, almost put it in boxes to Goodwill or given it away as a gift. But I never do. I keep it with me and read it over and over again.

I brought it here with me, one of the few books I stowed away in my backpack, and the other night, I was struck by a section of his essay *Walking*. It is about an African hunter who describes a dead antelope's skin as perfumed with the scent of trees and grass. Thoreau says he wishes people were like that, that we were so much a part of nature that we smelled of it.

My mother did. I have no doubt. If you would have run a blade along the inside of her arm, her very blood would have smelled of the tundra, of Labrador Tea and blueberry leaves, of caribou hide and sun-warmed moss.

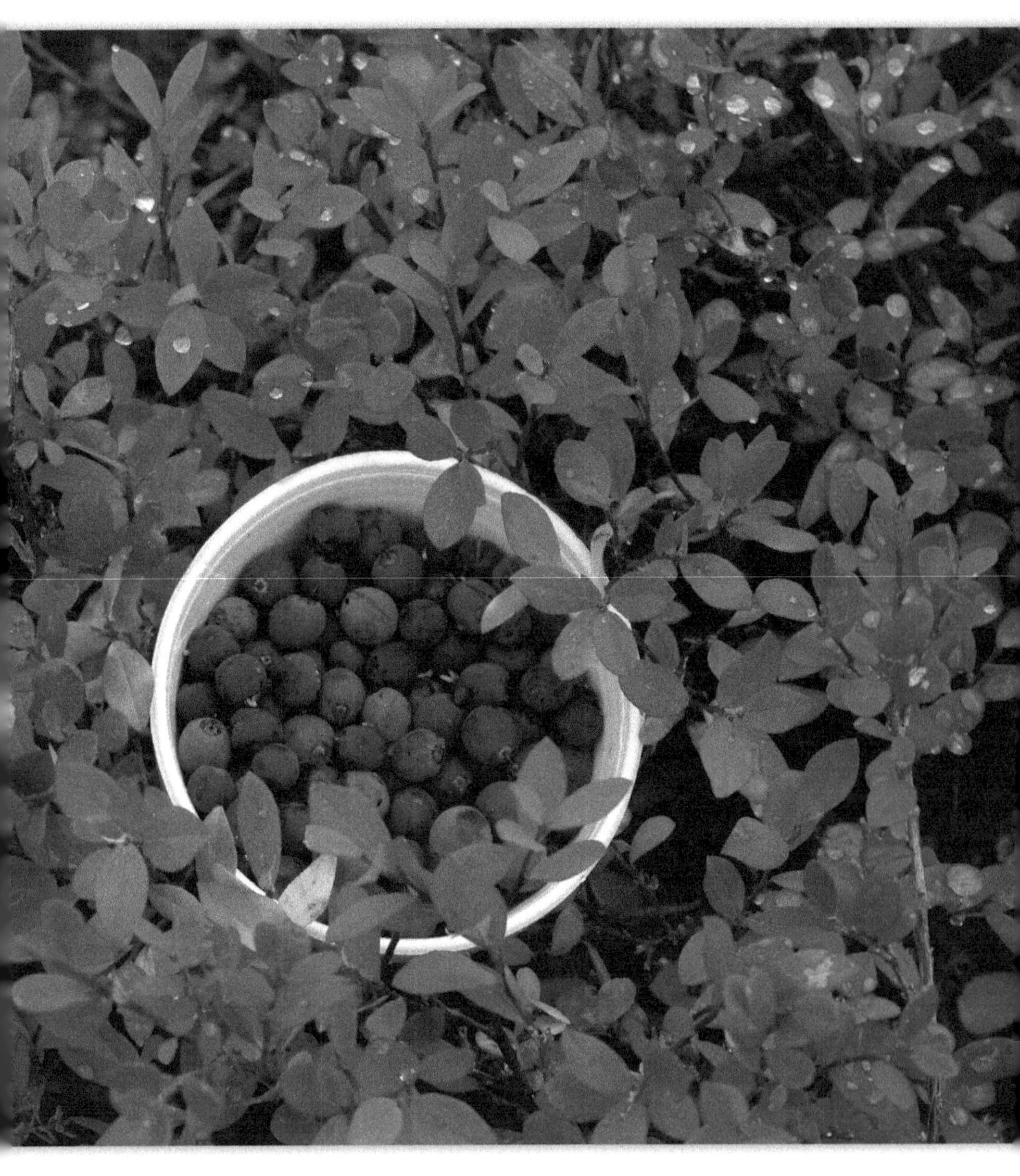

Fall's Bounty, Don Rearden

And Then the Earth Moves

MARK ARVID WHITE

Good Friday, 2004.

Old knees feel the strain of my climb, but I press on without you. A few more steps. There.

I stand on the slope of Pillar Mountain, near the spot where I stood trembling forty years ago, watching boats in Kodiak's small harbor toss and bounce like so many pieces of popcorn in a pan of hot grease. The ground was jolting, rolling, all reality unhinged in minutes of madness, all the earth roaring like a brown bear cut off from her cubs. Some boats got away to the deep sea, riding out the coming tsunami with barely a concern, while their sisters capsized or smashed through buildings, some lifted and dropped a mile or more from the safety of their berths.

Now the harbor lies calm. I stand upon the hill for several minutes while you wait in the car, and I wonder how to break the news of my cancer.

Kentucky girl, we have bobbed in waves before and felt enough tremors in our twenty years of marriage, but I know you have never felt the ground move for so long and so hard.

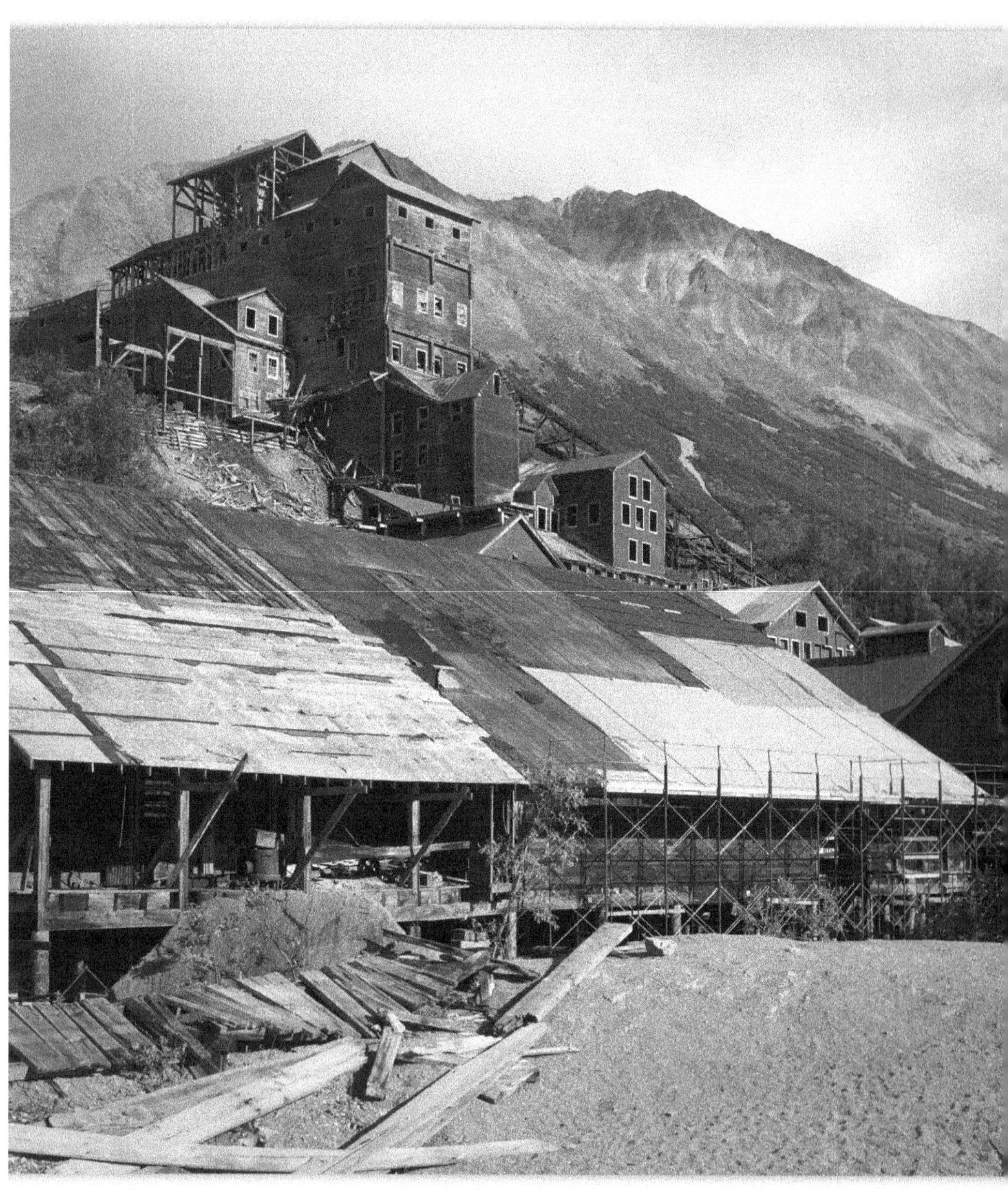

Kennecott Mine, J. T. Thomas

Redoubt's Ash

BRUCE ORTON

Redoubt's ash came in every snowfall and rose in the drifts like grim gray strata in the coldest winter for years. Moose starved and moved into towns to get away from wolves. One sat at the only stoplight in Wasilla that winter for six weeks, too tired to budge. People brought veggies from Carrs, and I think she made it.

I lived in a big log home looking down on the Little Su and cut down birch trees that had been there since Baranof, so that moose might eat the buds. Fifteen lived in my yard for four months, too tired to care. My dogs left them alone, the tired moose rested, and peace reigned in the wilderness. When I'd fire up a chain saw they'd come like cats to a can opener. Twenty-three stood in a circle as I cut a tree, and as I finished the felling cut, an earthquake quivered down the spine of the Talkeetnas. Dropped it right where I wanted, and the moose moved in to feast.

That spring two calves were born in my yard, though Fish and Game proclaimed one-hundred-percent mortality in our borough. I hope Redoubt waits for summer this time.

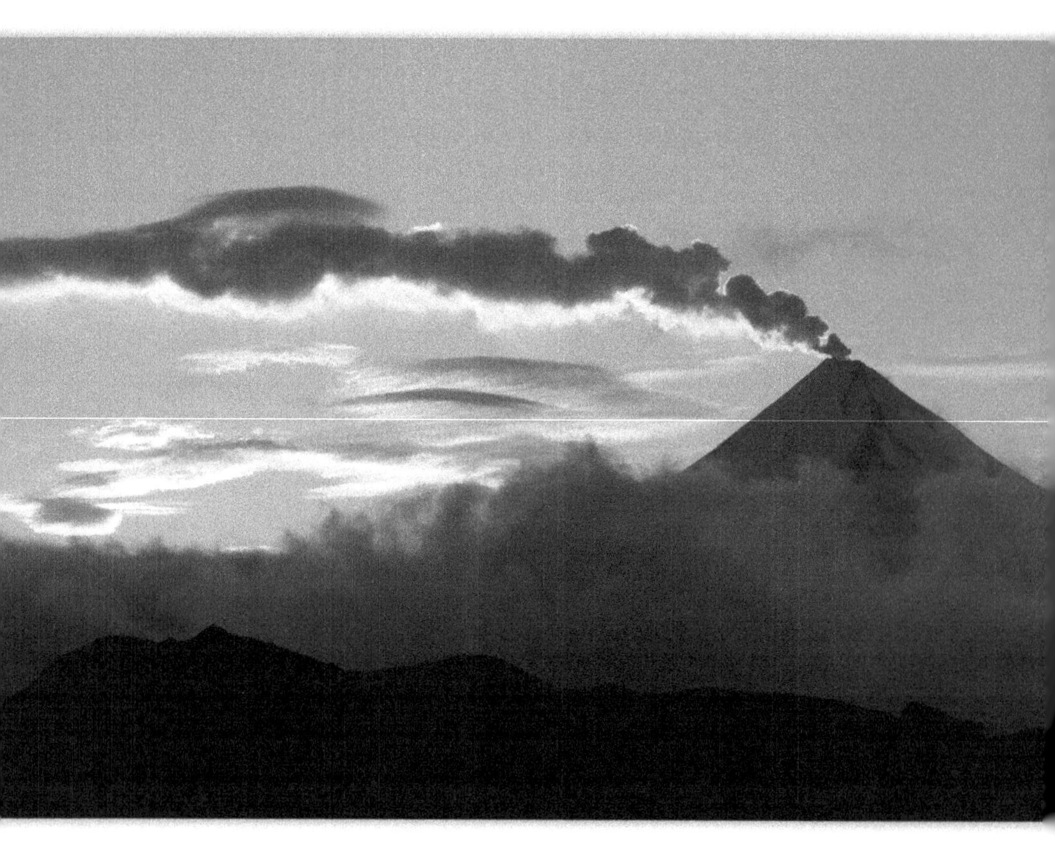

Shishaldin at Sunset, Cyrus Read. (Courtesy of the USGS/Alaska Volcano Observatory.)

Hunger Mountain

STEVE KAHN

The week started with Jesse's complaints of sore feet and a tender stomach. On the seven-hour climb up the mountain he lost his rifle's clip and banged its scope against a rock. The bull caribou we were stalking disappeared hours before we crested the final ridge. Then Jesse missed a Dall's ram five times.

The first I heard about his gall bladder troubles was shortly after he vomited and just before a casual mention that he'd had part of one lung removed. Nice surprise.

The spooked sheep had bedded down two ridges distant. I suggested we descend to camp, eat, sleep, and then return early the next morning. Jesse shook his head. "You'll never get me back up this mountain." I knew he was right.

I cast around for a place to spend the night—a small depression on the treeless ridge allowed respite from the wind. From my pack I pulled dry socks, a space blanket, a wool cap, and a *Sitzkissen*, an inflatable German seat pad. I handed the items to Jesse. "Try to get some sleep," I said, as I put on my thin slicker and looked for a place within the hollow to lie down.

Guides try to perpetuate a myth about the profession: John T. would carve off a chunk of raw liver just removed from the gut pile, swallow it, smack his lips, and offer some to his hunter. Mike W. smeared moose urine all over himself so he would smell like a bull in rut. I didn't go that far—mostly I tried not to shiver in front of my clients.

Lying on my back I watched the stars but soon the jab of a rock below my right scapula convinced me to try another position. I rolled onto my left side. Something hard pressed into my thigh. I dug in my pocket and removed my measuring tape and a match container. Dampness crept through my wool pants to my hip.

Jesse started to snore.

We'd had a cookie apiece for dinner. I was cold but mostly hungry. Fishing around in my jacket, I produced a stick of gum. Bits of paper stuck to it as I peeled off the wrapper. I worked the wad in my mouth counting seconds—twenty chews with the right molars, twenty with the left, twenty with the incisors. One minute. It was a hell of a way to kill time. I tucked my hands into my armpits.

Jesse snored wildly. My stomach growled and I kept thinking how, wrapped in the space blanket, he looked like a huge baked potato—and under his chin the white T-shirt, mocking, like a dollop of sour cream.

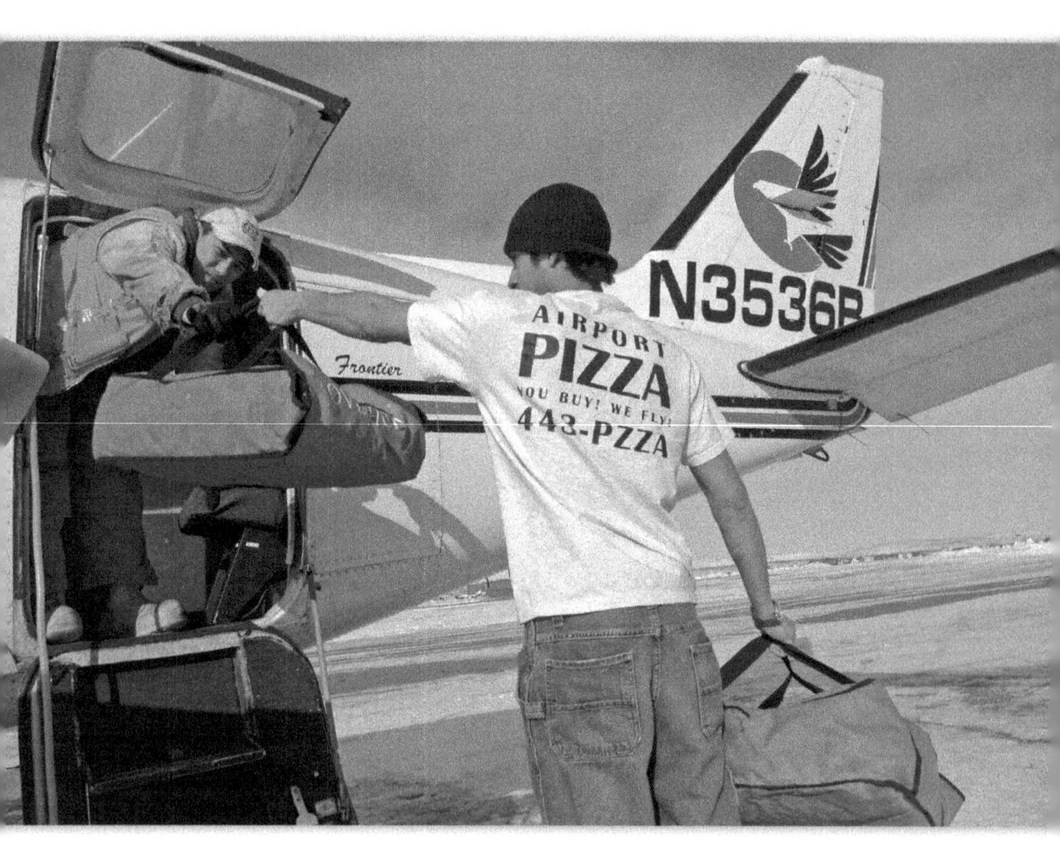

You Buy, We Fly, Laurent Dick

Tikchik

MARY COOK

We drag our raft onto the river's edge and scramble up the bluff. Fall has stained the tundra floor crimson, splashed the cottonwoods a startling gold. A young caribou stands motionless within shooting range. Kathy positions her rifle and takes aim; one shot and the animal drops. I cannot take my eyes off the still, brown form. It occurs to me that I never heard the gunshot. I'm startled when Kathy grabs my arm.

"I've been hunting all my life and I'm still not sure if it's right to kill things." There are tears in her voice, and when I hold her she feels shaky and small.

"I'm so glad you're here! I feel better having you here." Kathy has been my angel-friend since the sudden death of my partner eleven months ago; I'm happy to give something in return, even if it's simply to bear witness.

Paul and Kibbons approach the animal quietly; Paul bends to touch a shoulder, the velvet of an antler. They give us a thumbs-up before returning to the raft for knives and game bags. Kathy and I walk hand in hand to the caribou, kneel by its side. Reverently, we stroke the warm fur, marvel at its animal perfection. Its death feels wrong and also absolutely right. I put my lips to the soft hair inside its ear and thank it for giving up its life.

The men return and we help them move the animal onto a blue tarp. Kibbons takes a knife and slits the caribou's throat. Blood oozes onto the tarp. I step back, then back again. I am flooded with images of Jon's death, his broken body lying motionless in a scarlet pool. There was nothing right about that death. I flinch when Kibbons cuts off the animal's head, cry softly as Kathy takes the knife from him and smoothly opens the belly from groin to chest. Paul sharpens knives, arranges game bags. Everyone is involved, except me. If I mean to eat this animal—and I do—then I need to help butcher it.

I wipe my tears and rejoin the group. Kathy is cutting into the chest. When she sees me behind her, she turns and offers me the bloody knife. "Why don't you cut out the heart, Mary?"

I take the knife and cut where she directs me; I am elbow-deep in warm blood. I remove the animal's generous heart and place it tenderly on the tarp. Gripping the knife a little tighter, I keep cutting until the butchering is done. It feels like honest work.

One minute we're standing and the next we've fallen forever. The truth is as shocking and natural as that.

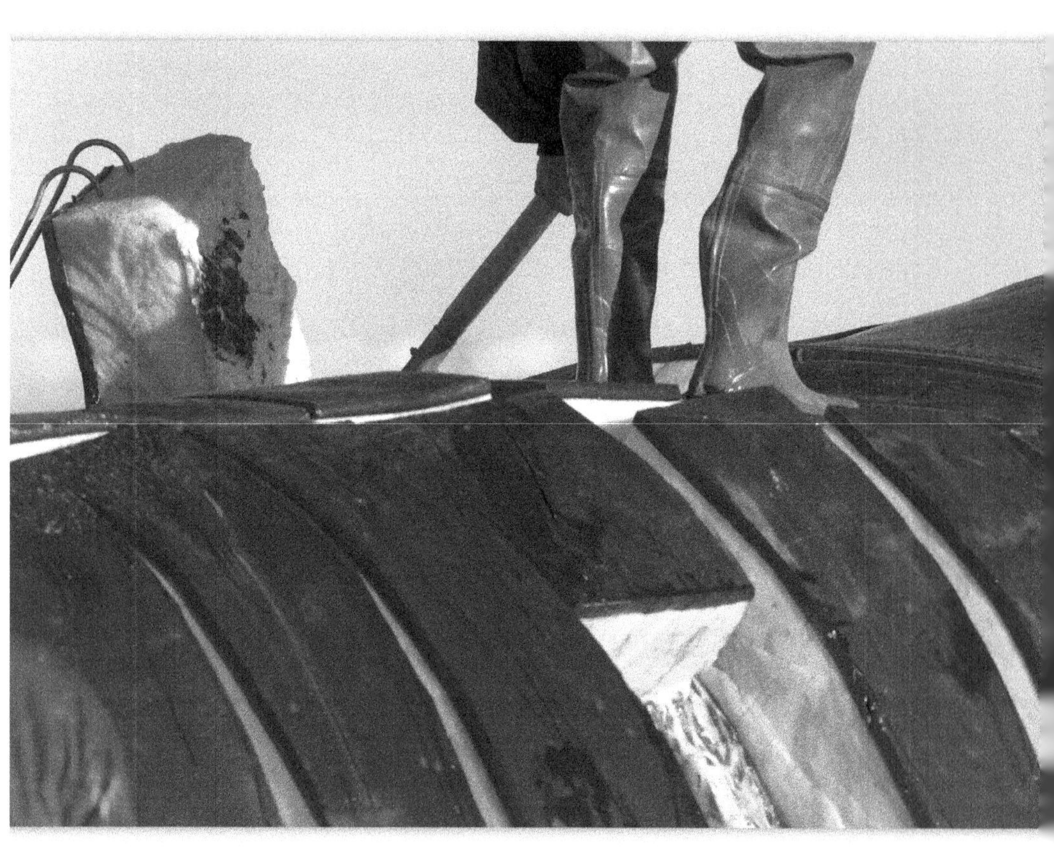

Bowhead Harvest, Patrick Endres

Fat of the Land

LYNN DEFILIPPO

Moose cracklings—that's what I like. Chunks of fat, picked from the intestines or carved from around the rump where a fat cow stores her winter calories, reduced on a low flame till only small globs remain in a clear, black pool of melted lard. I love the slow sizzle in the skillet, anticipating its lavish taste, the melting of salted and crispy bits in my mouth. It's pure cellular nourishment, a calm, happy fat that pads the belly and jiggles the thighs. Willow and tundra transformed. So succulent.

One September day at the end of hunting season, a creamy hunk, about the size of a soccer ball and wrapped in a plastic bag, was plopped onto the kitchen table. My husband chuckled as he hefted the blood-smeared package. "You wanted fat, you got fat!" The mass of congealed energy impressed me with its smooth whiteness. Slowly, reverently, I sliced through it, stopping when the knife met resistance. Peering through the pale cleft I saw something reddish, a kidney nestled so comfortably there, surrounded by what was not long ago warm gelatinous fat, solidified now, parted several hours from the animal. I lifted it out.

That kidney tasted like piss. Even the dog wouldn't eat it.

The kidney fat was excellent though, and melted down cleanly. Intestine fat came in smaller pieces and left more cracklings in the pan to nibble on. Most fat we kept for sausages, mixing the ground greasiness with meat and seasonings, one part fat to two parts meat. Cranking down the lid to the sausage maker, squeezing the mix into casings, twisting between the filled links, then greedily frying up a few to sample. If you prick a hot sausage while it fries, a stream of juice will spurt out, arcing over the pan, and burn your hand.

Now you know how I gained weight those winters living in Nome, eating moose cracklings I rendered often for fat to fry a burger in, or fat to make a roux for soup. And this fat fest went on while snow drove in horizontal sheets on dark, windy days with so little light that I hardly spent any time outside. I stayed in the house instead, eating fatty sausages and thickened stews.

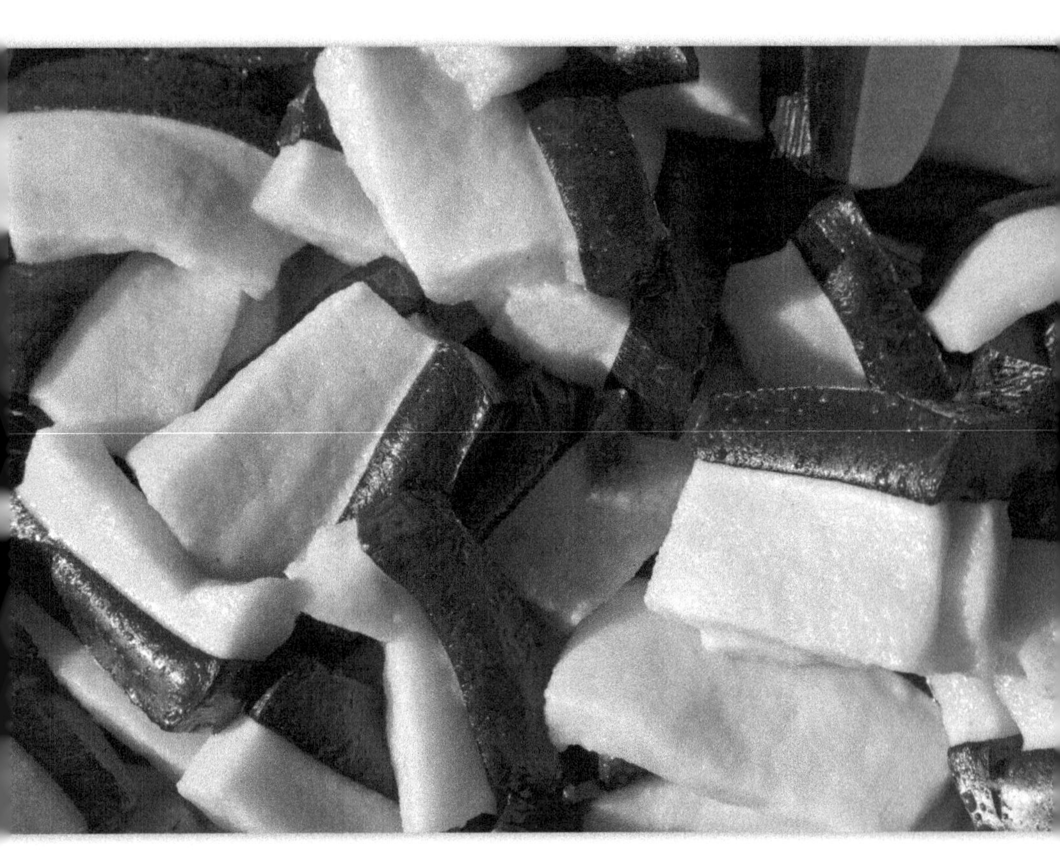

Muktuk Tidbits, Patrick Endres

Soul Food

CHRISTINE BYL

The first time I saw a coastal brown bear on the Sound, I was tightening lag bolts on a viewpoint bench near the Alaganik Slough, looked up and caught sight of what must have been the biggest male in the Cordova district. But when Dave joined me and we watched it feeding on sedges along the slough's bank, he said it was just a juvenile. He'd lived in Cordova for years, and he laughed and called me easily impressed.

Unlike the smaller inland bears, those opportunistic omnivores with a hankering for the occasional carcass, coastal browns bulk up because most of their summer and fall calories come from salmon. Spawning stream banks are littered with half-consumed fish, tails and backbones left behind as bears rip out the bellies, rich with eggs and organ meat, and heads, thick with brains. Eagles and gulls peck out the eye sockets of abandoned skeletons and, always in search of more, trail the bears on land, the sea lions on the water, and the fishermen in their orange Helly Hansens filleting out on the dock. In the course of an average salmon's spawning ritual, my naturalist friend tells me, the fish benefits one hundred and thirty-six species. Like the Biblical catch made sufficient for five thousand, most salmon feed more than one mouth.

And not just ursine mouths, or avian mouths. Coastal people take cues from coastal bears, growing full on what's near. A midsummer potluck dinner in Cordova offered the following dishes: sockeye salmon fillet, king salmon croquettes, pickled silver salmon with onions, pink salmon dip. Mountain goat meatloaf, salmon roe, black bear steaks, moose burger, salmonberry jam, blueberry pie, salmon milt on crackers. In one Crock-Pot, there was stewed alligator brought back from someone's trip down south, the only meat on the table not shot, caught, gutted, or wrapped in Cordova within the last nine months. Except for half a package of hotdogs, which the kids, like scavenging gulls, scarfed down with four-dollar-a-bag white-flour buns.

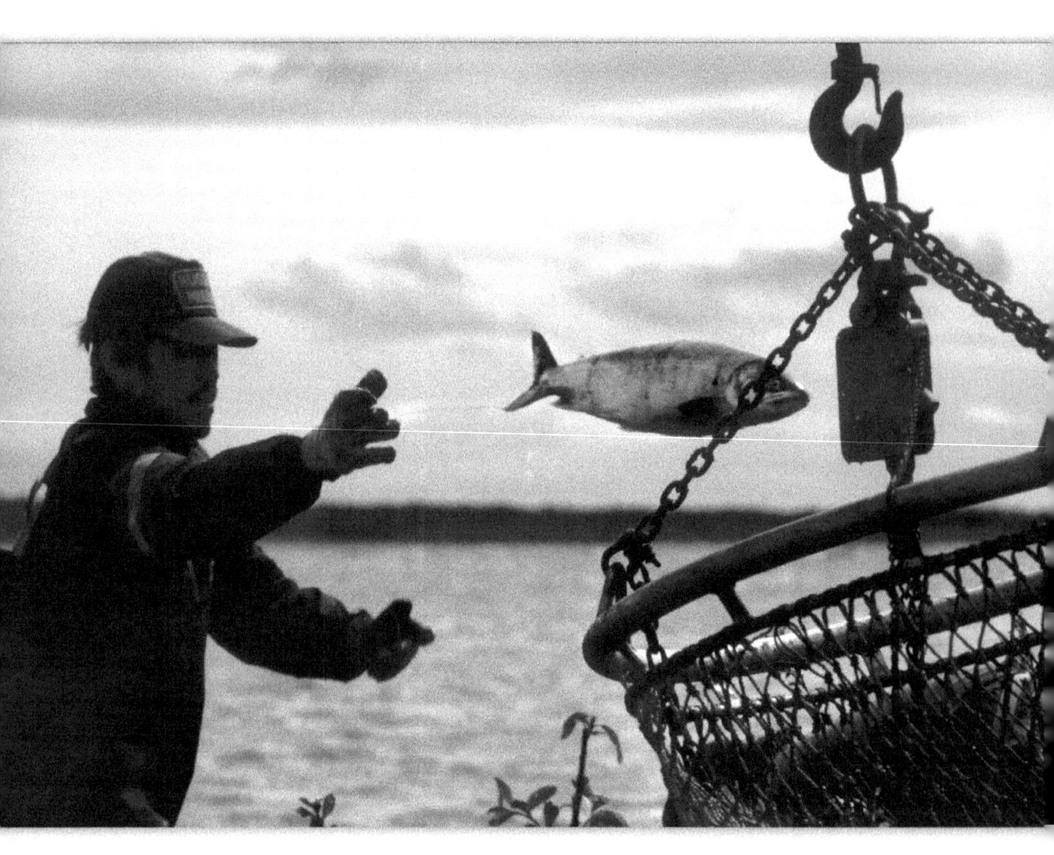

Fishing—Yukon River, Robert Drozda

Our Just Getting Going

JEREMY EDWARD SHIOK

This is how the best days begin: bacon, scrambled eggs, black beans simmered with cilantro, toast burned to perfection, leftover salmon grilled the night before, strong black coffee for coffee drinkers, strong Earl Grey tea for tea drinkers, juice if we have any, sourdough pancakes from the Mason jar on the back of the oven, nachos.

Dry socks hanging above the woodstove, XtraTufs folded over below it, gloves and wristers clipped to the wall, sweatshirts warm with smoke and smelling like dried salt and jellyfish, bibs without holes in the crotch, a stiff-brimmed hat, sunglasses.

On the beach: full gas tanks, a tote full of ice, a clean picking skiff to pull in on a flat calm sea, the Yamaha's roar on the first or second pull, my favorite hook right where I left it. Just offshore, the holding skiff, still in the water and low with the weight of reds picked the night before.

Out at the set, all things where they should be: anchors, buoys, attitudes. In the net, salmon as far down as the eye can see, and to our surprise, the tender just on the edge of the horizon toward Uganik Pass, their all-night trip to town and back done earlier than we planned, the crackle of their call to *Eskimo Pie* like something from much farther away: a float plane, maybe, or a camp over in Viekoda Bay, or some other universe.

But they're close, within sight, and seeing them we know they see us and won't bother calling. We drive the gear, pick the fish, drive the gear, pick the fish, double back—no time for ice. By the time the tender rounds the hook and their wake hits the king kegs, we're fully loaded, two skiffs on a mission, weighed down and racing toward the center of the bay to unload, sea spray in our faces, that Shelikof air deep in our lungs, those frequent thoughts of obligations back in town and bills that need to be paid and beers we wish we had and the women we'd drink them with if we could, fade away.

We are totally alive in the moment, no past to hang heavy or future to loom large, just a present tense where the salt and the sweat, the fish guts and the cool water rinse one another away. There's no better present to be living in, and if we had to describe it we'd say simply, *It's all good*, because in that instant it *is* all good, there is no bad, no there or where, just here, where our just getting going is getting along fine and soon will be gone.

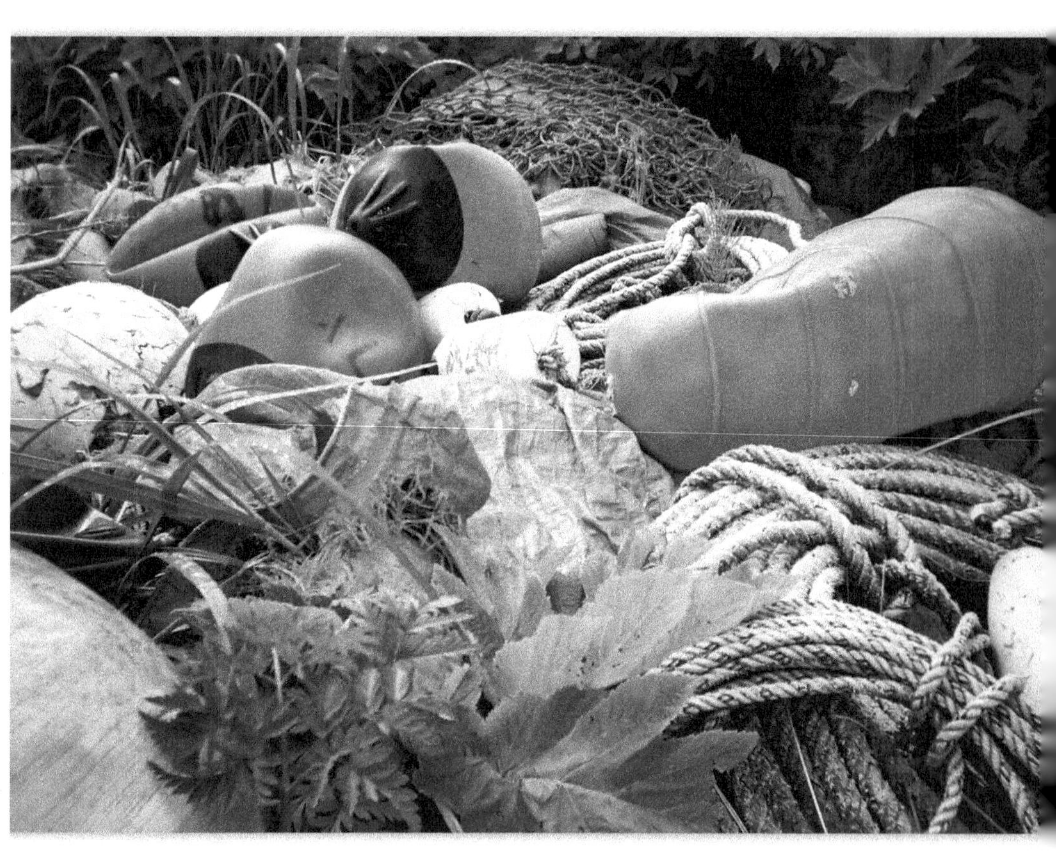

Buoys, Jeremy Edward Shiok

Mrs. Weasley

SIERRA GOLDEN

I used to beg butter from this woman. I'd been on a fishing boat for four weeks with a week's worth of groceries. She was redheaded and cheerful and plump. She ran the *Quaker Maid* with her husband and sons, and although there were only two sons, they seemed like an entire brood of skinny redheaded versions of her. When she started baking us cookies and cupcakes, I imagined that they were the Weasleys, lost and somehow far, far from London in the watery wilderness of Southeast Alaska.

Two years later and at forty, she was in the damp pitiable building that the cannery calls a gym. Unfinished, it housed a basketball hoop and ten three-quarters-inflated orange bouncy balls with jack-o'-lantern faces for the children of Mexican cannery workers—perfect for the fleet of fishermen that had appeared in the afternoon with nothing to fish for and everything to drink to. A violent game of dodgeball erupted that night, and she wasn't just there; she was in the thick of it, holding her own against twenty twenty-something, bearded, burly, slightly sauced fishermen engaged in a pissing contest of dodgeball. *Whapp!*

Years ago, in Juneau, she had dug from the garbage a red wagon and painted it into a Coast Guard ship for her toddling son. She told me how, after eighteen years in Alaska, visiting Tenakee Springs on the Fourth of July became her first moment as an Alaskan: she found the same wagon, spattered with ripe salmon berries, covered in crepe paper streamers, rusted but still with the clean lines of a Coast Guard ship. *When I find my garbage all over Southeast,* she said, *I know I am home.*

She neglected to mention the treasure she found, refurbished, and passed along.

Puddle jumping, I contemplate this woman: I am a poseur, enjoying the phosphorescent glow of Alaska in the summer before returning to the Lower Forty-Eight to write about its magic, embracing all the amenities that world has to offer. She, on the other hand, is the poetry of my poems. She is the acceptance and innovation that transforms towns without sweet potatoes, people without computers, miles without cell service. She makes us forget, for a moment, our inhibitions, lets us play like children in the rain, like boys in a gymnasium. My toes are wet in these puddles; she went swimming in them. I begged for the butter, and I thank her for the wisdom: accept what you do not have, and do something better without it.

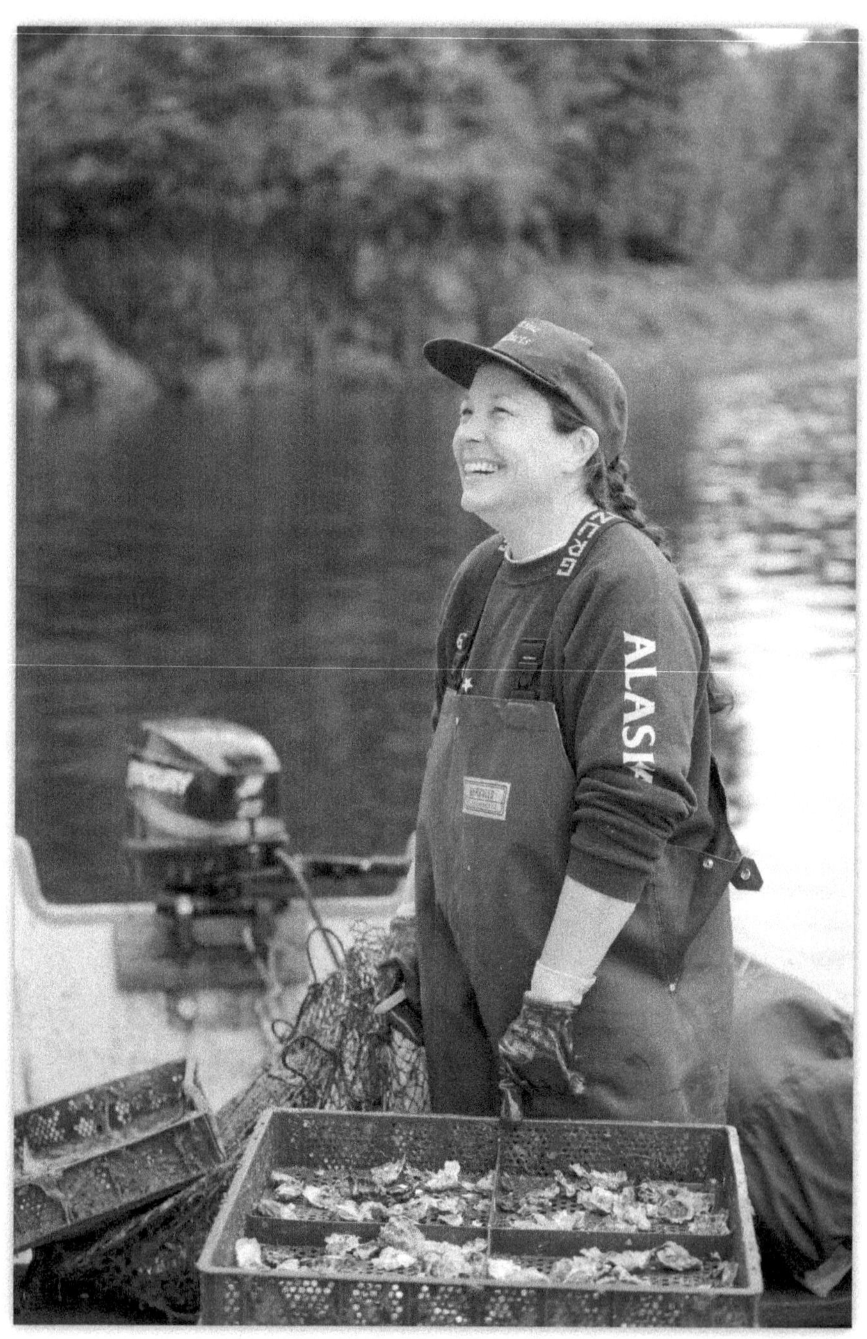

Oyster Suzie—Prince William Sound, Patrick Endres

Specialization

(Hammer Museum, Haines)

ELIZABETH BRADFIELD

I hadn't known I'd needed proof until I entered, parrot squawking by the door, bells along the jamb struck by their little clappers.

Long-handled hammer for posting signs high—Sale—Lost—Wanted—Circus—Vote. Hammer for mining gold, its handle sheened (dim hope polished) by the hand's swing and swing into dark ore. Wide and softheaded hammer made to pound hemp and tar into planking, to ready a hull for the slap of breakers.

He said time lay like a thing in need of shaping. The hours between ship dockings, when he was paid to grab the lines or cast them off, were too short to drive home, too long to idle on the wharf. So he brought his collection. Found a friend's empty frontage. Arranged and invited.

There is a wall of hammers for lumber and one for metal. One for rock. Three-clawed hammers. Ball peens. Tiny mallets to beat the rims of empties in bars—not to break but to lift the sound of thirst into the air.

I pick up a hammer for chipping fossils from rocks. The wood is warm, the metal head cool. There are lineages, divergences, stories hidden that someone with training can make sense of.

Once he drove his collection across the continent, pistons hammering, to the Smithsonian. Returned with the mannequins now posed in a back room, plaid shirts and suspenders, picks and sledgehammers. You can see, he said, the places where he had to saw them up to fit them in the van, where he put them together again.

Reassurance. What care reveals through its accretions. So many ways to beat sense, beat shape, beat attachment and separation.

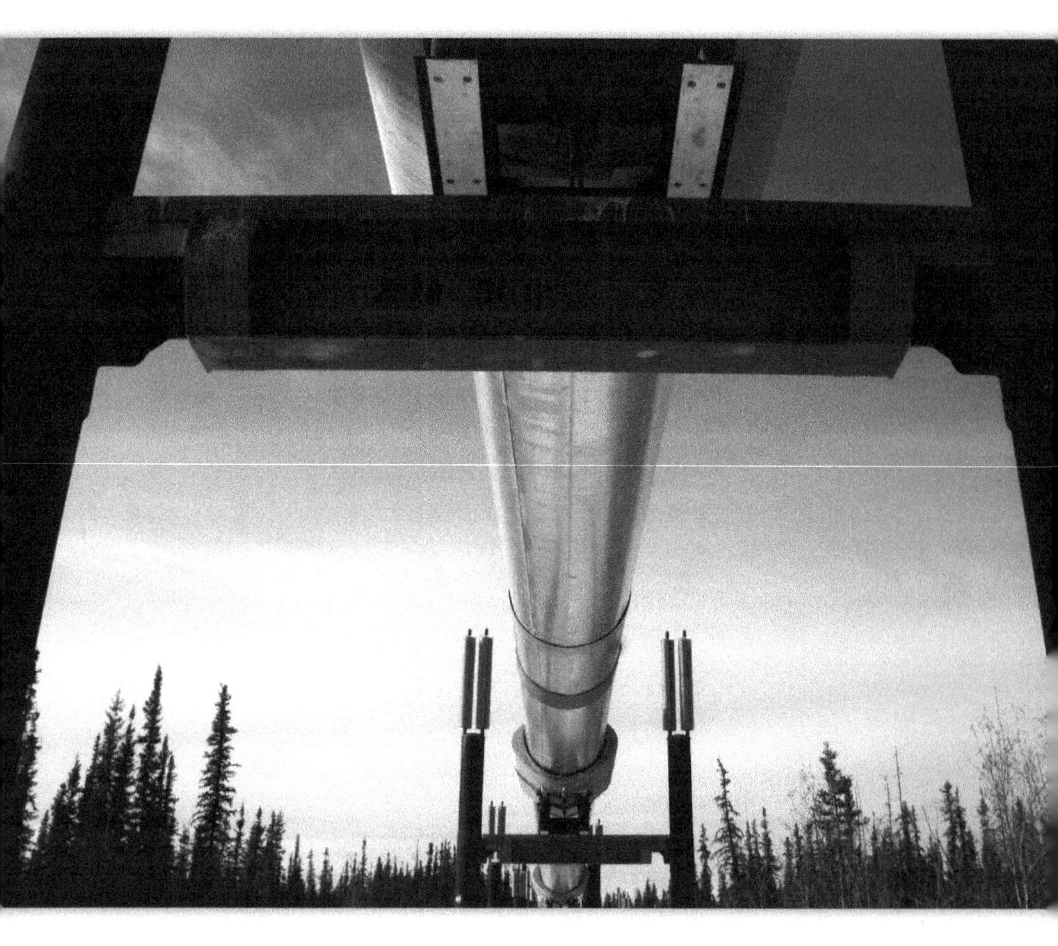

Crude, Robert Drozda

Outside of Eden

DEIDRE ELLIOTT

A college scholarship lured them south: she, the oldest daughter of a Russian-Aleut businessman from Ouzinkie, and he, the third-generation son of Filipino cannery workers from Kodiak. That first evening they sat, stunned, on the tiny balcony of their student apartment, staring at the dry riverbed of the Santa Cruz. Midnight and still 110 degrees in Tucson.

In July, they tried to summon up the chilly mists of a northern ocean. Wearing tank tops, shorts, and flip-flops purchased that afternoon from a Mexican market, they tried to conjure winter on Marmot Bay; they tried to imagine the cocoon-like feeling of parkas, mukluks, and mittens topped with wolverine fur to wipe snot from frostbitten noses.

During the stifling August heat, they thought of summer evenings back home when, by the light of the midnight sun, men finished roofing houses at 3 a.m.

In September, he got a job roasting chiles. He welcomed the change from cannery work where he had had to operate the fish head cutter with one wrist chained to the machine to avoid slicing off his own hand. Still, chiles stung his eyes and pungent fumes permeated his clothes.

In October, she baked fish pie—golden crust, rice, onions—but, alas, filled with canned salmon. They pined for the crimson flesh of wild fish from their home waters.

During the dry November heat, they ignored the orange blasts of Sonoran sunsets and recalled the dancing turquoise green curtains of the aurora.

In December, they gazed across the flat rooftops of dull adobe churches and sighed, remembering the blue, onion-shaped dome of the Russian Orthodox chapel where they were married.

In January, they cried when a skinny postal worker delivered photographs of their rotund relatives, laughing next to idling snowmachines.

In February, still trapped beside a waterless river, they purchased a clock radio that simulated the sound of ocean waves (though they realized the crashing electronic surf mimicked Southern California waters and not the chattering current of Kodiak).

In March, while the rest of Tucson whooped and hollered at the rodeo, they sat silently, transfixed by the latest drama at the Iditarod.

In the desperation of April, they taped plastic sheets across the bathroom door and crouched naked in the tiny shower, attempting to sweat the desert from their veins, sauna-style, but the creosote wands they struck each other with didn't produce the necessary, repentant sting of birch.

In May, they threw their possessions inside a U-Haul and sped across the still-dry Santa Cruz. They turned the AC to high. They could almost smell the ocean and feel the rocking of the northern ferry that would carry them home.

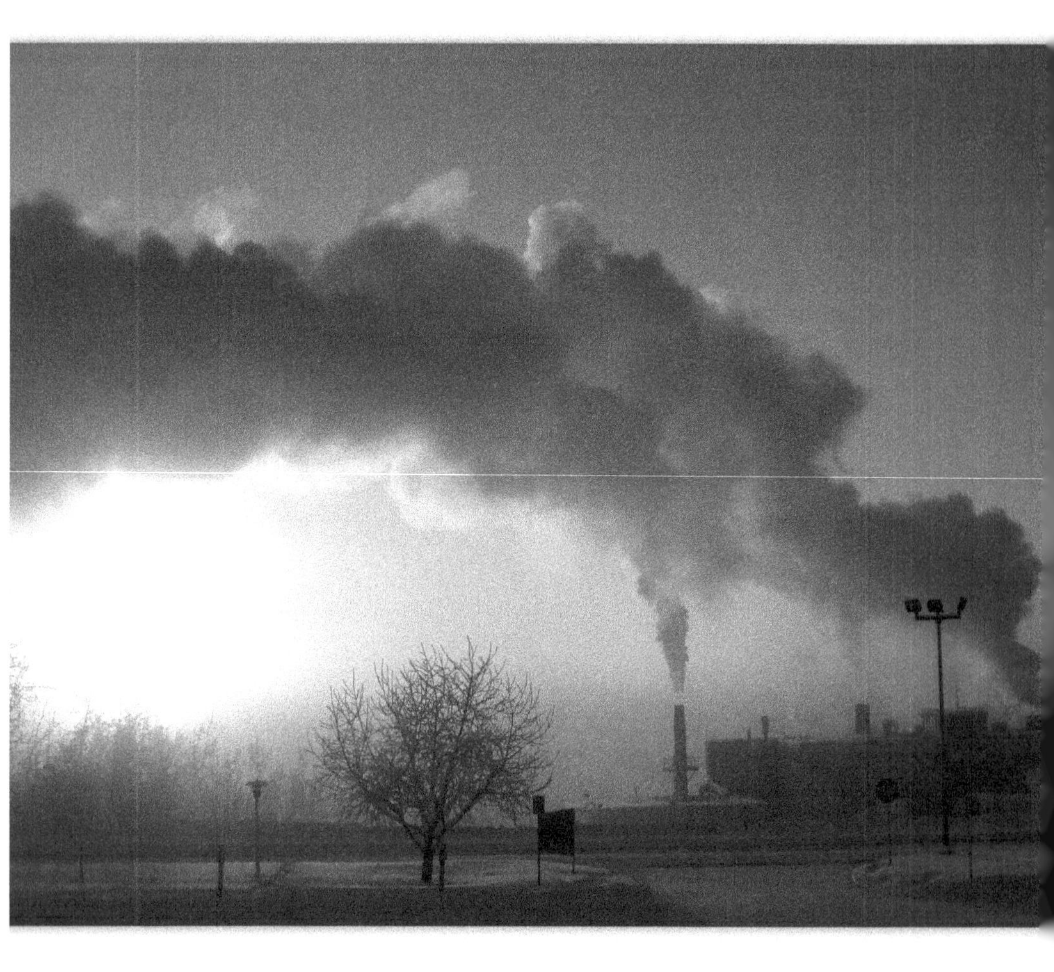

Fairbanks Fresh Air, Melissa Guy

Wind

LYNN DEFILIPPO

We stand facing into the wind. Black feathers of her long, loose hair lick the air behind her. The sky stretches out, around us, embracing the tundra, which rolls from here—the base of Anvil—to Norton Sound, roughly one mile away. The sea is a glimmering blue stripe along the horizon. We don't talk much. We breathe and wind washes over us.

I took my eighth-grade language arts class out here today. Suffering from spring fever in a windowless classroom, we went for a walk back behind the school. It was a small class, a dozen students, and we headed off through the tailings piles to an easy trail up the mountain. Enjoying the sunshine and warmth of an early spring thaw, we weren't teacher and students, just people. Girls talked in small groups of two or three, boys threw stones into the mining ponds. One skip, two skips, three skips, four. The air was fresh, the breeze steady and cool.

I walked with a young Native woman from Wales. She had transferred from the village to Nome mid–school year. A thoughtful writer, her essays were well organized, and her poetry, sad and beautiful, spoke about losses in her family. I came to know her the way I came to know other students from the Bering Straits villages: slowly. Shy, quiet, and often keeping to themselves, these students taught me how to listen, observe, watch for subtle cues.

The young woman and I talked about the wind. I don't remember exactly what I said, probably something obvious, something about it being strong or cold or unrelenting. That first year in Nome I was always braced against it, collar turned up, cap pulled down over my ears. I would not venture outside without a windproof layer. On this blustery afternoon, my companion walked hatless, at ease. She is of this place, rooted in the land, if not in the town.

She spoke with quiet contemplation and longing about Wales. How she and her cousins would catch gale-force winds with their jackets held high above their heads. They would ride these gusts on ice skates across a frozen pond just outside the village. I imagine them laughing, speeding across the ice, the wind their playmate, the Bering Straits their home.

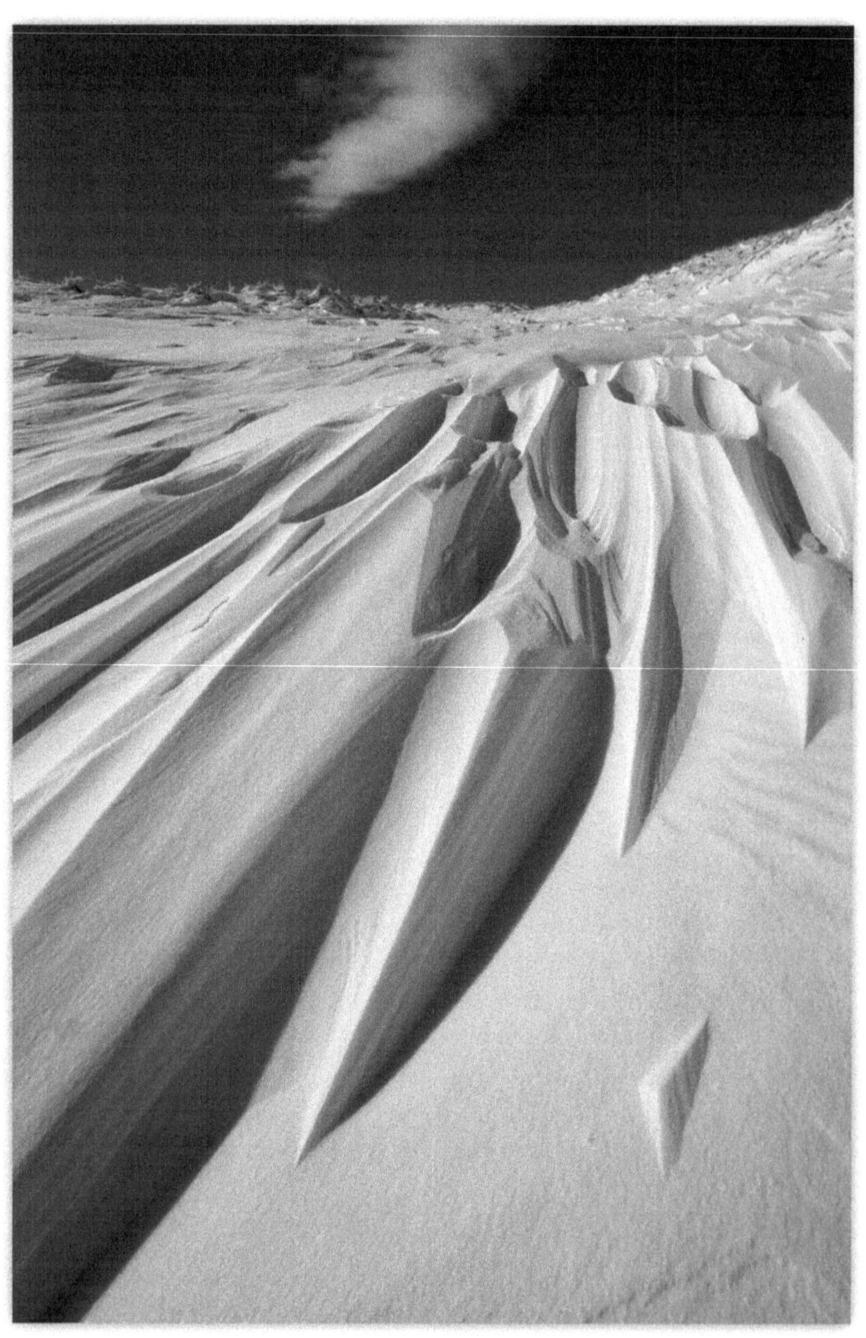

Elements, Ron Perkins

Letter from the Bush

TANYO RAVICZ

I lead a kind of watchtower life here, with an all-around view of the animal works and days. A varied thrush hops over the moss, a butterfly clinched in its beak. The hares stop to inspect me, followed by a foursome of skittish deer. A silver-maned fox watches from the trailhead, flicking his ear as I chop wild chives into my boiled potato. Fox sparrows chink; chickadees flock. I dine outside in the evening when the hermit thrush sings his watery song. It's the loveliest song in all the woods, a swooning, melancholy air. Oh, if you were here it wouldn't be half so melancholy! I was surprised to see a yellow pine grosbeak—the female—and am looking out for her consort. I'll tell you the truth—a brown bear has made Swiss cheese of our inflatable boat. It will take some patching. Would you believe my body has gone into building a bird's nest? I fell asleep one sunny day in the moss. Waking, I found a bird tugging the hairs out of my hairbrush and making off with them! Do you hear the eagles whistling? They descend and shrill and spiral above one another in a kind of sky ballet. Spring fever is here. It reminds me of us.

You haven't changed your mind about coming? Don't! The walls and roof are up—heaven's a leaky roof compared to this one. So you see, our cabin is growing. But some days, I just have to get out on the country, and there's no help for it but to go. Sometimes I'm heartsick with wanting to climb the mountain: it's the distance that separates me from you. Up there I'll be near you. Up there is the awful joy that says I'm alive.

My exemption from solitude, I long to hear your voice and the children's laughter. We'll be like the nesting eagles that guard the barnacled headland and shriek and wheel low over the intruder. How dizzy I am! I kneel in the thick vegetation and part it with my fingers, bringing my lips to the elusive berry. My toes burrow the earth, I wake to the blazing fireweed, and thoughts of the world don't sadden me. The wildflowers hear me coming and twine around my legs. They use me to carry their seeds—I don't mind. The water makes such a din! A pale-bellied salmon jumps three four five times, a kittiwake swoops, a whale rolls his fluked barrel to the sun. I stretch out between the waves and waterfall, the living divide between fresh and salt—yours truly—littoral oddity—champion of the biological sublime.

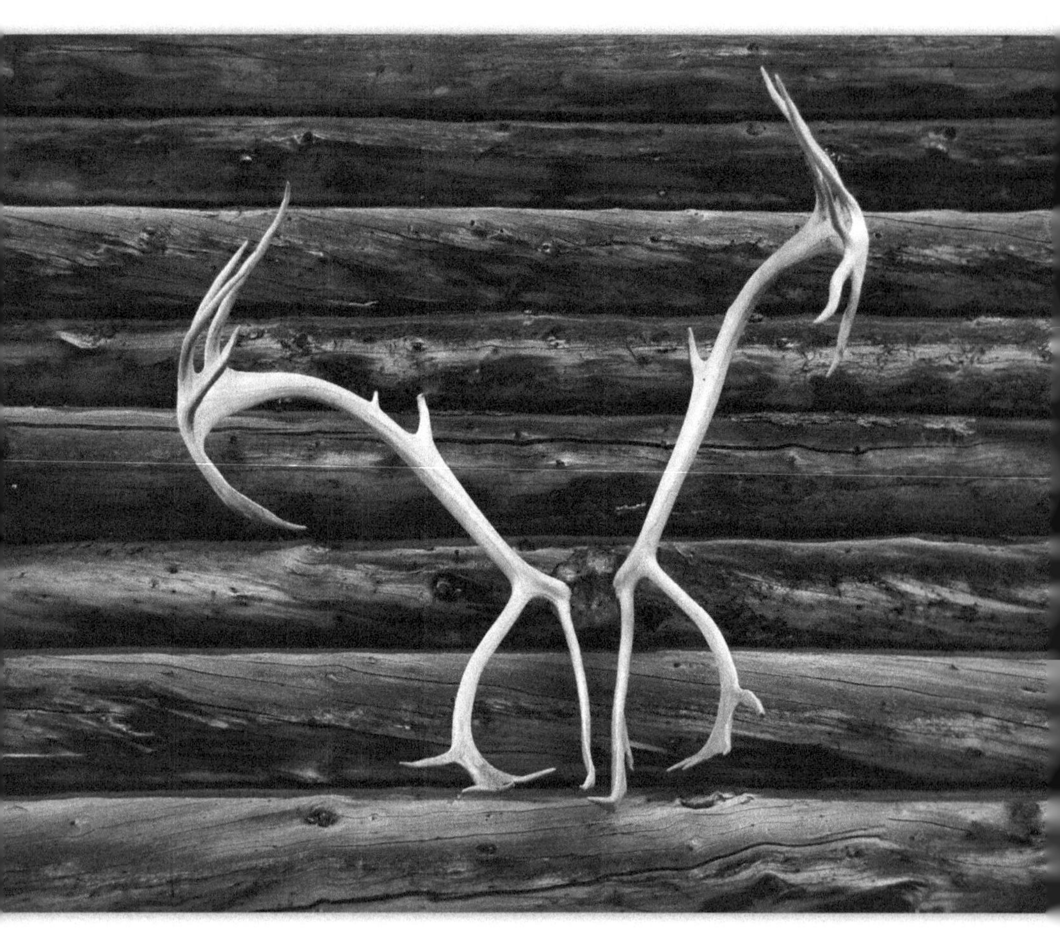

Caribou Antlers at Wiseman, Scott Page

57 Reasons I Love Valerie

(by Go-boy)

MATTOX ROESCH

You—

1. sewed me a sealskin wallet
2. guzzle pop
3. have a thumb that clicks from a fishing accident
4. drive a boat way up North River
5. (*when I asked you to marry me last night, you laughed*)
6. collect birch bark
7. hum hymns
8. wear T-shirts inside out
9. know the old Eskimo ways enough to joke about them
10. know the old Eskimo ways enough to keep them alive
11. (*last night your answer was no*)
12. refuse to treat dogs like people
13. believe Jesus will return as a woman
14. called *The Price Is Right* "monkey wheel"
15. say *crook'd* instead of *crooked*
16. (*when we held hands early last night, walking to the boat, and it was perfectly silent, I could hear you smile*)
17. never zip your backpack shut
18. sure always "been get that good kind"
19. repeat the family stories
20. (*just before I bent down on one knee inside the flatboat, while we floated, you fixed the fuel pump—that's why I proposed*)
21. respect the elders
22. mastered mathematics
23. spell *anthropomorphic* and know what it means
24. pick blackheads
25. volunteer for Elders Lunch
26. (*when I asked you to marry me last night, you had a red Popsicle stain around your mouth*)
27. cooked an omelet out of potato salad, and it was horrible
28. go AC Store for Ding Dongs
29. never drink
30. never judge
31. believe the Apostle Paul had issues
32. hate starting campfires
33. love bacon
34. cry during action movies
35. (*you didn't cry last night*)
36. wear size twelve
37. check *other* on applications under *race*, and write *winner*
38. notice hands
39. consider nudity to be more than sexual
40. bookmark pages with stickers
41. (*you drove the boat home, and didn't look at me the whole way*)
42. distrust TV
43. subscribe to *People* magazine
44. left the village for college, returned to the village for life
45. contradict the idea that living in the village is for failures
46. (*you landed the boat on shore, then ran to your car in rubber boots*)
47. accidentally wave at people when you drive around Anchorage
48. skied to college classes
49. lose your sense of direction easily
50. (*I haven't seen you since*)
51. claim computers are a fad
52. gauge a society by how it treats its elders
53. have experienced insanity
54. (*so maybe you can appreciate how insane I was last night*)
55. once broke my windshield
56. later fixed my windshield
57. (*will you take another boat ride with me tonight?*)

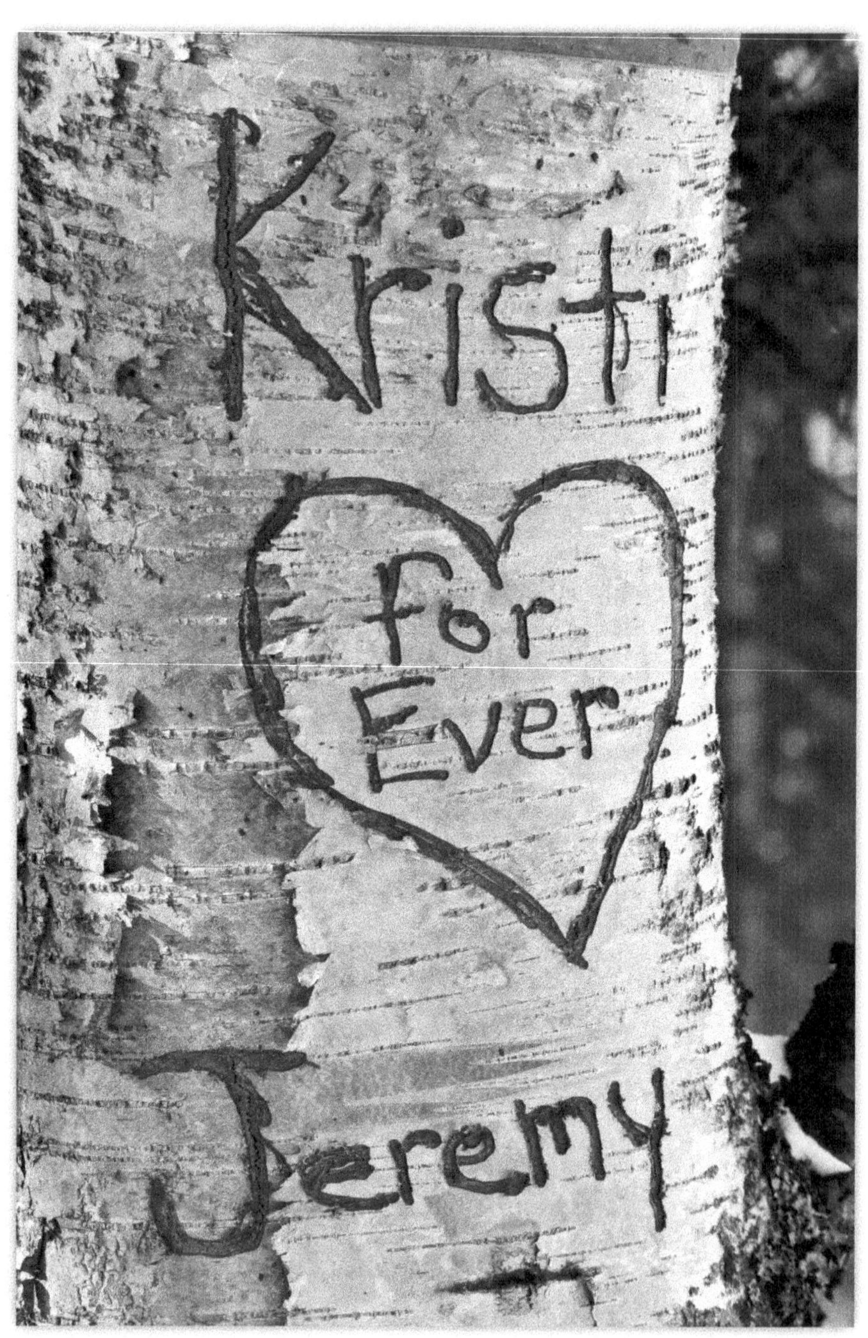

Forever, Jeff Manes

Mistress of the Blue

CELESTE BORCHARDT

She is the perfect mistress. Always ready to receive him. She takes him places no one else can. Astride her, he soars. Cockpit—an apt description of her pelvis.

Being mere mortal, I could not compete. I tried. Wrapped in her legs, I became a member of the Mile-High Club. Repeatedly. But she was his soul mate, I merely a wife. The dispensable one, the one sent back down to the mundane functions of terrestrial life.

What does she give him that I can't? What does she feel like under his hands? Isn't she hard and cold, to my softness and warmth? Can't he see her for what she is—high-maintenance, fickle, and expensive? I take care of the household and the children, am dependable, and affordable.

I should have grasped the significance of his relationship with her on our first date.

Saturday night in Kotzebue, Alaska. Dumbstruck and vibrating with nervousness, he drove to the airport. Within sight of the tarmac, he relaxed. For hours, we walked from hangar to hangar, while he effortlessly expounded on the features, capabilities, and performance of the airplanes.

On our wedding day, members of our community attended both our marriage and the funeral of a local pilot who had flown into a mountain in bad weather. It was as though she was mocking me. "See, I'll get him in the end."

She's almost taken him from me twice. Once, when she quit in midair, and once, when he flew her into the ground in a blizzard. He knows the danger of consorting with her. Yet he returned to her as soon as he was able. Does the risk excite him?

She is a mistress of illusion. She presents as a solid machine with color and mass, containing a heavy engine with a powerful thrust. Then she begins to vibrate, propellers spinning until they become a blur, like scarves whirling around a gyrating harem dancer. Transforming as she leaves the ground, she becomes lighter than air. Her skin darkens to silver-blackness. Then she disappears into the sky, as ethereal as the clouds. The men she leaves behind want only to be with her. Those who have enjoyed her tell tales of their exploits.

To withstand the buffeting of a marriage to a pilot, I have become grounded. I accept my destiny. Either he will fly away with her into the sky, and never return, leaving me earthbound and alone. Or she will spurn him because he has aged and is no longer fit for her. Then, it will be *my* lap he lays his head in, though his dreams may be of her.

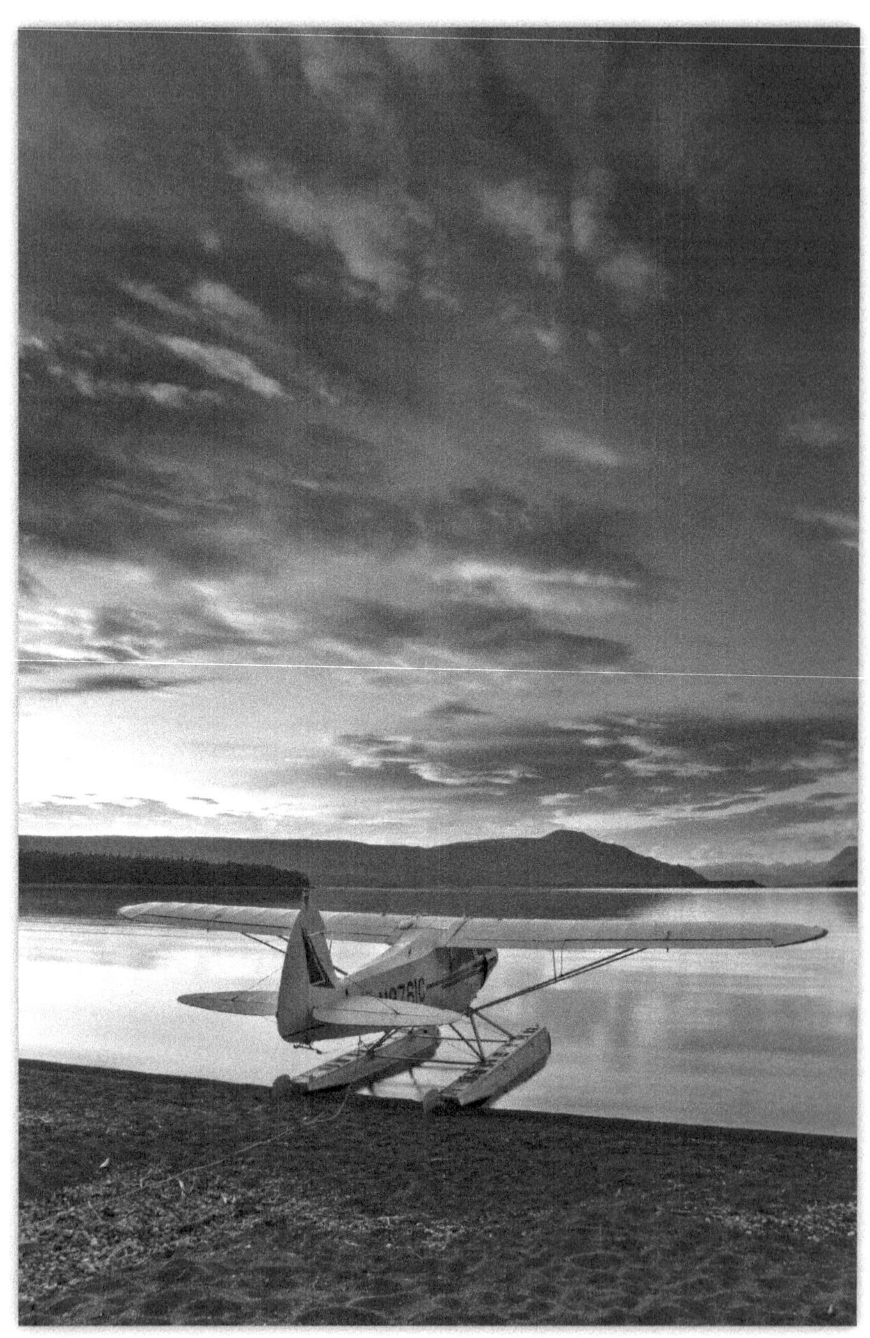

Super Cub at Dawn, Patrick Endres

Coming Clean

MATTHEW EVANS

My boots glide through the dry, airy snow, the upended grains tumbling aside with a muffled *whoosh*. The stars radiate against an inky night sky, while the flawless layer of snow sparkles in response. In the silence, mesmerized, I can't help but think of her.

We hadn't really met until I got to Alaska. It started out innocently enough, some short walks, maybe a day of downhill skiing. For me, it was nothing to be concerned about. My wife was busy with nursing school, and I just needed to fill up my spare time. Besides, our marriage was strong. Yet every year, she would come back into my life, and every year it got worse.

It was her beauty that attracted me first. She was radiant, her complexion lusciously smooth. She dazzled. I couldn't help myself, I just wanted to get out and be with her. Sure, she had a dark side too—even harsh at times. Yet that was the challenge, living with her wild and unforgiving ways. I began to spend more time with her. Pretty soon, it was long snowshoe treks, overnight backpacking trips, and cross-country skiing. I never thought I could be so happy. But amidst all the fun, seeds of guilt grew.

Gazing up at the heavens tonight, I know I have to come clean. I've decided I will go straight home and tell my wife. I can't keep it a secret any longer. I have to tell my wife of seventeen years that I am really and truly in love with winter in Alaska.

I know she won't be happy. The hot sun has her float in contentment. She stays with me in the Great Land mainly because of her serious fishing addiction. But she has no such vice from freeze-up to breakup.

Through the years, we've talked of going Outside in the cold months, somewhere sunny and warm. And to be honest, I'm not willing to give up my long marriage for this newfound love, so I'll probably go along with it. But I'll fight.

I'll fight to stay a little longer than just the arrival of termination dust. I'll try to be here when the cold takes hold. I want to hear the world muffled by a night's heavy snowfall, wake up to a virgin blanket glittering in the sun, and feel my senses tingle in subzero air.

Sure, I'll enjoy the heat, swimming outside in January, and having a mai-tai on a lanai somewhere. But I can't promise that, as I'm lying next to my beautiful wife on a hot sandy beach, I won't, every once in awhile, close my eyes and dream of *her*.

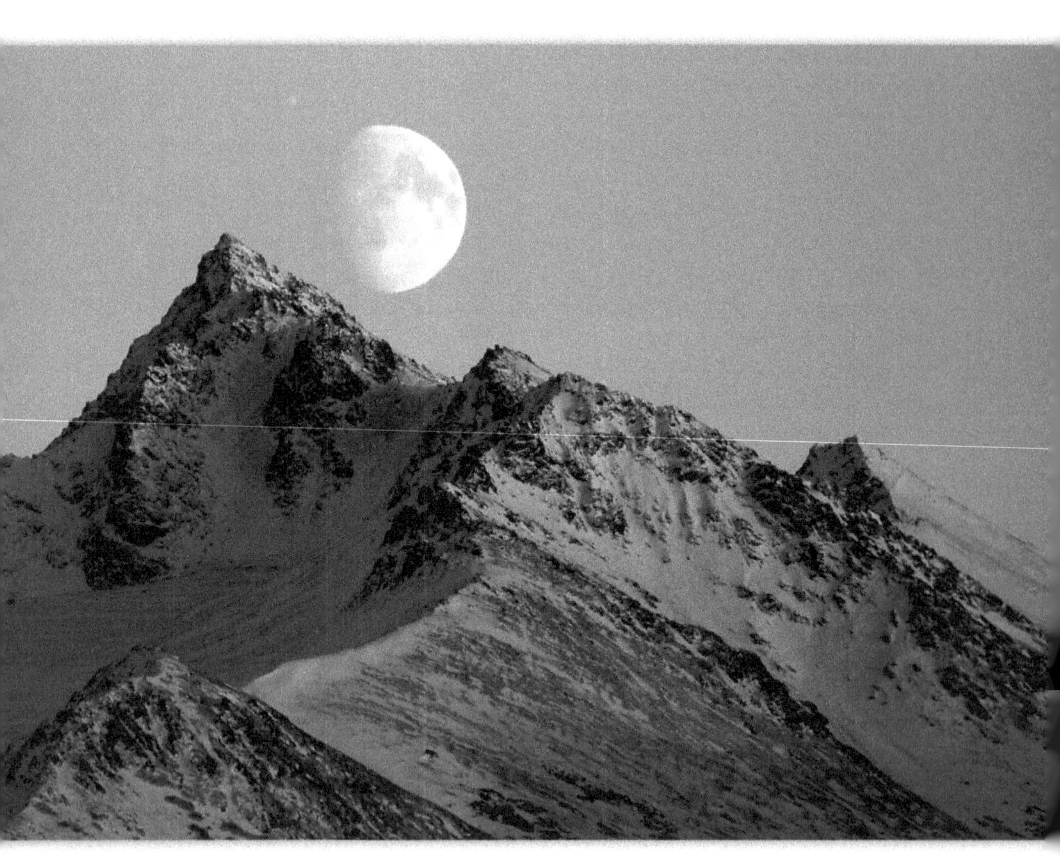

The Sweet Night Light, Bob Butcher

Eclipse

JULIE HAMMONDS

On the night of the lunar eclipse, they'd driven out to Eyak Lake in separate cars and parked behind a screen of trees. Now she stood beside him, watching the earth's red shadow eat the moon.

Of course they were not touching. After all his confessions of longing, Wyatt still hadn't touched her. Wanting him was an ache in her—he made sure of that, always half-promising, then pulling away, only to return once he sensed her learning to live without him. He'd reel Diane back into his life and make her need him again, then take off. When he slid back into town, he wouldn't call but let her run into him on the street, a jolt to the heart.

He was in a reeling-in phase, she guessed, the nearness of his body pulling at her like the moon pulls the sea. He'd called and said there were snow geese on the lake tonight, and would she like to go out and watch the eclipse? He was right about the geese, of course. Wyatt was always right about these things. He knew tides and weather, where salmon were running, how to catch king crabs. No matter how long Diane lived here at the edge of Prince William Sound, she knew she would always be an Outsider. That's what drew her to him from the first: his intimate knowledge of this place.

The road they'd taken to Eyak was her favorite. Farther out from town, the highway balanced on a knife-edge between the Chugach Mountains and the ocean, running between black spruce and across salmon rivers before ending suddenly, deep in the wilderness. Driving the long highway only to arrive nowhere didn't trouble her. She believed the road was its own reward, and drove it as often as she could.

They were the only ones watching the eclipse at Eyak that night. She listened to the geese honking to each other, the neighborly sounds of creatures bedding down. But when the moon faded all the way into shadow, the geese ceased to call. A shiver passed through her, but not of fear. She stood next to Wyatt, waiting for something to happen. It was a night of mysteries: the eclipse, the silent geese. Surely tonight, he could reach for her hand, and mean it; he could pull her close and not let go.

That was back when she still thought he loved her, but wasn't brave enough to say so; before she figured out she'd been fooled. Back when she believed she could never know such secrets as when snow geese were passing by, except through him.

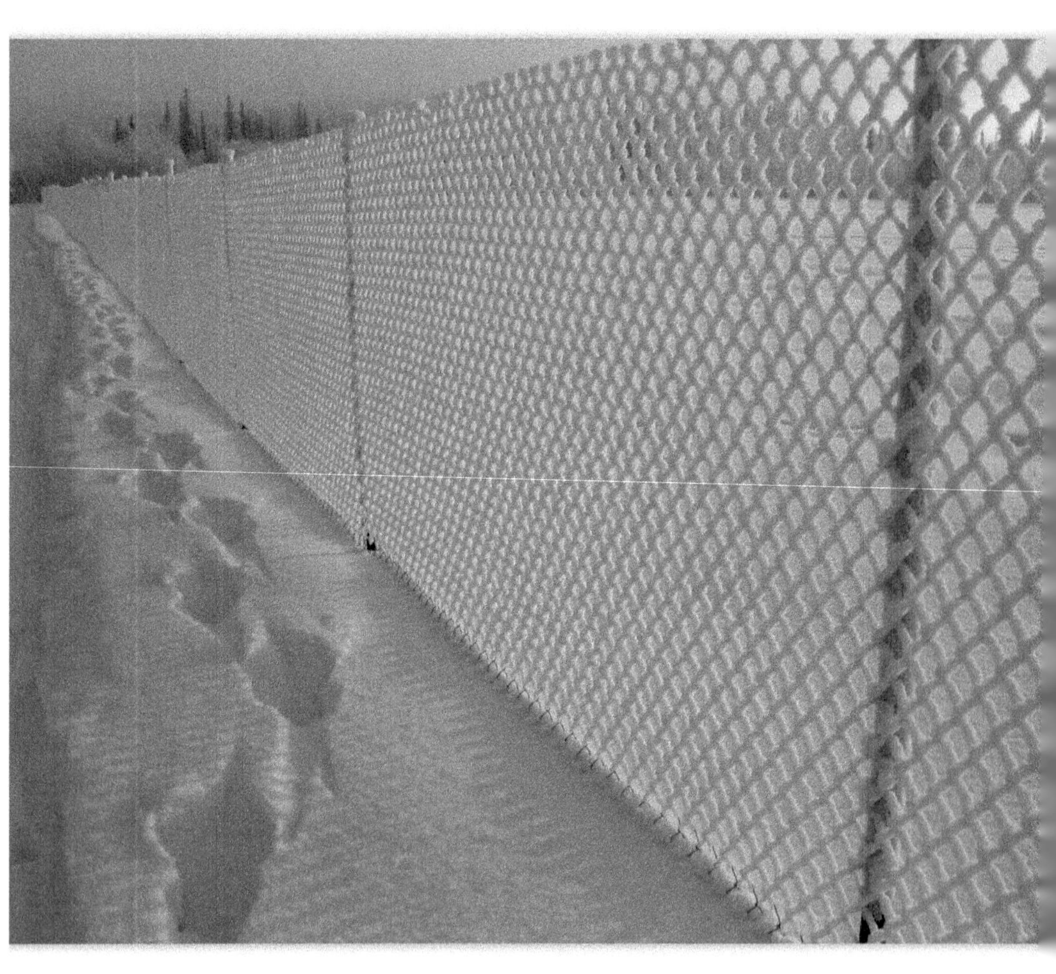

Closed Range, Michael Engelhard

Coffee Talk

MARY COOK

A foggy morning at the airport coffee shop. As I ready the espresso machine, I curse the weather. No plane, no donuts; no donuts, no peace. It's hell being the "coffee shop airline." If they're not complaining about the poor quality of the donuts, they're complaining about the lack of donuts. Half those guys are going to need a wheelbarrow to tote their bellies in if they don't lay off the donuts. But that's not for me to say.

Paper napkins flutter to the floor when the first customer pushes open the front door. He lays a trail of mud from door to donut case.

"No donuts? How come there's no donuts?" He shoves the ball cap back off his forehead.

"Maybe because the fog is down to the runway and the flight from Juneau is on weather-hold?" I slide by him and start a pot of Kirkland's finest.

Soon the coffee shop is filled with middle-aged men with too much time on their hands. Stories are repeated so often that after six years, I can recite them myself. I envy my coworker who is deaf in one ear and almost deaf in the other.

"Hey Russ, did you see Marcia jogging down to the dock yesterday? I bet she and Jonny are on the rocks." Gill sips his coffee and makes a face—he claims the daily brew is always as old and bitter as I am. Ha, ha.

"Yeah, and it wasn't the first time neither. As soon as the ladies start jogging you know they're either having an affair or getting ready for a divorce."

Stu comes in and heads for the donut case; he stops short when he sees the empty shelves. I make him a hot chocolate with extra whipped cream to ease his pain.

"Stu! Nice hat! Is it made out of dog hair?" Scottie looks admiringly at Stu's knitted cap.

"I don't know, could be. I'll ask the wife."

The phone rings. "Wings of Alaska, this is Mary."

"Can you tell me if Joe Johnson's car is parked in the lot?"

I drop the phone and walk to the west window. When you live in the bush it's easy to tell who's out of town by whether or not their car is sitting at the airport. Joe's beaten-up Honda Civic hunkers next to a Ford truck with no wheels. The airport parking lot has become something of a DIY used parts yard. (Note to self: don't park too long at the airport.)

A roar fills the coffee shop as a Cessna 207 rolls to a stop on the ramp.

"Mary, your plane's here! Get out there and unload our donuts!"

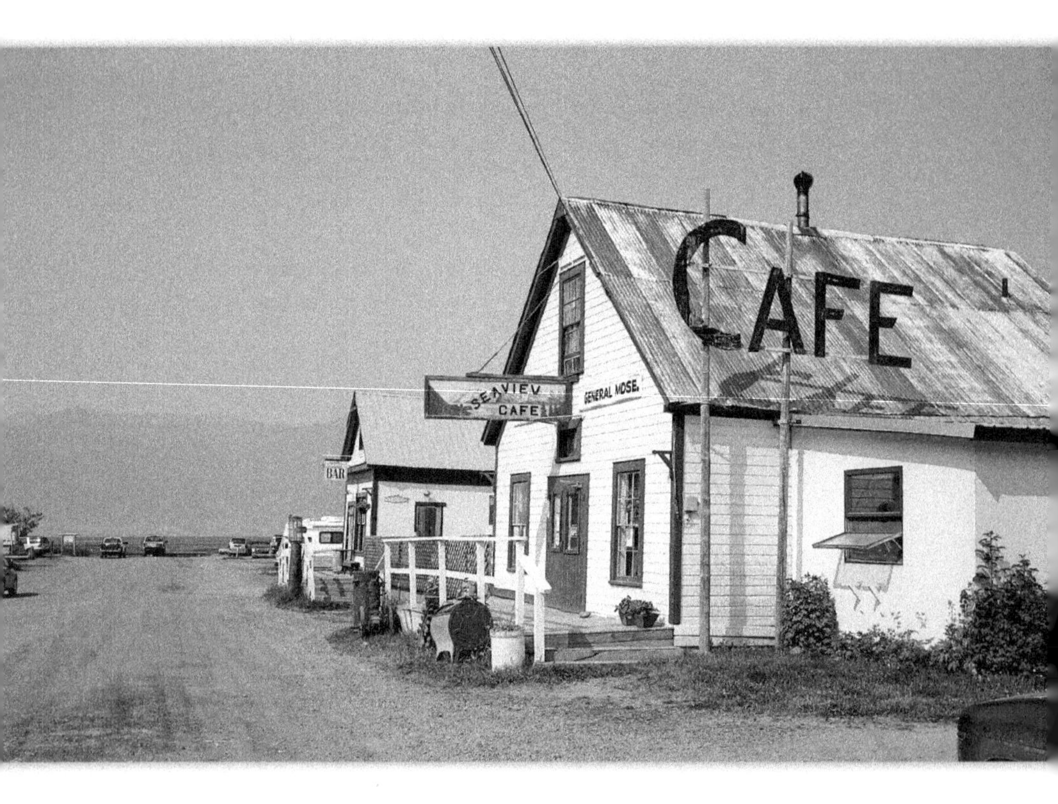

Hope, Alaska, Stephen Nigl

You Don't Lose Your Woman

ROSEMARY AUSTIN

Anyone could see he was no pretty Lower Forty-Eight yuppie mountain climber here for a guided trip to conquer Denali, the Great One. Not one fluff of fleece on his body as he leaned against the bar in Talkeetna, looking at a painting of the mountain with little flags marking locations of climbers on its flanks. No North Patagucchi for him. Nope, he was all Alaskan. From his Ketchikan sneakers to his worn-in Carhartts, his red-and-black flannel shirt, all the way to his stocking cap, loosely knit of tan marled yarn, thick, like what someone would wear if they were spending a lot of time out on the water in the wind. His face was unshaven, tan and windburned, because he had, in fact, been out on the water. He lifted a beer to his lips and took a long drink. He made a face, puckering his lips, and paused, holding the glass in the air as he rested his elbow on top of the bar. The best IPA was like him—bitter. And he had reason to be.

After returning from a season on the boat, a short season at that, he realized the adage his buddies had joked about was true. He'd lost his turn. His woman was gone. Karen had packed up all her things and moved in with Wayne. He took another drink. Well, he thought, though he could have said it aloud, and maybe he had because the bartender, Gus, looked up and nodded in apparent response when he heard, "Well, guess this is how ol' Wayne felt when she left him and moved in with me."

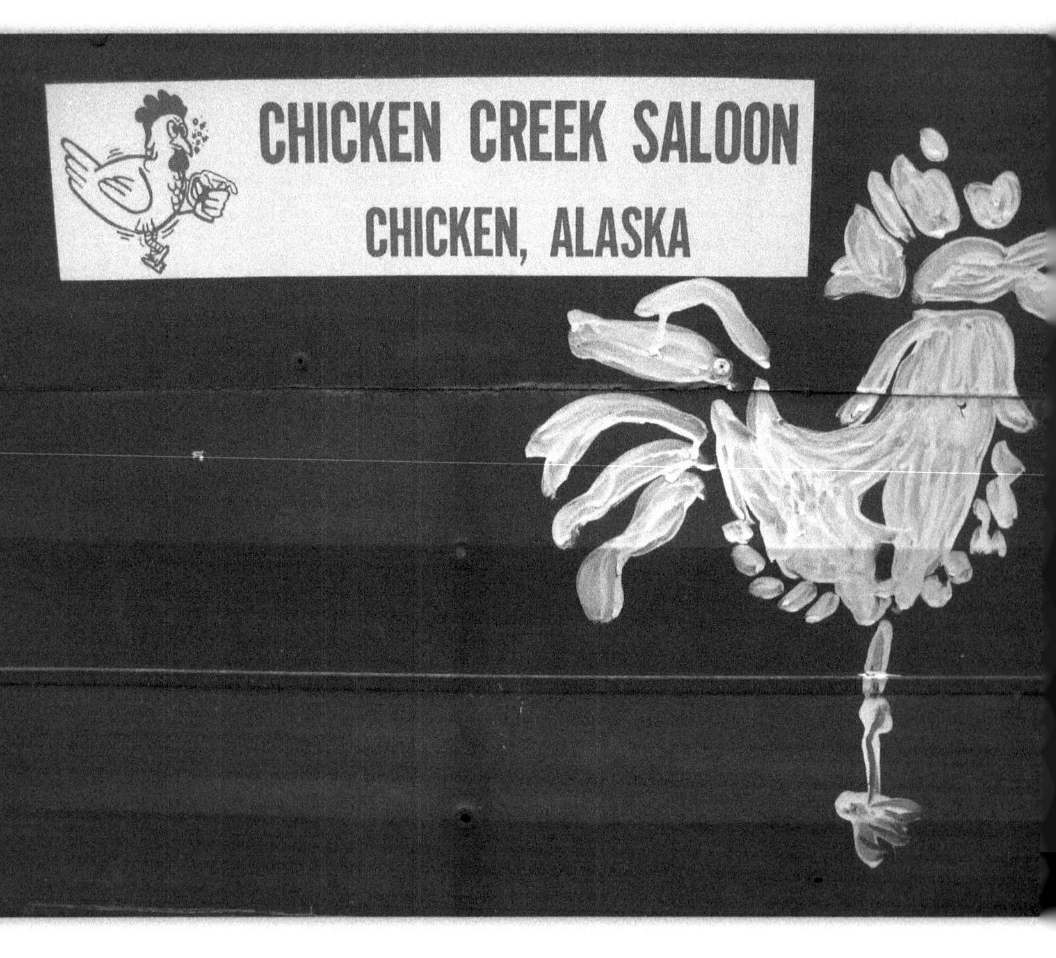

Attractive Chicken, Tara Wheatland

Tough Times on Denali

MICHAEL ENGELHARD

At the Talkeetna airfield, Laurent and I gulp down balmy air, staring in disbelief at a world that wallows in tender greens around the parked Cessna.

After stuffing our faces with real food—pizza and salad at the McKinley Deli—we amble to the bunkhouse for a shower. A glance at the half-blind mirror convinces me that I've lost ten years and about twenty pounds on the mountain. We relish water hot enough to raise welts before charging the historic Fairview Inn like polar explorers would a mirage. But wonder of wonders: this safe haven does not dissolve. I open its hefty door to find the place packed, though it's only four in the afternoon. For a minute I just stand immersed in cigarette smoke and warm humanity, flabbergasted by the den atmosphere. The current of voices, the clinking of bottles and glasses overlaid with women's laughter, the bellowing of climbers glad to be alive, run contrary to the mountain's composure. Climbers outnumber the locals, working hard on hydration. You can tell who is outbound from who just returned. The latter look burnt, raw—reduced, somehow, to an essence. I try to read failure or success in the lined faces. Regardless of outcome, Denali has honed edges in everyone, edges that cut into new and lasting truths.

The rounds keep coming, and I don't know who's buying. By the time dusk—or what passes for it on summer solstice—dims the windows, our waitresses have kicked off their shoes and no longer run tabs. As the home planet wobbles precariously on its axis, racing back toward winter, I become nauseous. Before I leave, I catch sight of Laurent atop the bar. Weaving like a bamboo wand in a gale, he plants a miniature Swiss flag on the summit of an oil painting of Denali, having a tough time with it. But till dawn at least, for him and for others in here, wild abandon will cloak memories, lodged firmly as ice screws, of a body laid out in a black rubber cocoon at 14,200 feet.

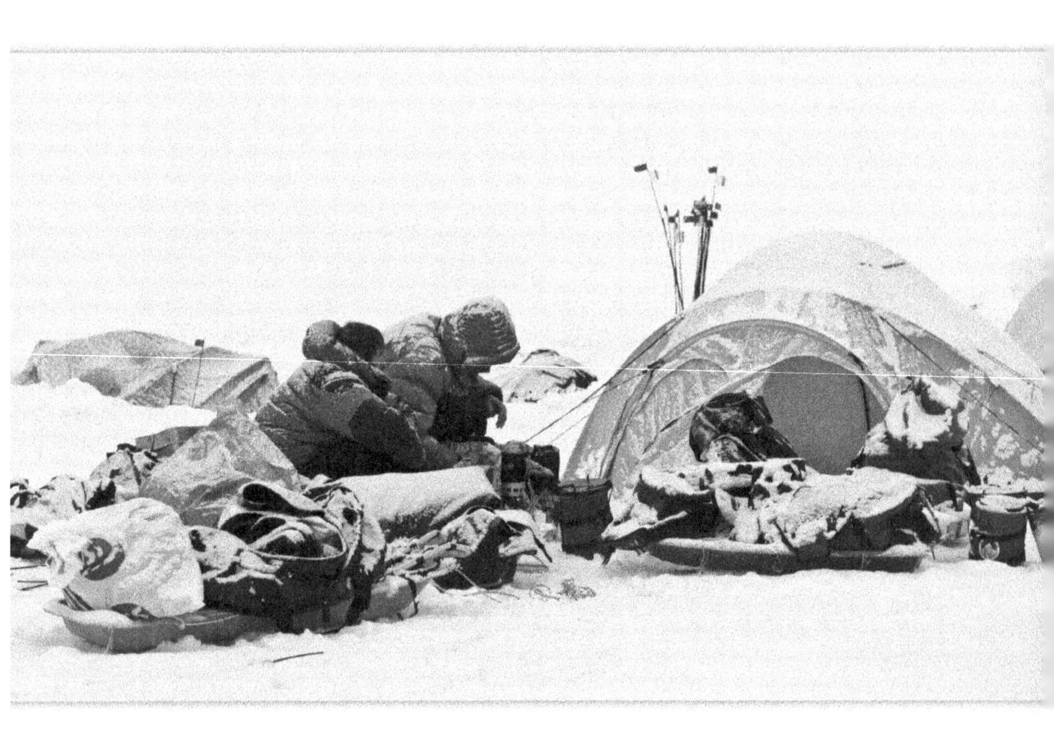

Whiteout, Doug Demarest

Here Comes Ol' Flattop

DAVID STEVENSON

In the dozen or so times I climbed Flattop last winter we didn't see any other hikers. In summer, the Glen Alps parking lot can be full, and all manner of hikers make the pilgrimage including sandaled kids, miniature yapping dogs, and an unusual number of semi-invalids—more power to them. It's the closest peak to most of Anchorage and more or less the easiest.

In winter it's a different encounter: weather, a sliver of danger, and solitude, the very qualities I value, if history is any measure. On Dimond Boulevard, one thermometer says 6 and the other −6. But it's really about the wind.

Once we leave the frozen road for the frozen trail we're moving single file and conversation is over. Every few hundred yards we huddle together to ask if we're still doing this. Apparently we are. Upward, each in a separate universe of wind and icy footing.

The last five hundred feet have too much snow to find what might have been a trail, and no one has been here to leave tracks, and it's been too windy anyway. We're all wandering more or less randomly. The gusts are strong enough to knock you off your feet if your balance isn't perfect. The wind is blowing ice under my glasses, which are fogged up from my breathing, and pretty soon, the wind *does* knock me to the ground, and I'm crawling blindly up the mountain. I remember a film version of Lear—in Russian—with blind Lear crawling over the moors bewailing his fate in universal moaning and English subtitles. I feel like that, except for the wailing part. Probably I'm not wailing only because I'm reasonably confident I could crawl all the way back to the car if I had to.

The wind stops for a beat, and the whooshing I hear is my heart pushing blood through my body at a manic pace, thundering in my eardrums. Above us the wind has blown a hole in the sky, and I see that on Peak Two a lone skier has made a dozen perfect turns down the otherwise untouched west face. Man, I think, that's a lot of work for a dozen turns.

Then I realize that I'm probably working harder than the skier was but will not soon be experiencing the pleasure of those twelve perfect turns. I must be doing it for some other reason. And it's not about the summit, a place I have been dozens of times in every possible condition. I am slow to arrive at the obvious, and, yes, I know it's a cliché: this is a form of daily practice, each step its own reward.

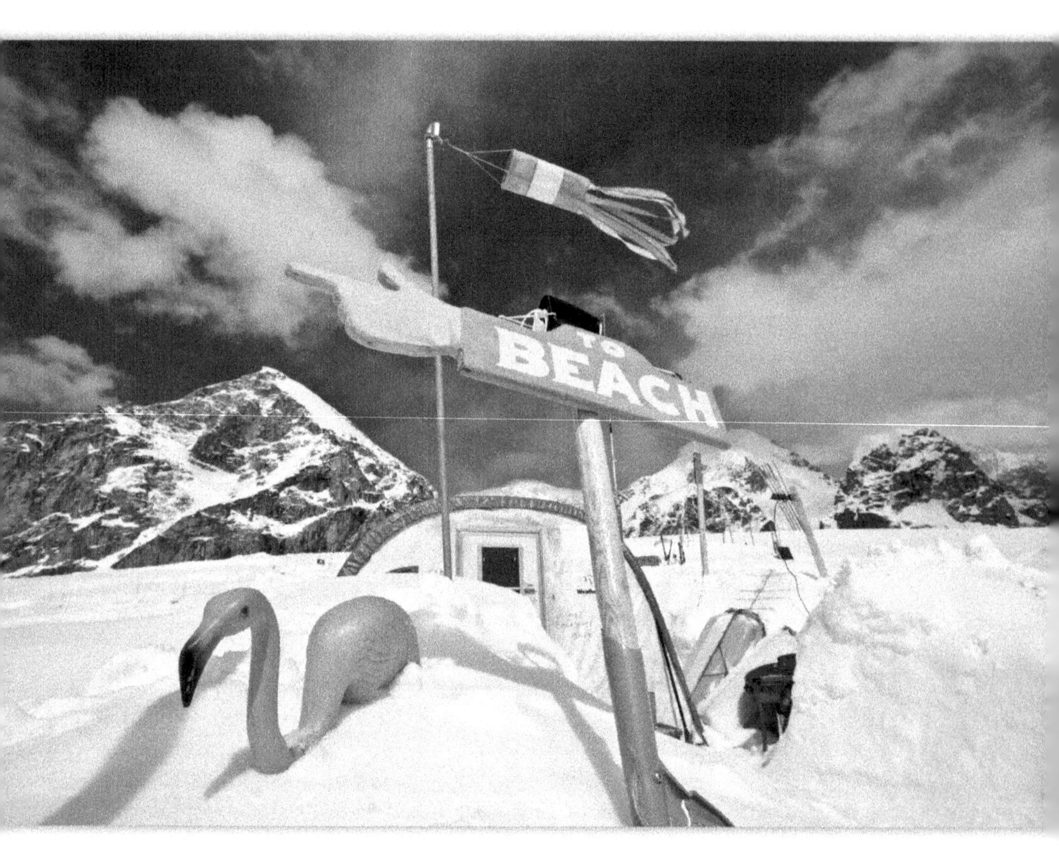

Kahiltna Basecamp, Doug Demarest

Blue in the Face

NABIL KASHYAP

This isn't where I'm from. I'm a visitor. I hold the hands of other visitors, help them onto the ice. I *guide* them onto the ice. Because the glacier is a good place to people-watch. To watch people watch. Watch out, I point, then the people point. Goosenecks cut by meltwater raked diagonally in dust. A waterfall, small and so clear you wouldn't see it but for its shadow. A crevasse, a cleft, something that leaves no room for speaking, something vast and deep and that blue.

They might squint even if there isn't any sun. The ice is hard to consider. I watch as little recognitions flit across their faces. But if they look too long, even as they check, recheck, the miniature versions, digital and dangling from their wrists, they will not recognize it. The ice isn't to blame, ice doesn't have color, nor does any water pooled on top. Not mere reflection, not the wavelength of any *thing*, this is the color of light examining the structure of the glacier, of light filling up the ice and spilling out.

How far down does it go, they ask. Of course I have my lines. The depth of the pond is deep, I say. Remember, there isn't much between *casual* and *casualty*. It's my job to think about that, the worst case. Personally, I don't think it would be the worst—oblivion isn't so bad—but you'd feel bad if you were caught courting it. One of the first signs of hypothermia is introversion, a turning inwards. Turning? Here, you'd be thrust, rocketed toward your core—crown of the head? behind the ribs? wherever—there must be a center, surely.

Most people don't shy away. They test the right crampon's purchase, edge closer. Yes, trust your feet. Yes, the spikes will hold. Hold on. A little back, a body's length at least. Go on. Wait. Mixed signals, I know. Not the first time I've been accused. So you're a little bewildered, that's fine. I'm struggling myself. I'm staring down an ultramarine hole roaring with water, trying not to be mesmerized. And I'm looking at you, gauging whether the lust in your eye is dangerous.

Like death, a friend once said. Her first time on the ice, and she was struggling to describe the color of a pool of water. Whether you arrived in a truck, in a chartered plane, on a bicycle, whether the sight of crampons thrills or makes you sleepy, whether you have cajoled your girlfriend onto the ice or were cajoled—makes no difference. With its singing voice, that color will call after you.

Careful, please.

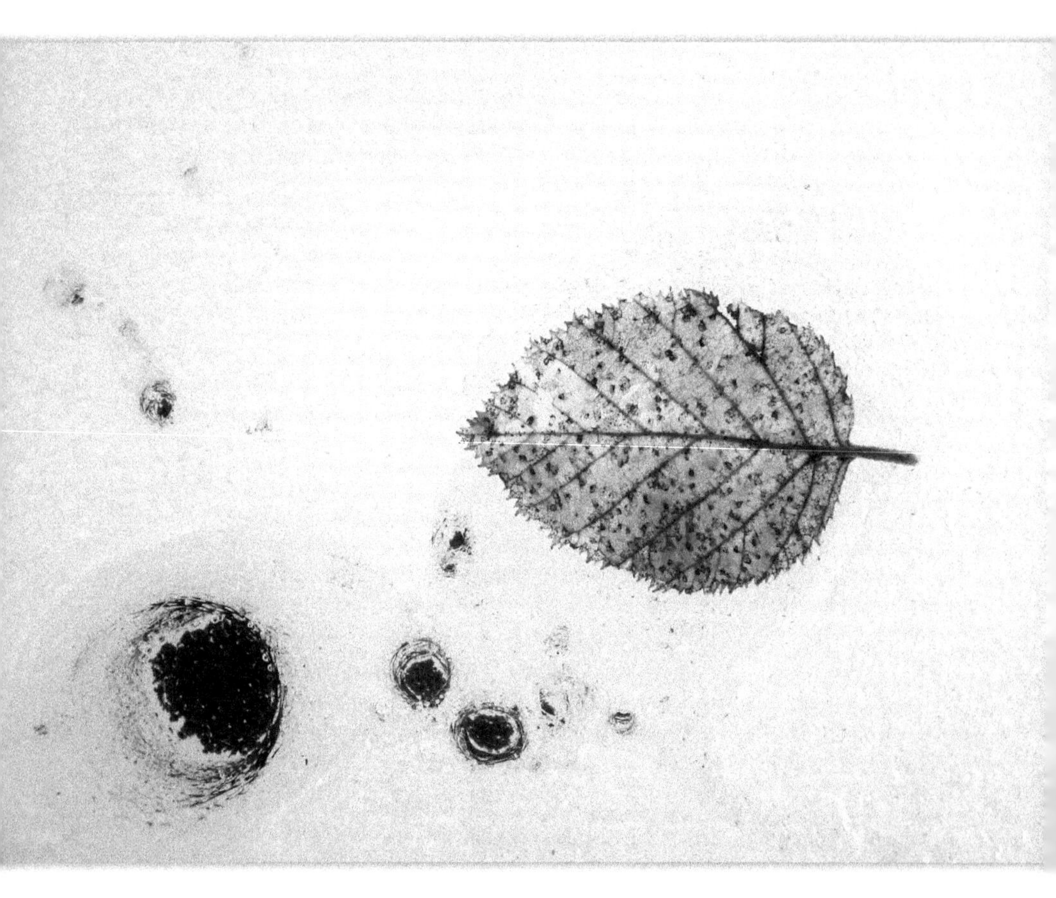

Nizina Glacier, Michael Engelhard

The Guide

JULIE HAMMONDS

Stephanie begins to regret taking this assignment as her clients relax by the campfire, waiting for her to cook the first night's dinner. The two boys—the bold one ten years old, the seven-year-old stuck to him like a shadow—are whining. "We're bored," the older one declares, and they run off to find sticks so they can bat pebbles into the ocean. It's a harmless game, but the shouts and plunks soon get under Stephanie's skin. Plus, now she's alone with Gail and Steve, and she still doesn't know what they're doing here, why these city people chose a guided trip to the bear-viewing station at Pack Creek over the chance to play tourist in town.

Now she needs to keep the boys in sight without messing up dinner. They don't make this easy, scooting up to the forest's edge for bigger sticks, darting back to the shoreline to take turns batting. Their parents relax on rocks near the fire, nursing glasses of wine, unconcerned. It's obvious the boys are Steph's problem, but being treated like a babysitter never sits well with her. She prefers to be valued as a naturalist, appreciated for everything she knows about the Southeast rainforest.

They haven't asked about the salmon runs, or the sheltering spruces, or even the patterns of weather and tide. Maybe watching bears along the creek tomorrow will tune them in, Steph thinks. It feels like that to her: nature humming along in its own quiet key, people playing their rightful parts if they pay attention. Maybe that's why the boys' noises bother her—they're out of sync with the music she wants to hear, shush of breeze through spruces, splash of silver salmon.

That's when she notices she can't hear them; the boys, that is. Absorbed in the drudgery of cooking dinner for five, she's lost the thread leading to their location. She looks to their mother, instinctively, but Gail and Steve have moved to the same rock and Stephanie now sees why they came here with a guide, her vision of herself as a babysitter firming into certainty.

Where are the boys? Stomach clenching, Stephanie scans the cove's forested edge, eyes tracing from tree to tree. She doesn't want to alarm her clients, but this is a wilderness, not a baseball diamond, and the boys aren't schooled enough in its dangers to go off on their own.

She still doesn't see them. Dropping her head, Stephanie draws a long, settling breath and sets down the ladle she's been using to stir the fragrant stew. "Gail, Steve," she says quietly. "The boys."

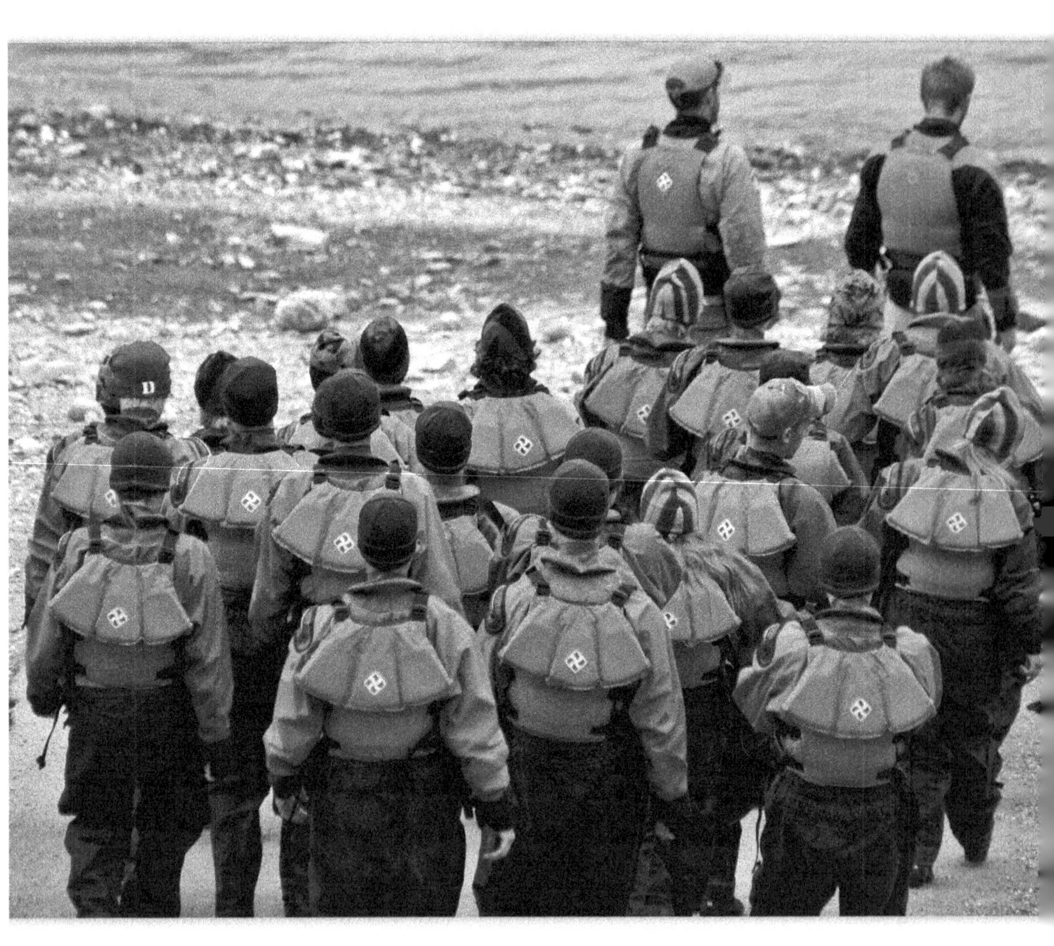

The Guides and the Guided, Laurent Dick

The Cold

ANNE CORAY

Long after Margaret left, Dehlia lay in bed, not sleeping. A great horned owl sounded in the distance: *whoo, whoo, whoo, whoo, whoo.* That would be a male, sending his five haunting notes out into the wilderness in search of companionship. Dehlia imagined him, feathers fluffed, ears upright, eyes slightly narrowed, perched in the wings of a tall spruce. She had never seen an owl with a mate, though she'd heard that they mate for life. But how solitary seemed their existence.

She recalled what she knew about the great horned: how they will defrost a frozen cache of prey by incubating it; how a brooding parent is often covered with snow; that their longest recorded life span is seventeen years, far longer than their average life expectancy. It didn't seem fair that a bird so well adapted to the northern climate shouldn't live to be a hundred, but, Dehlia thought, it wasn't any better for the bears and moose. And what did fairness have to do with anything?

She climbed out of bed and wandered to the northwest window. A cloud passed, exposing a half moon and a jumble of stars. She touched the line of frost on the bottom of the pane. Her fingertip burned and she held it to her lips, sucking gently to relieve the sting.

In the distance, the outline of Lost Mountain traced the skyline. At three thousand feet, it stood apart from the surrounding hills, a dutiful sentry at its post. It was not the most spectacular mountain in the country; the eastern peaks were higher, more rugged, of stronger, more durable stone. But Lost Mountain held a special charm for Dehlia, despite its wistful name. *Dghhili Shtunalgguk,* the Dena'ina called it, literally "Mountain Where She Lost Her Way." The story was of a six-year-old child who had been separated from her parents and companions when she fled camp in the middle of the night after a terrifying dream. It had taken three days to find her.

Back in bed, Dehlia ran one hand up and down Phil's side: the sheets were smooth but cold. She pulled another blanket up from the foot of the bed and hugged her T-shirted arms to her body. *Loneliness,* Margaret had asked, *How do you fight it?* And for the first time Dehlia sensed that her world, her defenses, were only illusion, and in the right circumstance all would collapse, leaving a hole so huge and raw that no soft words, no flannel wrap, no images of swans or ermine or snowshoe hares could fill it.

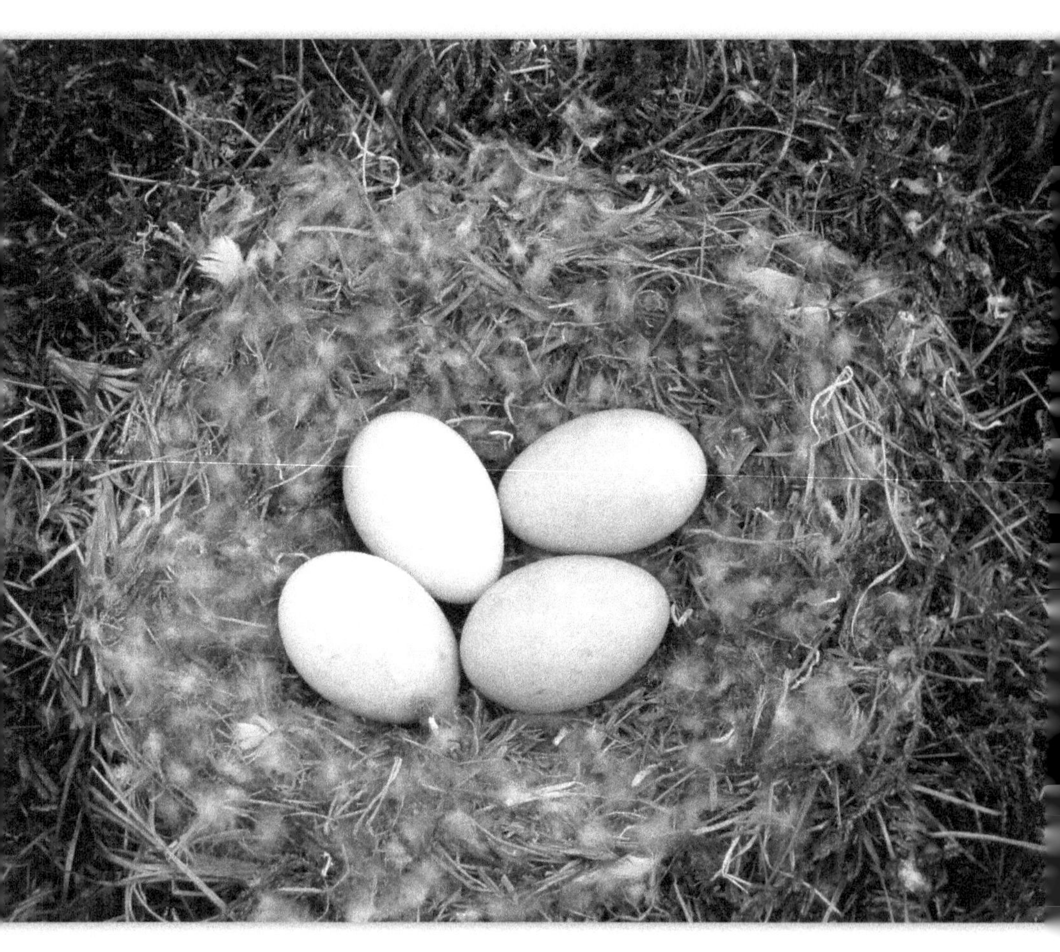

White-fronted Goose Nest, Adrian Gall

Grimshaw on the Ice

KATEY SCHULTZ

Three months on the ice and the thought of three more made me skull-duck crazy. After a while, you start to see white rainbows. There are more shades of white here than polar bears. Sunset white and sunrise white. Ice white, blue white, and just-about-to-crack-open white. Egg white, dark white, pus white . . .

We made a game of it after Grimshaw hit his head. "I'm seeing white," he said, then realized his mistake. He meant fake white. Wrong white. The kind of white that dances a two-step in front of you while you clutch your forehead and try to remember what happened.

Specialists on the island were few—we liked to call it the island to feel exotic, like one morning we'd wake up to cacao trees and amaryllis, a dozen monkeys beating their chests. I bribed our only surgeon to take a look. He puckered his cracked lips around a flask and tipped his chin to the ceiling. Clicking his tongue after a long pull of whiskey, he leaned over Grimshaw, who looked like a pile of damp clothing in the bunkhouse corner. The surgeon unfolded the corkscrew on his Swiss Army knife. "This ought to relieve some pressure," he said, then laughed wickedly. He hadn't been right since his first winter.

"Get out," I told him, kicking the door as it shut behind him.

Grimshaw squinted at me and moved his arms slightly, as though trying to hoist himself from the bed. Slowly, I lifted him up and angled for the door. A petrified ox could have moved easier than the two of us. I nearly dropped him. Two hundred twenty-five pounds plus subzero gear and work boots heavy as ice blocks. Even my best fireman's carry wouldn't cut it.

Later that night I salvaged an old wheelbarrow from the junk pile and heaved Grimshaw out of the bunkhouse. His head bobbled like a puppet's as I wheeled him across the ice, one leg dangling over the side of the barrow. The heel of his boot clapped an embarrassing beat against the metal.

Fifty yards from the research station, I stopped to let Grimshaw have a look at the sky.

"Look," I said. "Look at them all."

"Star white," he said.

"You nailed it," I told him. "The Captain says you're gonna make it, Grimshaw."

"Liar," he said. He rolled his eyes in their sockets until his gaze met mine. He might have smiled. "Don't let them put me in the pile, okay? Wheel me someplace else."

The next morning Grimshaw was gone. Dead white. Ghost white. Now-you-see-him, now-you-don't white.

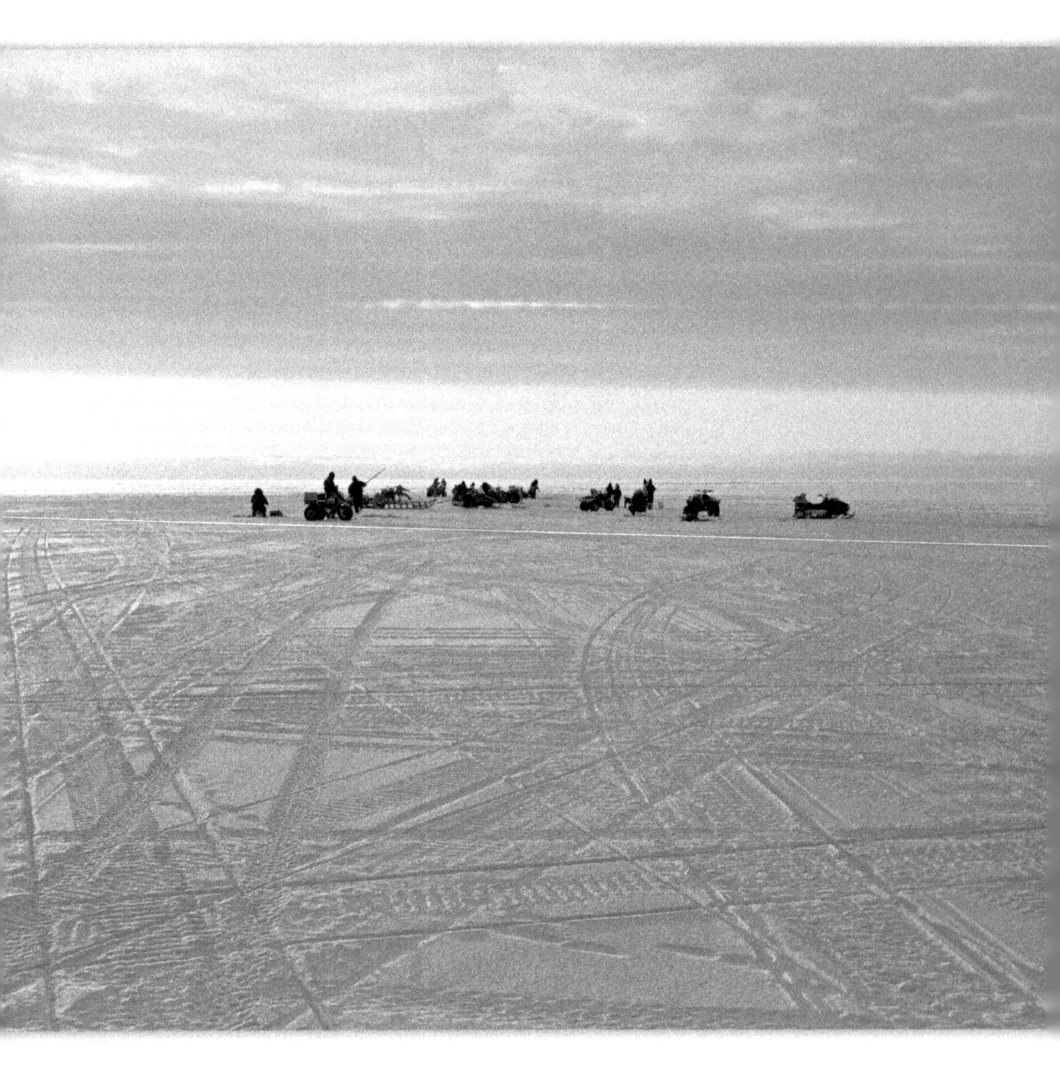

Fishing for Tomcod, Dennis Witmer

Matanuska Green

REBECCA GOODRICH

Psst! Want some weed?

Sure I did, we all did. Craved it. But you had to be smart.

We tromped the snow behind the corner of the dorm, behind some dead trees.

What you got?

He pulled off his ski mask, giving the filter a reflexive little tap. The best. Very, very fresh.

That's what they all say, these dealers.

Never frozen, he assured me.

I eyeballed him as he slid the package from the armpit sleeve in his jacket, his briefly ungloved fingers fanning like a raven's wing.

Sometimes you could tell if they'd been using their own product by their skin, their eyes.

He urged me. Try a pinch—It'll make you feel like it's 1985.

Course I tried it. It was free, wasn't it?

I chewed. Slowly. Swallowed. Savoring. Tried not to sigh.

What's the point of origin?

He just crossed his arms, puffy in the parka. Smiled, eyes clear as the sunrise coming in six weeks.

Good stuff, isn't it? Pure water, full spectrum light, if you know what I mean.

I was still teasing the taste through my mouth with my tongue. Feeling it work on me, even that little bit. Oh, yeah. I started looking for my wallet. It was somewhere in my recycled wool backpack. Finally I shook everything out, trying not to lose anything in the long twilight of winter: stainless steel water bottle with filter, only a little banged up. Stainless mess kit. Old cotton napkin. Red-flavored lunch bars. My e-thingamajig, bookmarked at *Silent Spring* and some other boring reading my girlfriend had given me. Air filter spares.

My guy was getting nervous with me taking all this time. Usually they offered, you paid, they faded. His nose dripped from the cold, just like mine. He slipped his mask back on, adjusted the carbon form to his face.

Oh it was good. Good. Authorities didn't like you to have this stuff. My girlfriend sometimes called them "The Establishment." Said it messed with your mind. Made you want things you couldn't have, things that were gone. Like what, I'd asked. Like the blue sky, she'd said. Then she'd cried.

I had just enough for the transaction. He gave me the little baggie—recycled, of course. He left and I stayed in the shadows, chewing my spinach leaves: Matanuska green.

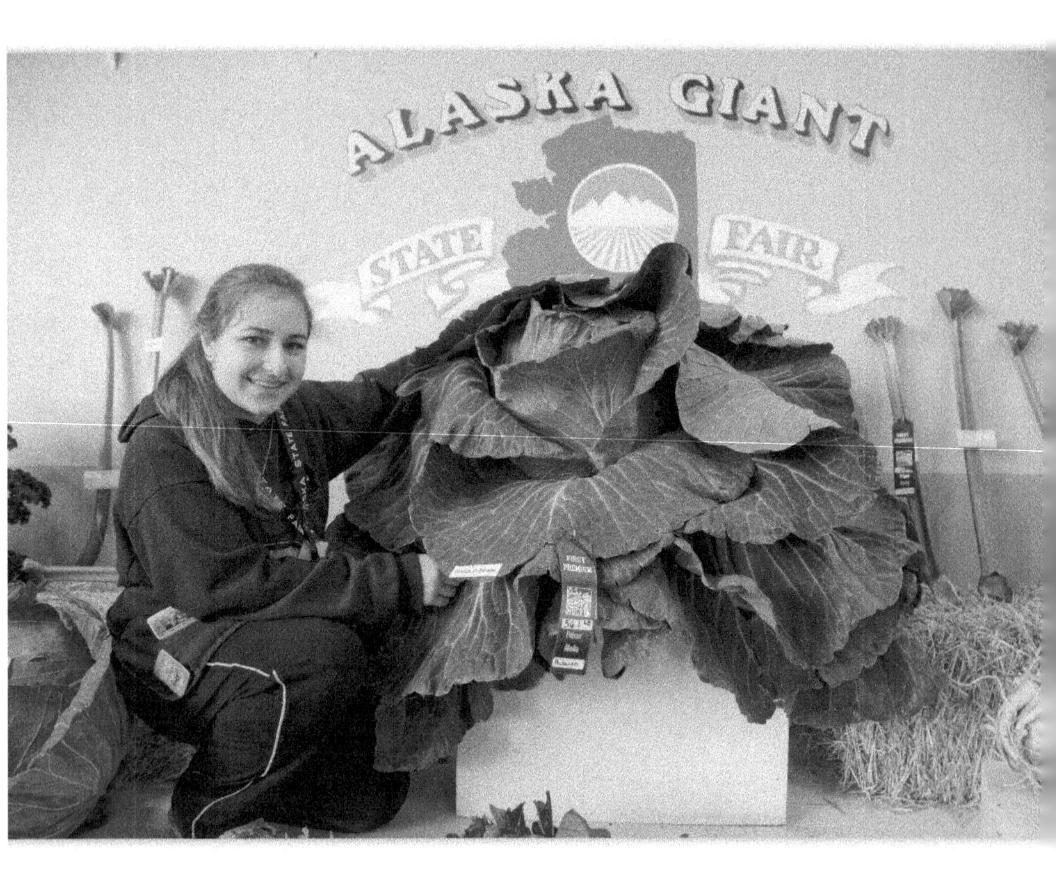

Alaska Giant, Patrick Endres

Christmas on the Fortymile

LOUISE FREEMAN

I was living in San Jose and longing for Alaska. I'd call Sam at his cabin outside Eagle and beg him to tell me a story. A true story. An Eagle story. In the long pause, as he considered which tale to tell, I heard the silence of the subarctic winter just outside his window. I heard the dog curling its tail over its nose and going to sleep despite the bitter cold. I heard the smoke trailing from the chimney into the still midnight air. He told me about the woman who was left alone in a trapline cabin on the Fortymile River for two weeks just before Christmas when her husband went to Eagle for supplies. They were down to beans and pancake mix. In the silence of his sudden absence, the eight-by-eight-foot cabin seemed empty, and the voles took over. At first the mouse-like creatures stayed on the floor. But without two people coming and going, dancing around each other just to get from the bunk to the door, the voles became bolder. They started running over the bed at night, scampering across her as she shrank further down into the sleeping bag. They scrabbled around in the beans. They scritched and scratched and chewed and gnawed.

Her husband was over a week late. She lay awake at night, hating the voles, unable to sleep for fear her husband lay dead along the trail. Then they got into the pancake mix. Their feet, white with flour, left little tracks across the table. That was the last straw. She took to sitting up at night clutching a big hickory knife. By the light of a candle, she struck. Chop. A vole lay in two on the table. It was simple. "Steal from me and you die," she said. Hack. A vole lay in three. It was a grisly tableau.

The woman huddled, sitting up, in a sleeping bag at the foot of a bunk bed, on the table in front of her a scattering of vole parts. She kept it up night after night until she was winning the battle. The voles were fewer and farther between. She would have kept it up, still, but one night, she caught sight of her shadow against the wall, a crazed woman with a large carving knife poised over her head, lunging forward to strike. "That's it," she said. "I've gone over the edge." The next day her husband returned and they had dry milk and sugar, cheese and butter, raisins and rice and even a couple of oranges, and the voles had gone into hiding again. It was Christmas.

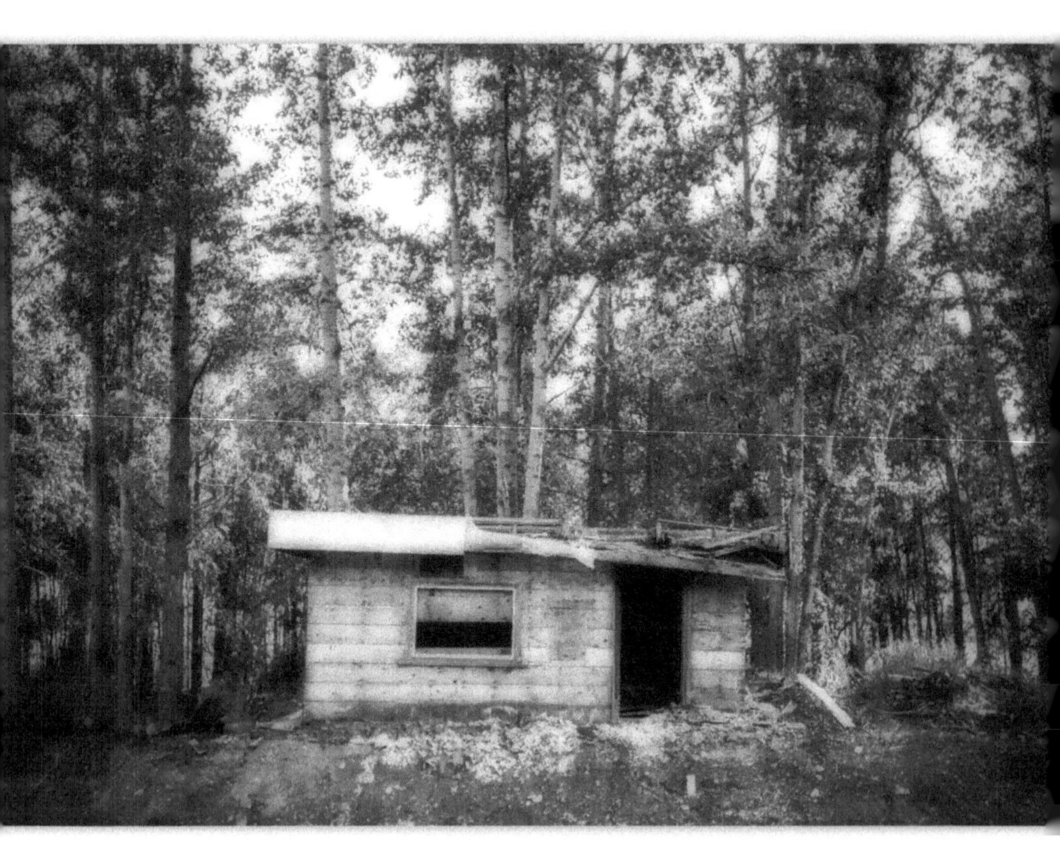

The Shack, Stephen Nigl

The F-Month

NITA NETTLETON

Lola chucked a dry piece of birch into the woodstove. She eased down into the old rocker and closed her eyes to listen to the wonderful snap and pop of her sleepy fire waking up. When there was enough light to see her hoar-frosted woodshed, she inventoried its contents from the kitchen window and moaned, "It's not enough."

Turning slowly on her bad hip, Lola carried a steaming bowl of oatmeal to her table and tried not to look at the calendar. "Probably still February," she grumbled to the molasses. "What's wrong with this month? Why does it have to be so cold for so long? What would be the big deal about warming up a few degrees? Something must be broken somewhere."

After breakfast, Lola stared at the woodpile again, willing it to be bigger. Firewood is life, she thought; it's not just comfort. It's as important as every single breath in the winter. She squinted at the crisp southern skyline, willing a mess of clouds to form. No clouds formed. She limped back to check the calendar: still February.

Two cups of tea demanded a trip to the outhouse. Lola put on enough clothing to be outside at forty below. "May as well stay out and do chores," she said in matter-of-fact resignation to her insulated pants, sweaters, parka, bunny boots, scarf, flap hat, and mitts. As soon as the cold air hit her face, she wished she'd started dressing sooner, and hustled.

Back from the outhouse, Lola answered a fluffed and frost-rimed raven that lectured her from the roof. "Oh, you know a thing or two, don't you?" In the woodshed, she caressed each frozen row of neatly split and stacked birch. Slowly, she picked up and stacked what lay scattered around the splitting block from the last time she'd been in there. The work loosened up her back and hips. She whistled an old tune that matched the rhythm of the work. Stooping one last time for her Swede saw and the tow rope of her red sled, Lola straightened up, took a deep breath, and turned to admire her home surrounded by a heartbreakingly beautiful crystal forest. The raven still sat on the roof, watching and nattering.

"You worry too much," Lola said. "I'll hit that nice deadfall down by the creek. Saw up a sled-full. Be back in time for my nap." She laughed, dropped the saw into the sled, and began to pull. Between foggy, sun-kissed breaths and deliberate steps, Lola admitted to herself, if not to the raven, that February was the most beautiful month.

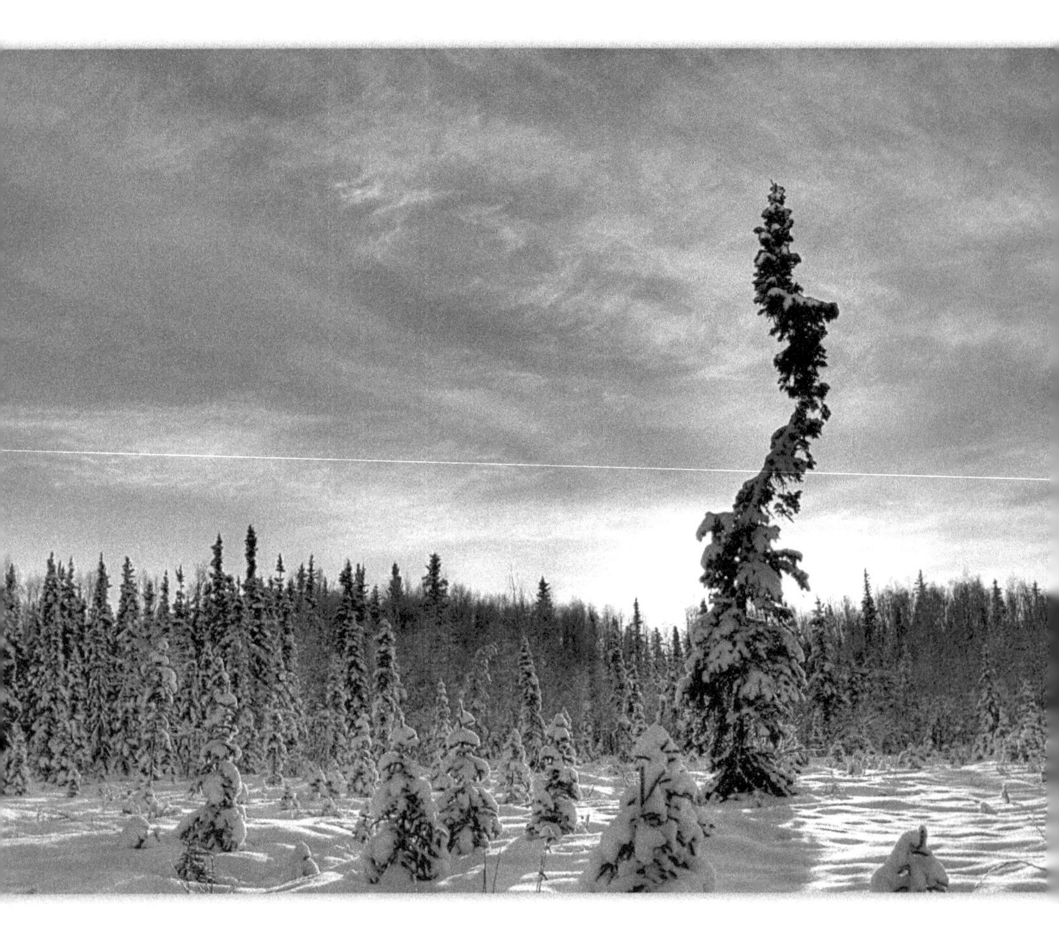

Crooked Tree, Tom Jamgochian

A Special Place

(with deference to Aldo Leopold)

CAROLYN KREMERS

The outhouse. Oddly, that's the first thing that comes to mind when I think of a place special to me.

Driving into town this January afternoon, I felt that arctic winter light, all pink and blue and yellow, like a watercolor wash. Peaks and lumps of the Alaska Range, sticking up like paper dolls. My faith that a moon would be rising as the sun sank (3:45 p.m., it must have been). And the memory of sanctitude, the promise of the day: sitting in the doorless, tilted outhouse when the moon dips down, exactly opposite, a peaceful, quartz-like globe with a face in it, about to disappear into the chilly morning behind Ester Dome.

Nightly, too, she glides—over Chena Ridge—a sliver or a half circle or, just once each month, full: soundlessly spilling her liquid light (if she's not obscured by clouds) upon the birch trees and the willow branches, the hillside and the sauna cabin, the driveway and the Subaru, the woodshed and the sawhorse, the moose tracks and the dog tracks, the squirrel's and the vole's ... shepherding my footsteps, up the snowy wooden stairs, from the cabin to the outhouse and back.

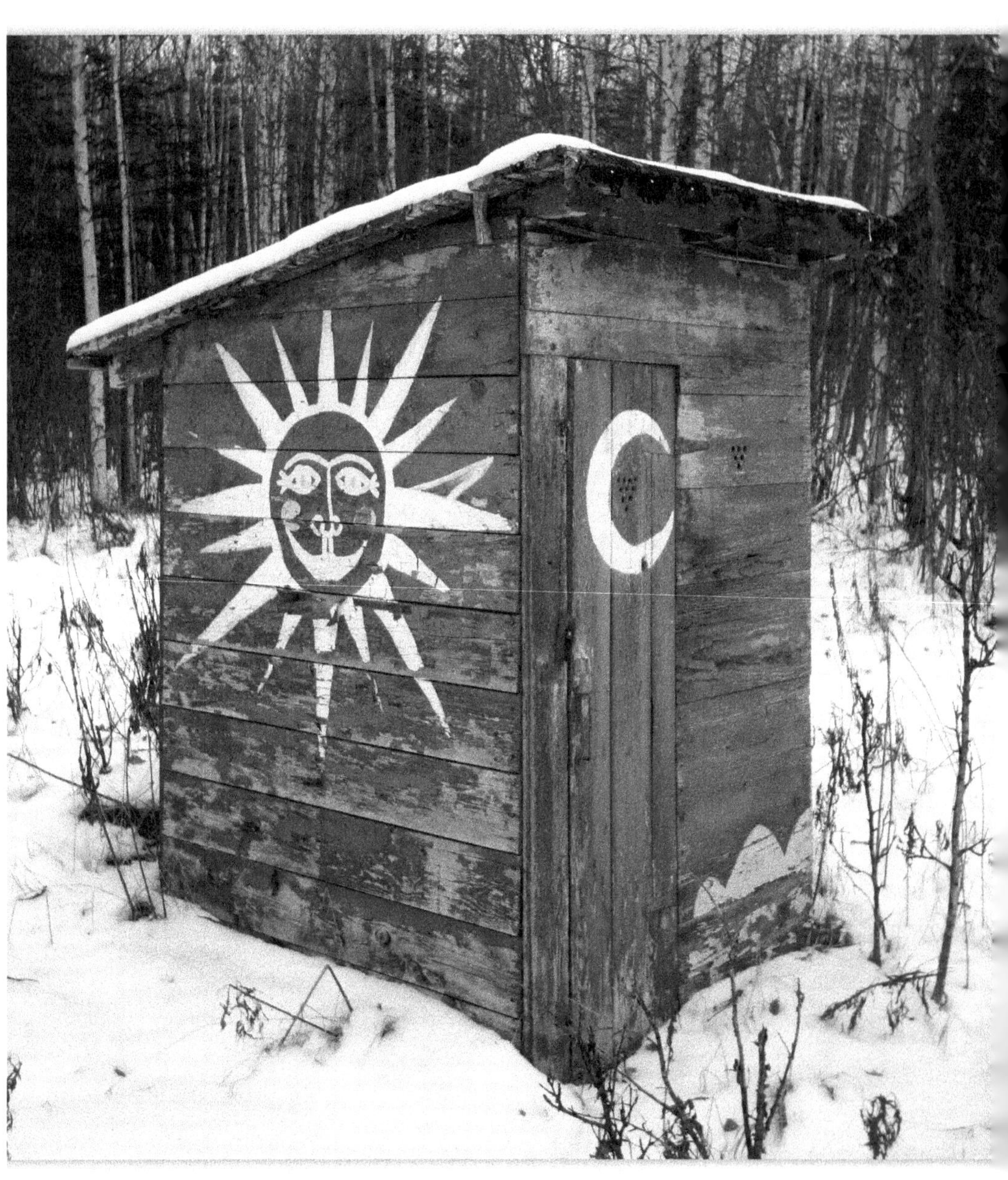

Sanctuary, James O'Rear

Yukon Rising

ALAN KESSELHEIM

"Watch for my boat," Dick Cook called, when we pushed off from the bank where we'd stopped to visit the renowned trapper. He wore black pants and flip-flops. His dogs had howled the entire time. Our three young kids wanted to go see them, but he advised against it.

"I pulled the boat up but it still floated off," he said. "It's got a load of lumber on it."

The Yukon River never feels headlong, but rather, a seamless, unruffled velocity that is revealed when one canoe takes off ahead and you look up, thirty seconds later, to find a distant speck on the water-filled horizon.

The first four days out of Dawson we camped on exposed gravel bars, bug-free and breezy. Then June rains set in. Clouds filled the basin. Even if it didn't rain on us, it rained somewhere in the gigantic watershed. Silt sandpapered the canoe bottoms. The river turned thick. Gravel bars shrank.

We began jamming a stick in the mud to measure the river's rise. Some evenings it was coming up an inch every hour. The forest was thick with mosquitoes, dripping wet. Sandbars went scarcer by the day.

One night we camped on a toe of gravel the size of my living room—a couple feet of freeboard, no more. We tied our packs into a willow clump and set our tents on the highest ground. Whole trees smacked into the flow from undercut banks, swung into the current. All night the root balls of mature trees ground over the shallows. At dawn our fire was three feet into the river, and half a dozen trees that had come to rest barricaded camp, blocking our way. We portaged over huge pick-up-sticks to start paddling.

Our canoes joined the parade of wood going downriver. Stumps bobbed to the surface, limbs rose like gnarled arms, eddies the size of city blocks spun rafts of wood. Clouds like rowdy giants in the sky cruised past, pounding rain that the kids cowered from under tarps while we paddled on. The nests of geese and sandpipers and killdeer washed away.

Two weeks out, at summer solstice, we stopped at Circle. It could have been New Year's: suitcases of beer poured from the store in a steady stream. Bush karaoke pulsed until 3 a.m. when I drifted off to the thirtieth drunken rendition of "Proud Mary."

In the full sun of dawn, surrounded by beer cans, I sat with some guy by the boat ramp. "Came up from the Flats for the party," he told me. "Found this boat in an eddy. I think it's Dick Cook's."

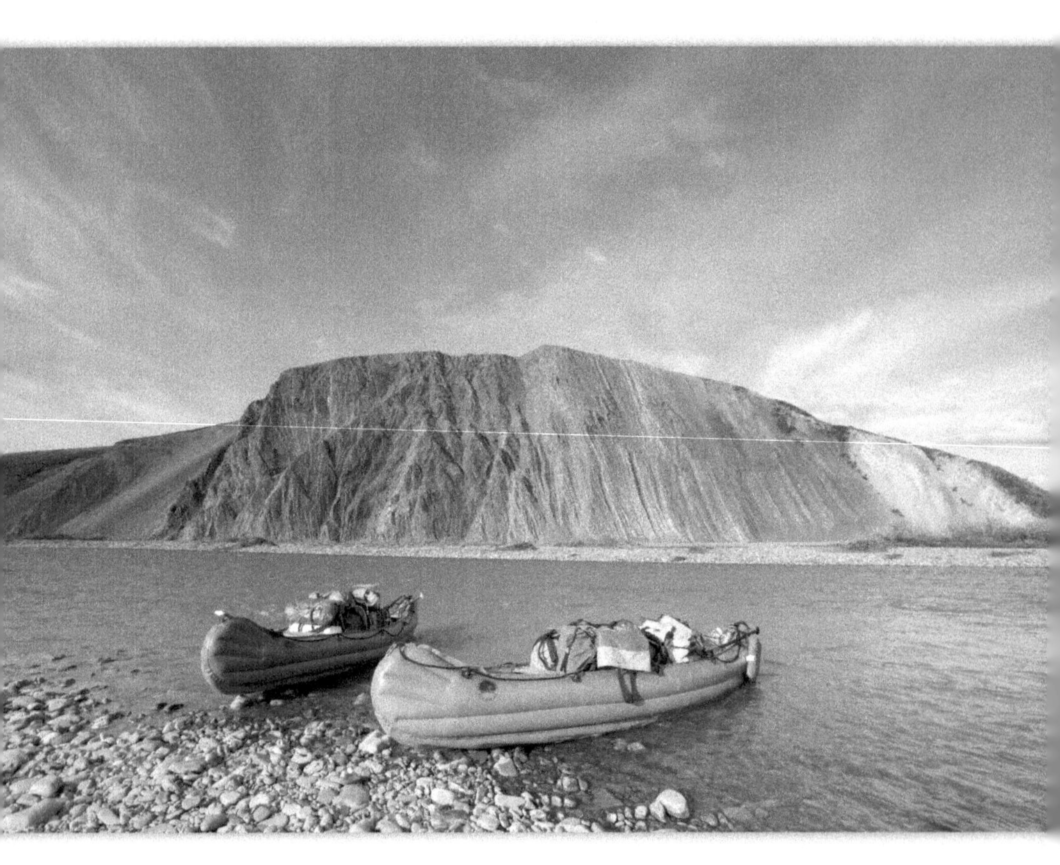

Nigu River Bluff, Patrick Endres

Turnagain

ERIN WILCOX

Pacific waters drift through the Gulf of Alaska, north into Cook Inlet, mixing with glacier melt as they hug the corrugated mudflats of Turnagain Arm. On a cloudy night, the sole explorer of this tidal plain picks his way toward Bird Creek's mouth. His fishing pole extends behind him. Waders carry his light frame across the muck.

The angler's name is Donald. He knows the mudflats and how to navigate them safely: keep moving, especially where the silt is wettest. He took a bet he could catch his limit at the end of September, when the last silvers trickle through. Technically, he lost at midnight when only two fresh coho lay gutted in the freezer. But the early morning hours, which he has never fished before, will provide one more slack low tide. He thinks of Cutter and Shaun taunting as they collect—*Double or nothing, Donald?*—and picks up the pace.

A gibbous moon peeks from behind the clouds, lighting his way. Donald's stomach grumbles, and he pictures his wife, Lana, leaning over the stove, scowling, sweating, stirring the stew pot. When she learned he was going back out after dinner, she said, *You promised to read 'Rora a bedtime story. You said we could look at the stars.* Donald stops short at the memory.

A slurping sound revives him to the present. His left foot won't come forward. He gives a little jerk, then a strong pull, which plants his right foot deeper.

He curses and twists against the mud at his calves. He tries to slip out of his waders, but finds them attached to his belt. His mind mires. From this point, the struggle appears choreographed, his movements sideways, forward, back, performed with a modern dancer's precision. Then, a sudden stillness as he realizes movement aids the enemy, which has him up to the thighs.

His heart pumps blood through awkwardly stretched legs. Donald looks to the bridge above, his vision blurring around the edges. He calls for help and waves his arms. Silt spills into his boots.

The mud smells of rich decomposing life and the contents of his bowels as they empty.

"Dammit, Lana!" he yells, "I hate your stringy stew!"

Then he laughs.

Eventually, the rising tide reaches him. Frigid water licks his waist. The moon slips behind a cloud, and he thinks, *it would be better if there were stars.* Like the night of Aurora's birth. Donald recalls that miracle moment when his daughter's body slipped from the cavity where he'd planted her, coated in brownish red. He remembers Lana's face, how she smiled with wet eyes.

He savors the crisp air in his lungs, and the sound of rushing water.

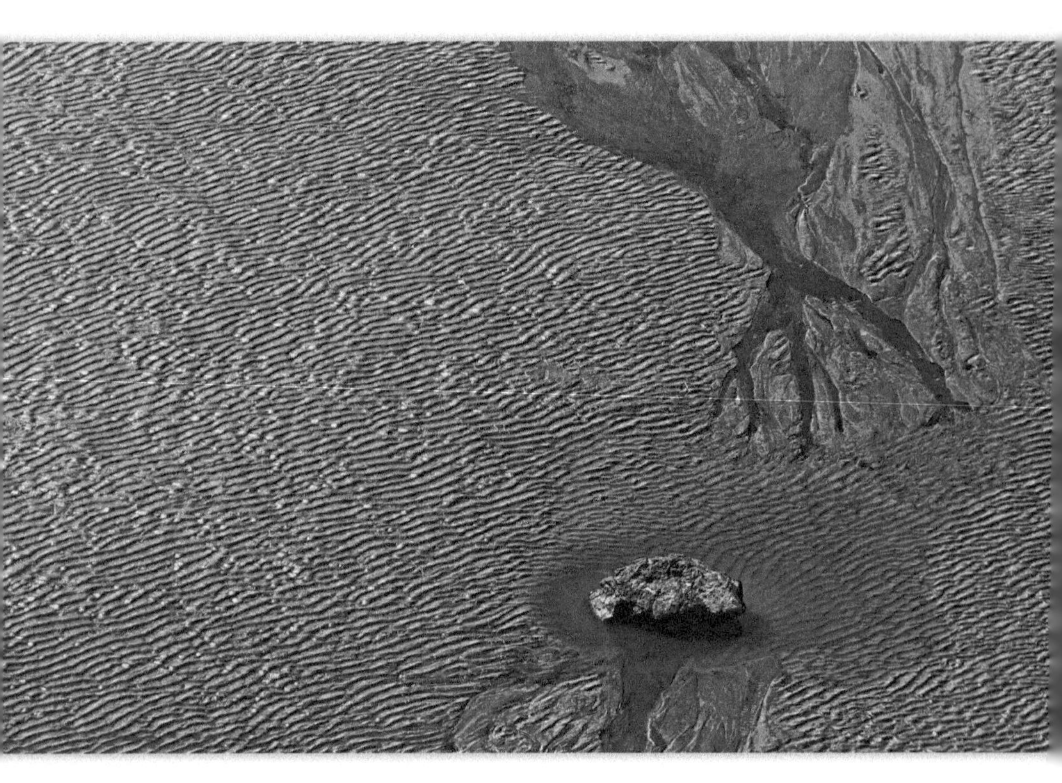

Tidal Flats, Keith Schuessler

Open Water

SANDRA KLEVEN

You better sit this one out. You don't have to go every time they call. Stay put. Give it a rest. Put your feet up. Who is going to notice you missing? When you see one of them later, don't bring it up. Don't ask how it went. They won't be thinking about you out there.

Like before, when that boy went under the ice. They will have other things on their minds. You remember how it is. How you found him that time, so changed by water. His face closed up like a seal pup. It's not something you want to see. You don't want to give that to the family. They knew him only by his size and some things he wore. You almost wish you never found him. But the families don't settle down at all until they have a body. Without it they are always looking, even for years. So you drag with hooks for two days, maybe three. Everybody giving up, still you try. Then you find him, so changed, like he was made of rubber or something like that.

Now this little girl missing under the ice. Just a baby. How will they find a girl that small? Maybe the current is slow where she went in.

How many times do we have to do this? Then, go to the house singing gospel, saying nothing. Who was watching that little girl, that boy? So little. Two years, three? You can't ask why they were playing out alone. You'll just make somebody cry. A question like that hurts someone who's already bleeding, sick inside with guilt. Let it go. Let someone else find that girl. Visit later, to sing "Amazing Grace." Hand them a twenty to help out.

In summer go to the graveyard. Look at the crosses. Read their names out loud. Say something sweet like, "Sure miss you." Or "You kids be good." Don't think about how it was going in. Just figure that they didn't know what hit them, that death was instant. Don't think of them frozen with terror reaching for a mother who was not there. Just say, "You kids stick together now." Don't look at the other crosses of other kids who died too young. Keep your eyes on the ground.

In summer you can go up there and think about this. Today, you better get going. Take some coffee. Extra gloves, too. Those guys will need your help if they are going to find that little girl. Gotta give her family some peace.

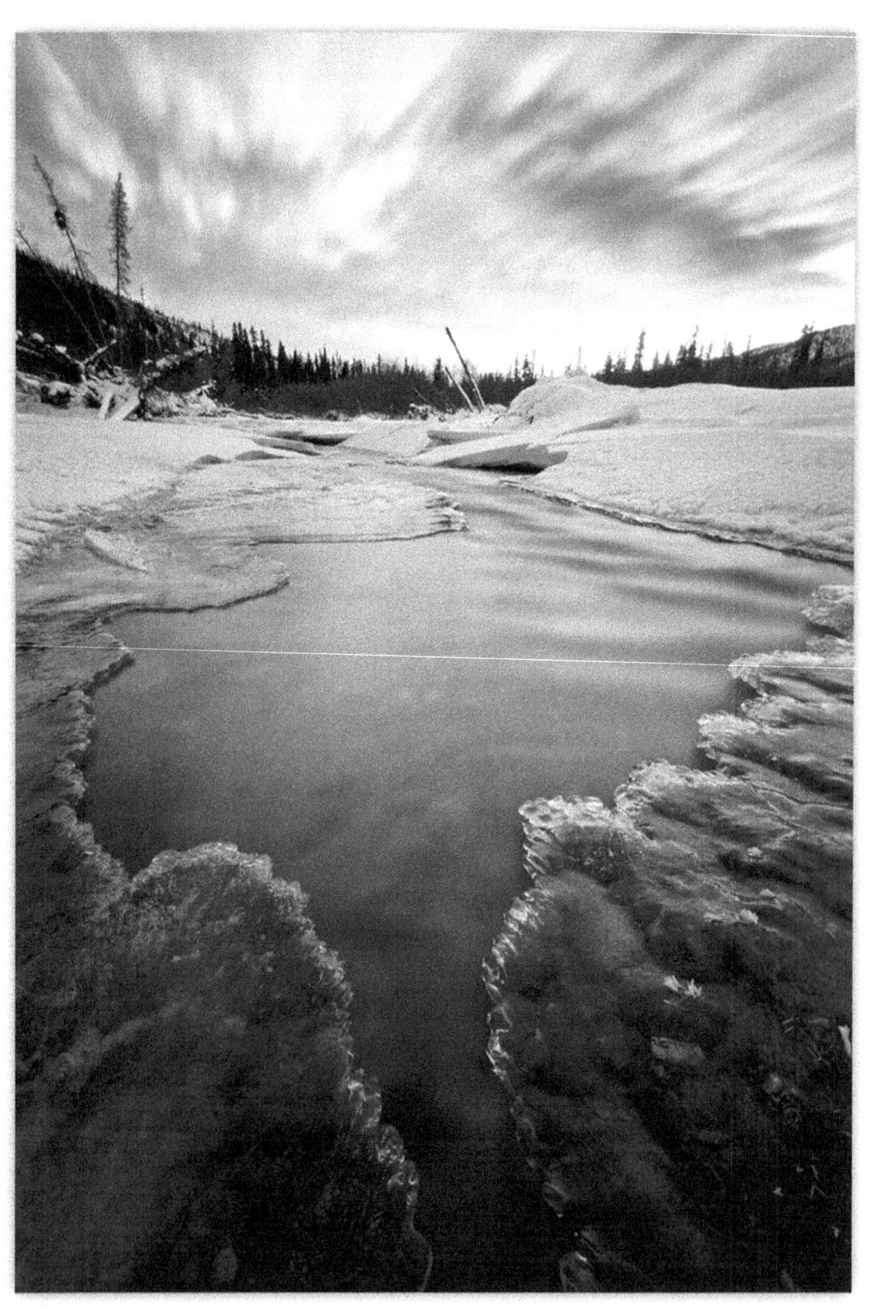

Thin Ice, Ron Perkins

Rink Rats

SCOTT BANKS

In Anchorage, on the Park Strip at the intersection of 9th and E Street, a hockey rink and a figure-skating rink glow under the overhead lights. It's 1961, which makes me four years old. One of my parents supports me by the elbows, trying to stave off the imminent collapse of my ankles as I teeter on a pair of double-bladed ice skates. I grip a cut-off hockey stick, but it's more of a prop than for a purpose. The ice squeaks under my blades as I walk more than skate across the ice. At the hockey rink next to us, men warm up for a league game. Pucks bang off the boards, muffled yells echo across the ice, and someone calls for the puck amid pregame warm-ups. I am not thinking about them—I just want to stand upright.

A hockey player who looks eight feet tall crosses to our rink, skates over, and passes a puck to me, lightly, barely propelling it across the ice and onto the blade of my stick. I concentrate on what he tacitly asks me to do. Everything in me focuses on that puck and on not letting the player down. I hear murmurs of encouragement. My parents have faded into the background. Something clicks, but the recognition of what that is comes to me only much later in life.

The rink on the Park Strip centered the Anchorage hockey world. Indoor ice didn't come to Anchorage until 1965, when the Anchorage Sports Arena was built at the corner of Fireweed Lane and C Street. "Arena" was an ambitious description for a metal structure that barely warded off subzero temperatures and held a thousand spectators. The building still stands, now an office supply store.

I'm looking at that outdoor rink through the second-story window of the building where I work, an office apparently meant to survive next to a hockey rink, with cement block walls to repel flying pucks. It's a powerful slapshot that sails over the twelve-foot boards and chain-link fence I knew as a child. But it can be done, because every spring, I find at least one puck stranded on the sidewalk out front. I check the rink a couple of times a day, pausing to see who's out there and making sure the ice has been flooded and is ready for when a bunch of rink rats gathers to play a game of shinny at noon. And when I see a kid barely able to stand on that ice, I want to be the guy to pass him the puck.

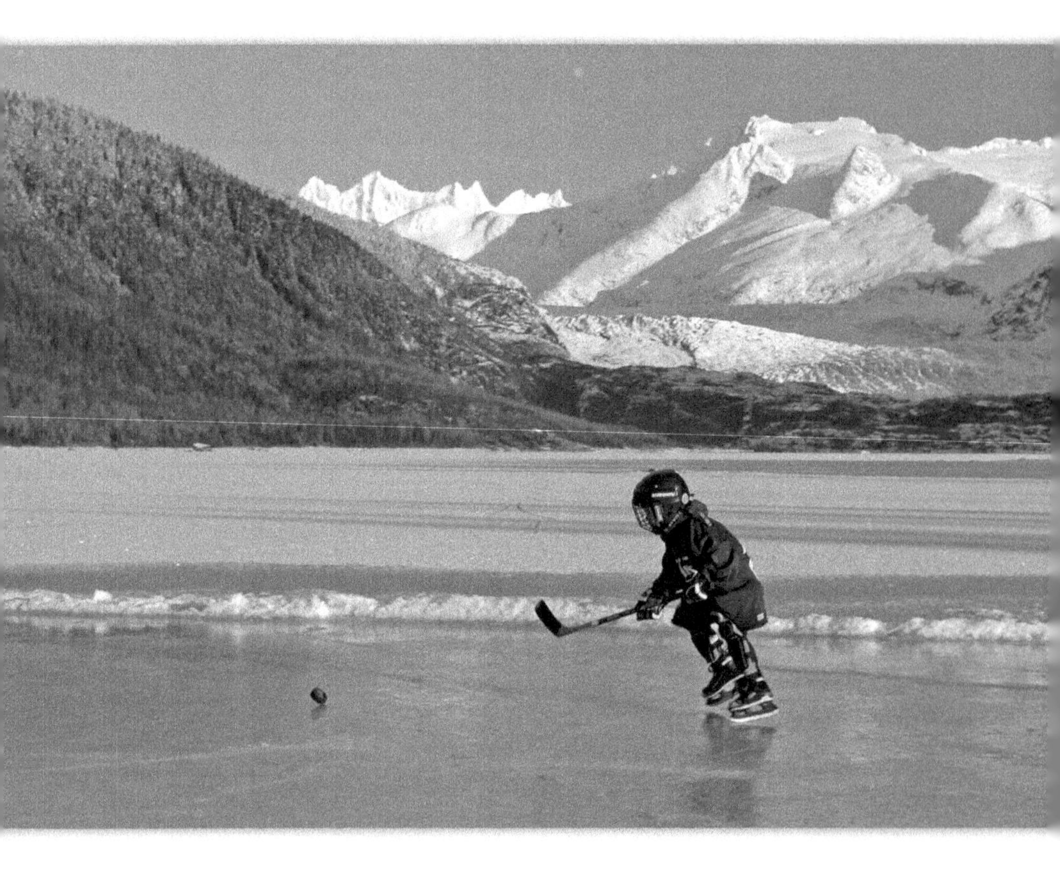

Hockey, Alaska-Style, Laurent Dick

Memories of Smokewood

JOHN JENSEN

In the mid-nineteen-forties when I was about eight, friends and I would sometimes go to Sandy Beach south of Douglas on warm summer days.

The beach is no accident of nature but was built up gradually by the Treadwell Mine pulverizing rock into sand. After a swim, the older boys would build a small fire on a rise above the high tide line. Shivering in the light but perpetual breeze with only a wet towel for protection, we might enjoy a toke on smokewood passed around. It was, well, *cool*, and safe from parents' eyes. Once I'd put a paper-and-candy cigarette between my lips before jumping into my father's pickup. He glanced at me and declared angrily, "Oh, tough guy, eh?" as I wilted back into the seat. He was flummoxed, he told me later, at how to handle what appeared to be the real thing dangling from my lip.

After an absence of many years, I found smokewood to be still abundant there. But what was it? The pieces nestled among seaweed, one to three feet long, not tapered, lighter than other wood, ranging in thickness from little finger to thumb, lacking bark or core, and, in cross-section, showing hundreds of evenly distributed needle-size holes. It undulates rather than curves in one direction, as do branches, suggesting a root or runner. I showed pieces of it to botanists, biologists, foresters, and experienced outdoorsmen, but no one recognized it.

The mystery remained until the day I happened past several cottonwoods and noted on the ground near them a ten-foot section with cottonwood bark but also the peculiar undulation that indicates smokewood. When I picked it up, it weighed about half of what I'd expected, and its cross-section revealed the unique hole pattern. The picture finally became clear: The Taku River undercuts a bank, toppling a cottonwood. Sun, rain, and ice strip the bark, river action breaks chunks and carries them off, tide tosses them onto a beach, and the sun bakes them into their even, dull-gray color.

For years afterward, on a chilly afternoon, I would choose a piece from my supply, light it, and stroll to what remains of the Douglas dock to watch the gulls and crows; perhaps read a little, sitting on a fisherman's net stored there, and savor the smoke. If you happen along the high tide line and spot some smokewood, break off a piece several inches long. Once it's dry, air moves through it easily. Wet it outside with your tongue to slow the rate of burning, light up, draw a little smoke into your mouth, and appreciate nature's abundance. The sensation is, well, *cool*.

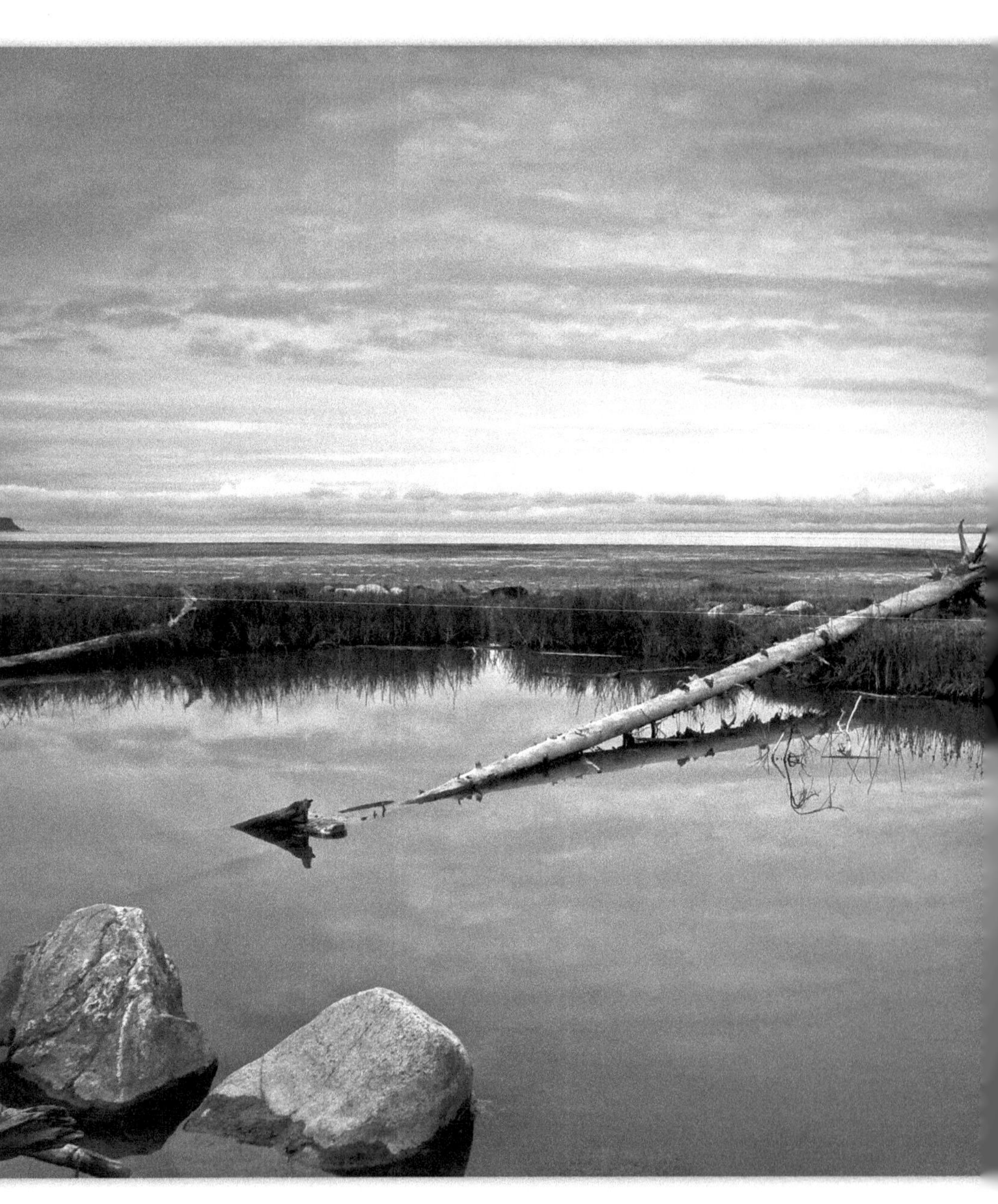

Fallen Tree, Peggy King

What I Knew on the Longest Day

(Fort Yukon, 1961)

MIRIAM BECK

How to mail the letters before the mail-plane came. The way back home along the empty track, barely a road, through the village. How to wheedle a ride from my sister, pedaling her bike toward home. The way she'd stand on the pedals, wobbling through ruts, while I straddled the fender, my feet held far from the spokes. To recognize the approaching sputter of my brother's motorbike. The taste of the tan dust as he passed us, *bip-bip!* on the horn.

To name people we passed, and sort them, White or Native. Their dwellings, often one room. The luxury of our log house—bedrooms for everyone, extras for guests. What the sign out front said: *Yukon Lodge*. To trace the rough-carved letters and name them. Where to find books, and how to examine the pictures or beg for a read.

The smells indoors: bread dough, cigarettes, smoked moose hide. That Mom and gray-haired Margaret would be working. Mom's voice blending with the radio, true pitch, a little sad. How to join in: *I found my thrill . . .*

How my baby sister would laugh at goofy rhymes and swiveled hips. That I was too long-legged to pedal her tricycle, but how to push her from the back, careening across the linoleum. That Mom would send me outside when I was rowdy.

That I should share the swing-set with *all* the neighbors. That sheets drying on the line made a maze. Where onions sprouted in an old garden bed. How to apply *Off!*

That five was old enough to use the outhouse, with its gaping hole. That the disinfected honey bucket indoors was for guests. Ways to sneak to it, unobserved.

To keep away from the riverbank—otherwise, spanking and disgrace. (Also, the irresistible pull of the river. Riverboats kicking up wakes. Mud swallows' quick maneuvers to catch bugs. Gray cobbles to plunk in the water. Fish wheels rotating empty for long stretches, then, suddenly, flipping salmon into the pens.)

Never to go near the men with pint bottles who lurched down the road. Not to be alone with guests. To stay out of dog yards without a grown-up. To run home immediately whenever I saw a gun.

When the next meal would be ready: soon. The way to gulp instant milk, ice cold, without breathing. That moose meat required ketchup. After dinner, how to listen quietly on Daddy's lap, so bedtime would pass unnoticed. That nobody could stay awake for all the daylight.

That in the branches of a willow shrub near the house, robins tended three blue eggs in a nest. The hope of it. Never to let the neighbor boys know.

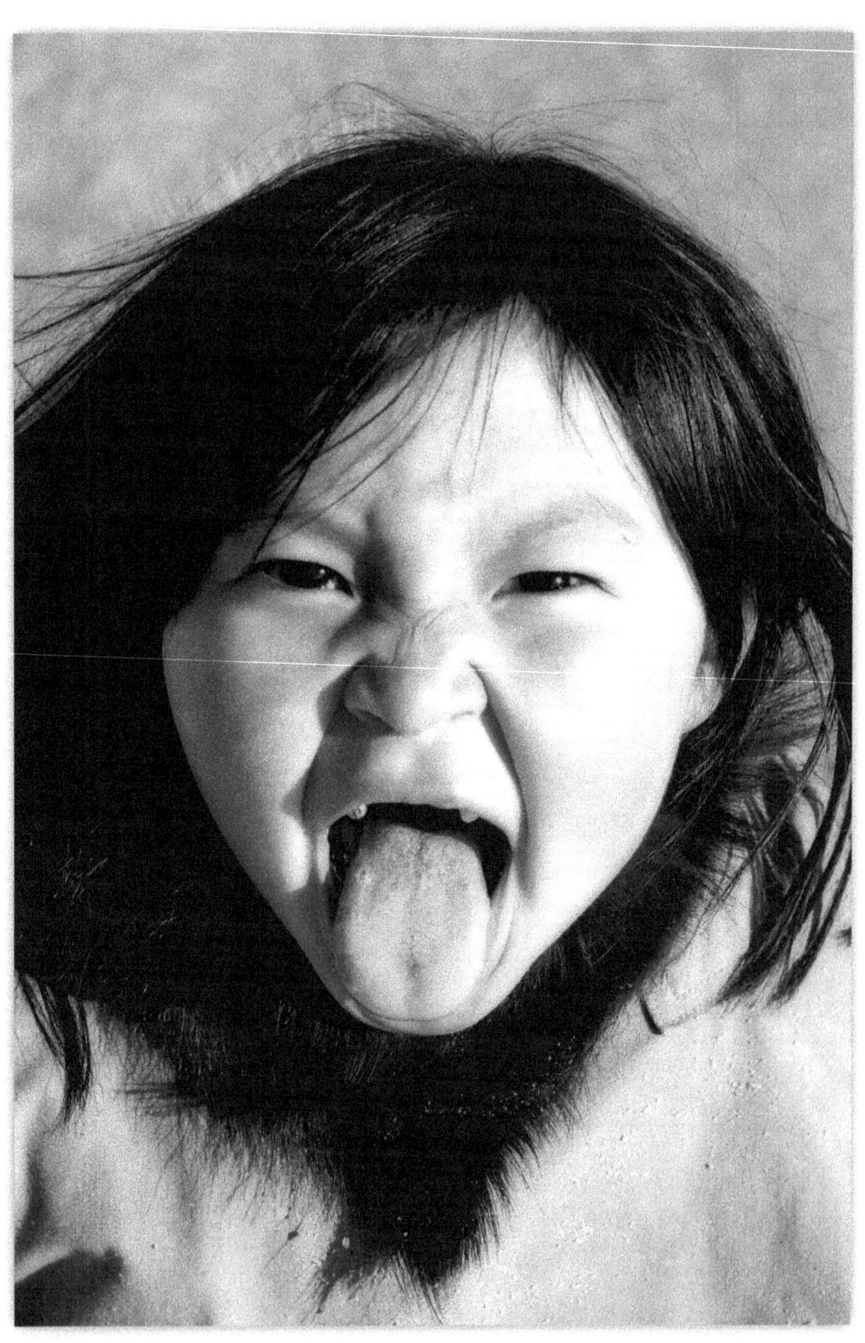

Uqaq (Tongue), Angela Busch Alston

Blood Ties

MICHAEL ENGELHARD

When I visited the elder for the first time, I found his mudroom cluttered with the implements of a bush life. Hip waders slumped next to snowmachine parts, dip nets, a shotgun, beaver-skin mittens dangling from a nail, and a chain saw that needed tightening. Two wolf pelts flowed from the rafters—complete with tail, legs, ears, and muzzle. Before I knocked on the inner door, I stroked the silver-tipped fur. Gaping eyeholes and the hides' steamrolled appearance left me slightly unsettled.

A dead beaver lay on the kitchen floor, half-skinned on a piece of cardboard, to keep the meat clean and blood off the linoleum. My host asked me to sit. His wife busied herself with a stew bubbling on the stove.

The Park Service wanted to know which of the nearby parks his people had used traditionally. If they could prove longstanding subsistence, they would still be entitled to hunt there, and even to trap wolves. On maps I spread across the table, he outlined forays that had taken him into the Brooks Range and as far south as the Yukon River. Bands of nomadic hunters had taken Dall's sheep and caribou from the mountains and plains for millennia—always in competition with wolves. The meanders he drew with colored felt pens resembled wolf wanderings on biologists' maps. The old-timer's eyes veiled with distance as he relived each mile on the trail. His crinkled, leathery face relaxed.

"That *teekkona*, he keeps caribou strong." A lifetime observing the animals had made this man a wolf expert and better hunter. I sensed admiration for the sleek, efficient predators under his words. With a callused finger, he tapped on their den sites and on those of bears, black and brown. Though he was too old by then to go on long trips, he remembered how to intercept wolves near their kills, which bait to use, and how to set and disguise traps. "They are smart, like us," he chuckled.

In soft, lilting village English, he spoke about respect. He untangled for me the web of taboos surrounding this animal, an animal whose spiritual power is rivaled only by wolverine or bear. When I mentioned beliefs I had come across in my research, he became serious. He nodded in recognition of an age-old kinship, stressing the rules that guide contact with wolves. To appease a dead wolf's spirit, caribou backstrap should be burned as an offering. "If you don't do this," he concluded, "he will turn on you." Unfailingly, disrespect would draw bad luck, injury, illness, or even death, to a hunter or his family. He'd wanted to pass all this on to a grandson who now lived in Seattle.

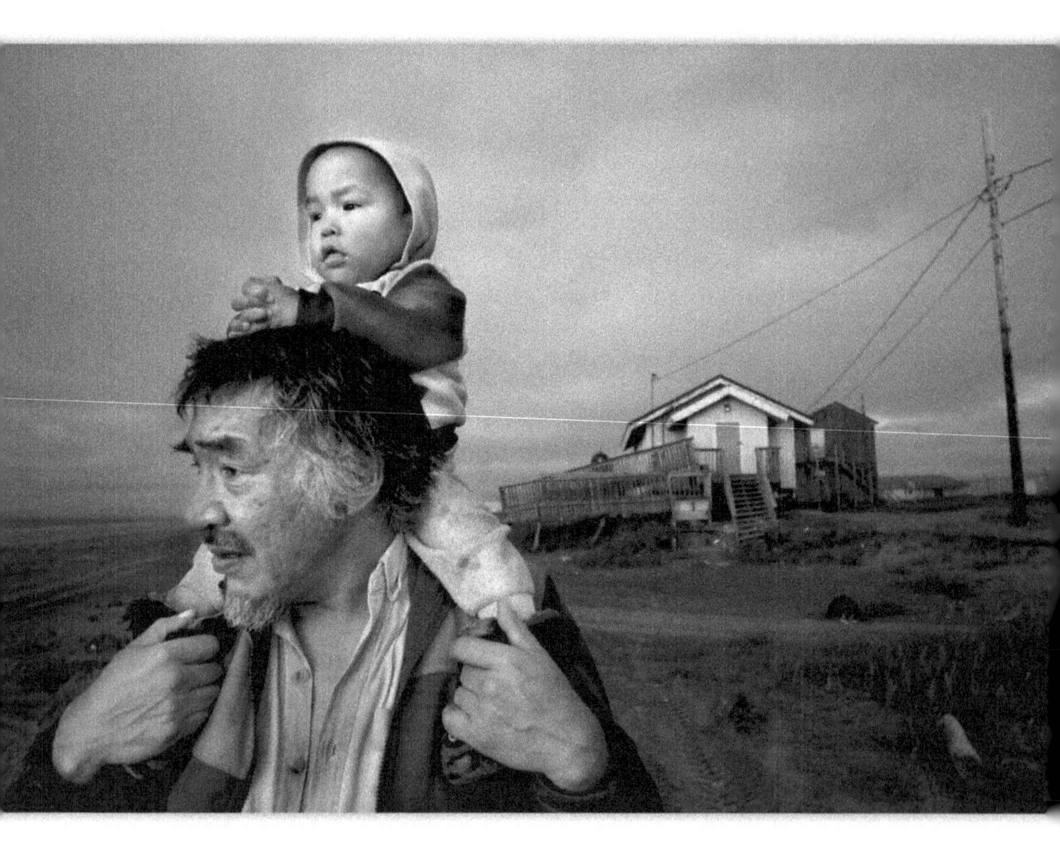

Father and Son—Shishmaref, Brandon Thibodeaux

Legacies

MIKE FREEMAN

I'd caught a break. It was cold enough to walk on snow and freeze the furs, but not so much as to be miserable. December, moreover, brings sheets of precipitation to Southeast Alaska, rain and snow, but they'd been delayed. I'd snapped dead willows in the meadow where even the weak sun managed to dry them. The jumble of kindling and stack of broken alder would be all I needed before lying down in the tent to sleep off the paddling and walking. In the black of the winterkilled day the feeble crackling wasn't much, but the flame gave more heat than I'd had in two days. I sat on the stump and put blade to tendon.

Marten aren't hard to catch but you have to spread out for them. Like most mustelids, they run a circuit. If you miss them it could be a month before they return, and I was only out for a week. Except during a cold snap or two, the rivers stay open here. I'd canoed from town, portaged from one delta to another, headed up some forested miles, then set one line upstream and another downstream, alternating checks daily. This was the fourth marten, along with a few mink.

The fire lapped at the dark.

Marten skin easily. The knife cut the thin tissue along the hamstrings, then ran from the armpits to the footpads, where I worked the forelegs free, popping claws. These animals live on the margin, hardly a dollop of fat. Pinching thumb to forefinger, I coaxed the tailbone, which came forth like a nightcrawler from wet ground, as did the penis. The rusted-orange fur loosed from the abdominal and shoulder muscles like a doll's robe. Cuts on the ears, eyes, and nose, and it was done. Rolling the hide, I tucked it in the cooler, to be stretched and dried in town. Frost clung to the other rolls, latched to the fur like bread mold. I walked from the spruce to the muskeg, carcass in hand.

Clouds had rolled in, fenestrated, windows smeared with stars. Pieces of Orion showed, the flank of Taurus, a corner of the Big Dipper—simple bits, like poetic fragments. I drew in a lung-full, pluming out air, then booted a hole in the crusted snow. Sticky meat slipped from my fingers; I sealed it with a foot's swipe. Ravens would have it in April, maybe a brown bear. I looked to the sky, the holes. Quiet ranged about the landscape. Those furs would likely end up doused in orange on some Manhattan sidewalk, neither party attuned to this equity, or to the ceremony I derived from the object of their antagonism.

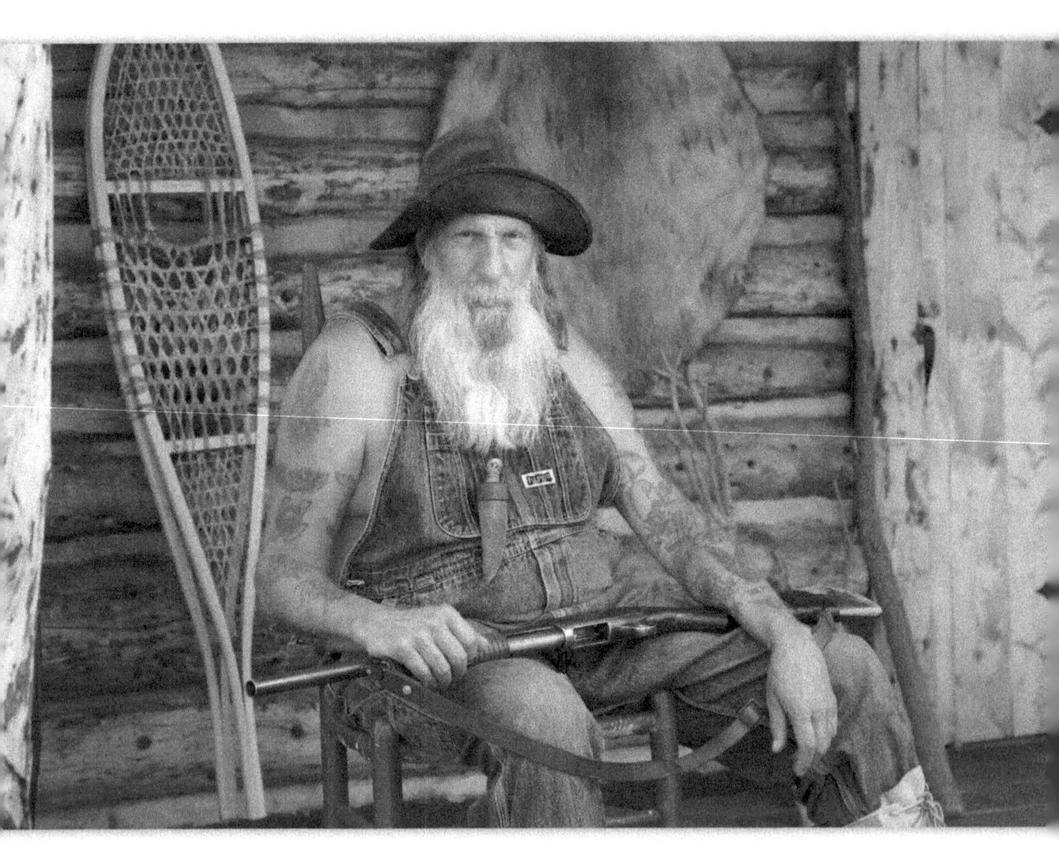

D. C. Smitty, Patrick Endres

Candles Don't Always Set the Mood

MAREI BENTON

On a weekday afternoon in Anchorage, Alaska, a shelf broke. This was not just any shelf, mind you; this was a loaded shelf. Before it broke, it was the top shelf of three, all of which held doe urine, beaver castor, and other such Tools of the Hunt that a private sporting goods store in midtown sold. Immediately after the top shelf buckled under its weight of liquid merchandise, it collapsed onto the second shelf, which collapsed onto the first shelf, which fell in one giant mess onto the floor. Glass bottles simultaneously shattered everywhere.

The smell was out of this world, a fact later attributed to the beaver castor. Even after the store's staff had finished cleaning the spill area, *even then*, customers would walk into the store, violently dry-heave and then run for the door, usually while offering a furtive *My God, what was that smell?* to their partners.

The store manager was desperate. This was no way to earn a living. Doling out the For Emergencies Only! money, he sent his two favorite employees to Walmart to buy scented candles. (These two were exactly the type you would expect to find employed at an Alaska sporting goods store—outdoorsy young men in their early twenties who frankly had never bought a scented candle.) The store manager had thought it obvious that they were to buy several candles of one bland scent. Because candles are so cheap at Walmart, however, the two returned with a bagful of mixed scents, including such pleasant aromas as Island Holiday, Spiced Pumpkin Pie, and Evergreen Forest. Frustrated, the store manager figured that the store couldn't possibly smell any worse.

The store manager was wrong. After lighting and strategically placing the candles throughout the store, the smell changed. Now it wasn't just Doe Urine, but Tropical Island Doe Urine; it wasn't just Beaver Castor, it was Spiced Pumpkin Pie Beaver Castor. It is hardly believable, but the store smelled worse. It smelled so horrifically horrendous, in fact, that the manager extinguished all the candles and closed up shop two hours early. The employees were excited to have a few extra hours at home. They didn't realize, however, that the stench had seeped not only into their clothes, but also into their hair and very pores.

For two days afterward, every time my boyfriend came near me, my nose would wrinkle and my eyes water at the lingering smell. You haven't experienced the real Alaska until you've tried living with a man who smells like Spiced Pumpkin Pie Beaver Castor.

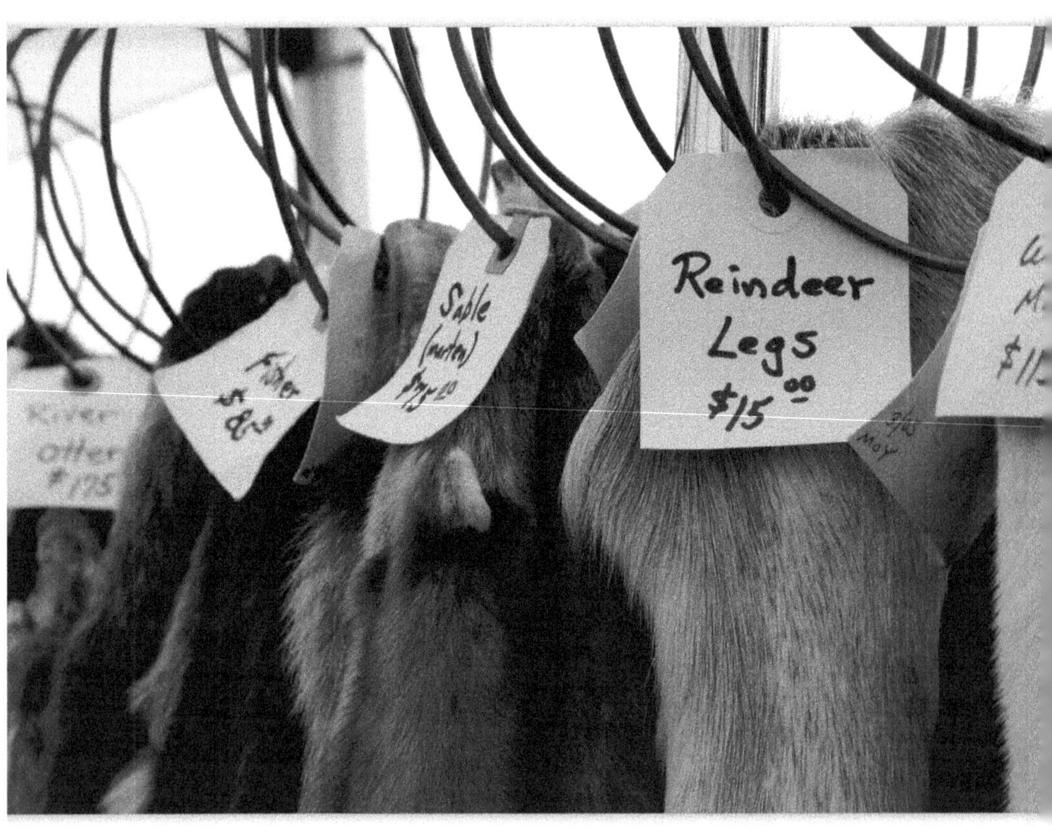

Inventory, Chris Heaton

Talking Wolf

BRUCE ORTON

Nothing like the heat rising off a kill in frozen air after a jaunt in caribou country. 'Course my bitch would say it's fresh snow on swollen tits before a big litter. I don't argue, Alpha Male or not. Domestic peace, and all.

Don't get me wrong. I love moose. Especially belly-up with a fat liver.

Cruised through Anchorage once. Ran the old lady through a backyard in heat. We had collie for Christmas.

I dig marmots. Really. Digging burrows in summer is how I met my spouse. Saw her doing it, walked up, took a sniff of her ass. Just call me a romantic, but love at first sniff is real. Hey dog, you know what I'm talkin'.

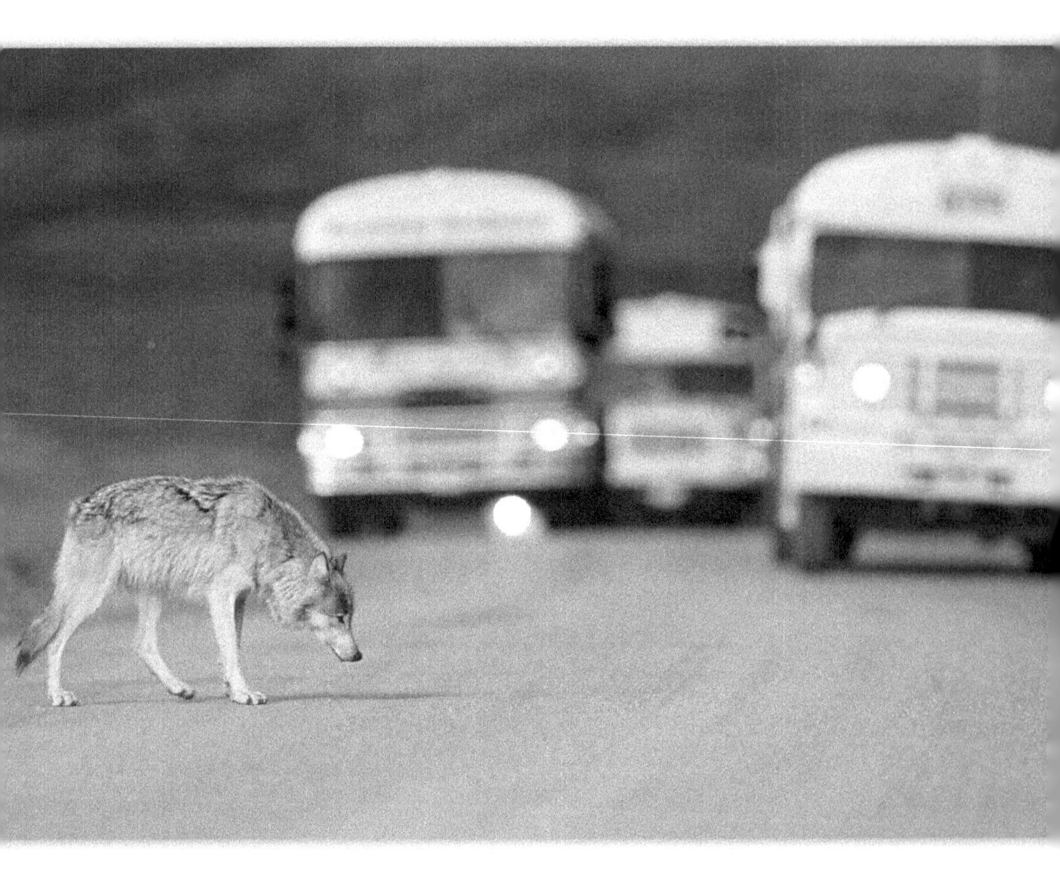

Right of Way, Patrick Endres

Hell-bent for Leather

NITA NETTLETON

Of all dog sports, skijoring is perhaps the most exhilarating and riskiest. I speak from experience and submit exhibits A and B: Chester and Violet. Wolf hybrid siblings, they came to me as weanlings against my better judgment. Thrown together, we three made the best of it.

They bonded with each other, but tolerated me to feed and shovel up after them and occasionally scratch an ear or two. Exercising involved a lot of running on my part until we discovered skijoring. I had skis and rope, got a couple of harnesses and explained the idea. Violet listened carefully and stepped into her harness without hesitation. Chester allowed me to wrestle him into a harness because Violet was wearing one. We took off.

There are few thrills to match careening along on skis behind two eager canines. We learned *right* and *left* and put in enough time to learn Esperanto from figuring out *stop* but generally didn't stop until the puppies were pooped. At that point, Chester asked to be carried home but settled for walking with no drag. We all got a good workout.

It was clear from the beginning that Chester and Violet communicated telepathically. Sometimes, I would be lucky enough to catch an ear flip or change in tail angle in time to crouch and grip the towrope more tightly. Other times, I wasn't. One dog would see something fascinating to the right or left of the trail, there would be a silent conversation between them, and we'd dart that way. You'd think they at least would have warned me, to avoid the skis and myself in a heap on top of them—but perhaps that was part of the fun.

One sun-spangled, squeaky-snow February day, we ran a trail to the northwest of the cabin, and life was good. We'd made several turns, and I thought we'd finally gotten our act down. Then Chester reached to his right without stopping. Violet and I could see he had something in his mouth. Something he preferred not to share with anyone. Violet took offense. I ceased to exist. Chester lunged away from Violet, she leaped onto his shoulders and knocked him down, I ran over them both. In the tangle of skis, ropes, and nasty little tempers, Chester held on to his prize. With Violet's help, I pinned him on his back and pried his jaws apart. It was a wallet. I looked for ID, Violet looked for cash. There was neither. It was just an old, empty leather wallet. Violet rolled her eyes and started untangling herself. I gave the wallet back to Chester. He carried it all the way home.

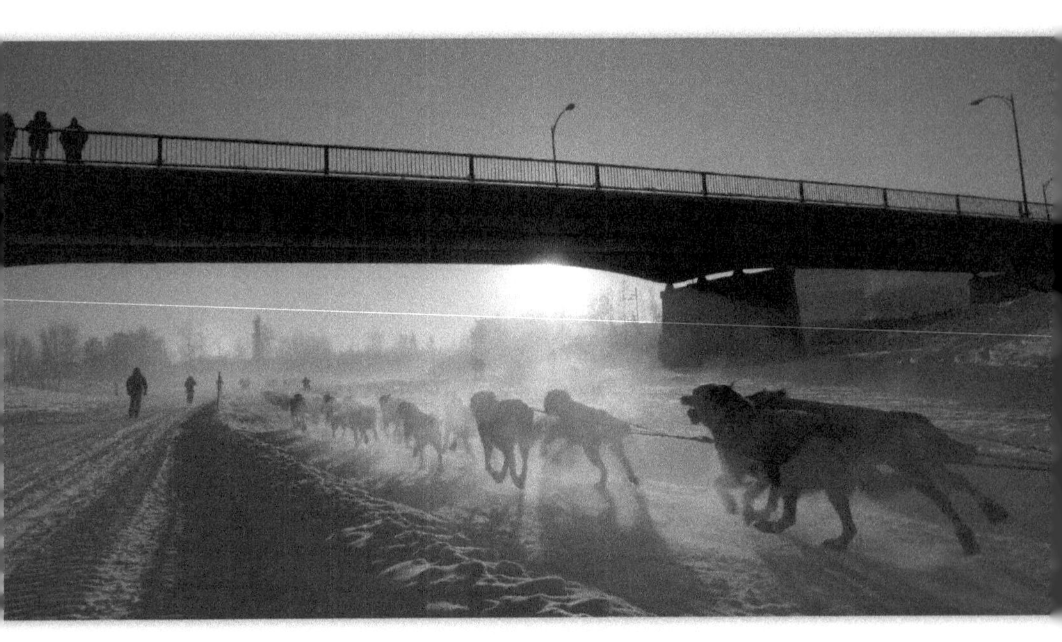

Yukon Quest, Kaitlin Wilson

Howling Dog

KATHY INGALLINERA

I pulled the old blue VW bus into the parking lot of the Howling Dog Saloon, just north of Fairbanks. It was June 21, 1992, and we had come to drink beer and watch the Midnight Sun volleyball tournament. I bought two Alaskan Ambers at the bar and followed Dave out onto the patio to watch the players and enjoy the late evening sun.

It was a warm, still night, and the sky was bright at 11 p.m. The game was good, but the cold beer was better. I went back in for two more.

I was startled when the loudspeaker crackled on. "Al Blake, please come to the bar." I didn't see any movement toward the bar from inside or outside.

"Maybe Al's not here," I murmured to Dave as I slid back onto the bench next to him and handed him his bottle. Ten minutes later the voice came over the speaker again. "Al Blake, please come to the bar." Again, no movement, at least from outside where the volleyball game was going strong.

A few minutes later the loudspeaker crackled to life one last time. "Al Blake, Fairbanks Memorial Hospital called. Your wife is in labor." A chair toppled over with a crash and loud footsteps could be heard in the bar, followed by the revving and then peeling out of a motorcycle from the parking lot.

"Must have been Al," Dave said to me.

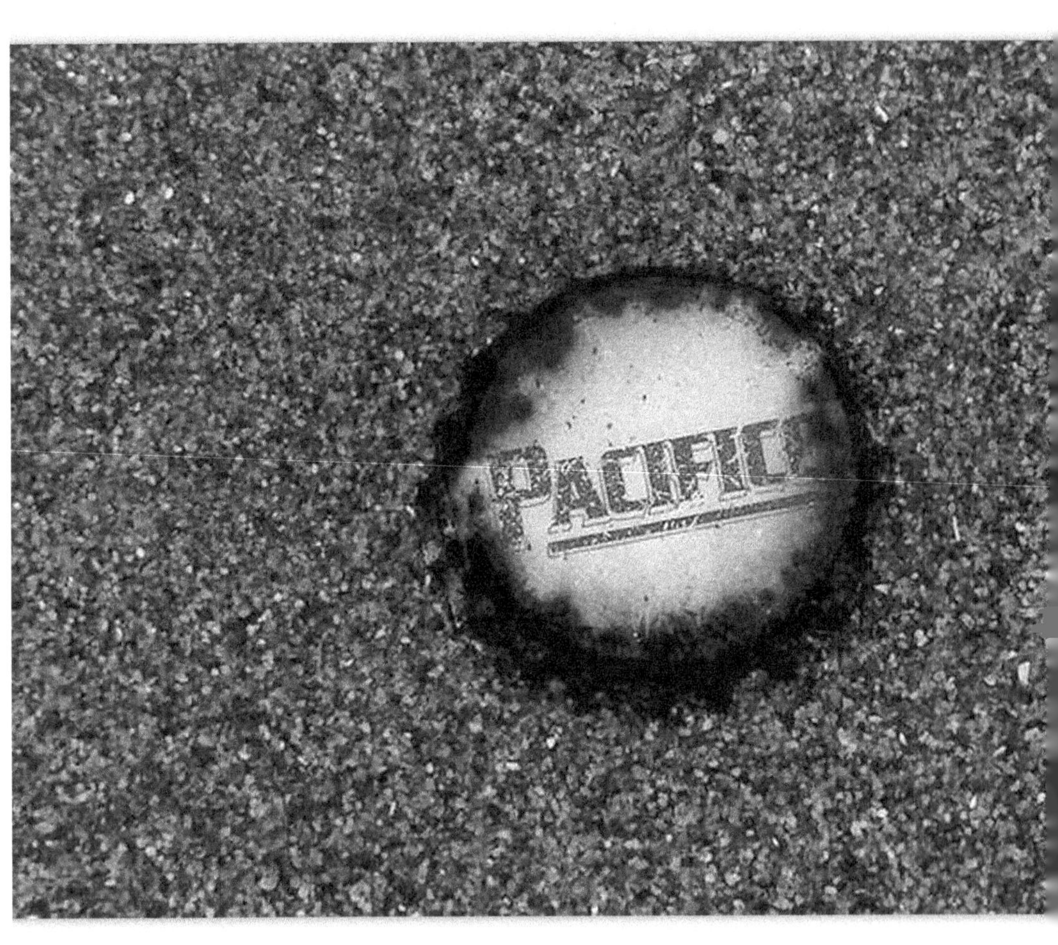

Flotsam—Settlers Cove, Karla Hayward

Northern Flyway

EOWYN IVEY

A hundred wild geese circle over the Matanuska alfalfa field, circle and cry out to one another and circle, until they drop and flap to the ground like weighted parachutes. The morning air is clean and good. A thin mist has settled in the lowlands, and the sun is still down in the bare birch branches. Nothing green yet, but Nick can smell it coming—furrowed dirt sodden with snowmelt, devil's clubs and horse tails pushing up through dead leaves in the woods, mosquito larvae hatching in the marshes.

He carries a cardboard box of beer in one hand and a .44 revolver tucked under his arm as he walks across the ground packed hard by trucks and tractors, past the silo and to the horse corral. The geese rustle in the brown-yellow grass clipped short by last fall's mow. The corral is overgrown and empty. They haven't kept horses in years. Four-wheelers get you farther into moose country and are cheaper in the long run.

He walks the fence line and sets a full can of beer on top of each post until he's got a row of six or seven. A prankster's grin pulls at the corners of his lips. He wonders how many shots he'll get off before the geese hit the sky.

Fifty yards from the fence, he sits at the base of a granite boulder, leans back into it. The .44 is cold steel, but the wood grip warms in his palm. He always liked this pistol. No screwing around.

He flips the pistol cylinder out to the side and holds the barrel between his knees as he loads it. It's going to be good. He imagines the bullet passing clean through, leaving everything neat, just as it was, except one hell of a hole where it will all pour out.

He aims, squints down the barrel, and pulls the trigger. Before he can blink, the can of beer explodes like a comic-book grenade. Silver shards of aluminum fly brightly over the fence, and beer sprays in a tremendous, glistening burst.

"Holy Christ!" And he laughs out loud. Laughs. Takes aim, shoots again. *So this is sobriety.* Since he was a kid, all he's shot is empties.

Once or twice he misses, but again and again the cans go like wet fireworks, and he laughs and wipes his mouth with the back of his pistol hand. The wild geese gather and squawk and take to the air in clumsy grace. Nick watches them as they fly over the treetops, toward the mountains.

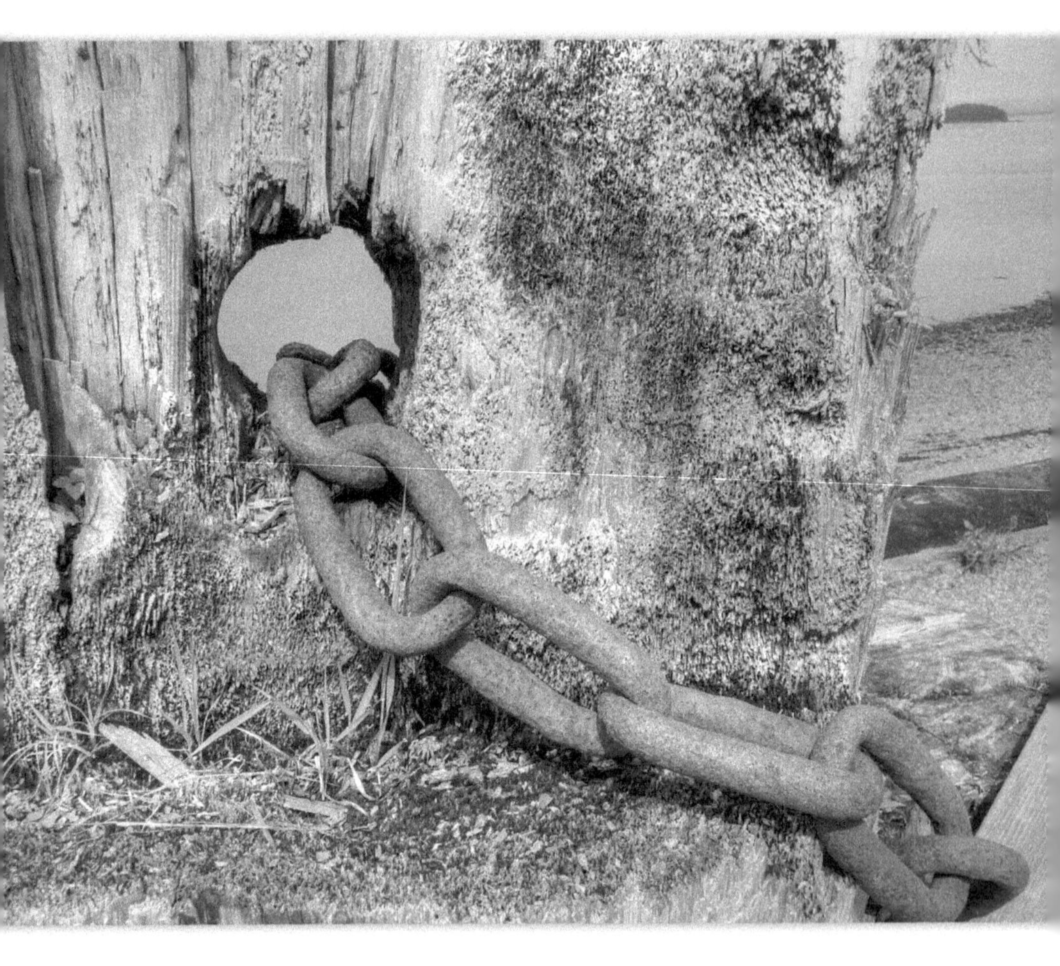

Rusty Chain, Mark McElroy

Village of Old Believers

KATHLEEN TARR

Sometimes, when grocery shopping in Soldotna, I would find myself standing behind a Russian woman from the Village of Old Believers. Old Believer women were easy to spot. They didn't look like other women in casual outdoor wear. They dressed on the frumpy side, in wide-cut skirts and frocks, white anklet socks, and flat, black shoes. Their hair was twisted in buns, braided, or tucked under a kerchief. Religious custom did not permit them to show bare arms or legs above the calf. These women never wore pants. Tourists who came to catch Kenai kings weren't quite sure what to make of the costumed people in the produce aisles.

They honored their past this way—the men in silver-embroidered tunics and long beards, the women in *sarafans*. Pious and defiant Old Believers had endured religious persecution for centuries in their homeland. They had survived the upheaval from migrations to China, Brazil, and Oregon. They shunned modern society, diversions like television and alcohol. In 1967, a small band of them had made their way north to Alaska, north to freedom, north to silence.

In today's high-speed, iPhone world, what secrets must they hold about how to live in quiet contemplation?

A part of me longed to be like them—on the run from technology—possessing a spiritual life so deeply felt, I, too, would obediently follow religious rituals in my everyday life. But I had no such commitment or grounding.

I would see the Old Believers with their quiet, well-behaved children in tow, and remembered how I once drove to their village with dear Moscow friends. It was Igor's idea to reclaim something of Old Mother Russia while visiting Alaska.

Katya, think of the historical ironies! We must drive there!

And so on a summer Sunday afternoon, three Muscovites and I were swept into the full circle of history. We sat sipping *chai* at Nina's luncheon counter in the Samovar Inn in Nikolaevsk. Russian *souvenira* cluttered the place: birch barrettes, fringed *platoks*, cheap *matryoshkas* dolls, a photocopied pamphlet, "How We Escaped Russia."

Desperate to make a sale of any kind, Nina popped in a cassette of Russian folk music and threw open the lace curtains: "Please, you want *knigi* (books)?" Hard times had befallen this fishing community.

To Old Believers, an unpredictable economy and petty politics had nothing to do with the essence of life. In setbacks and tragedies, in mystical beauties and joys, a "yes"—a holy "Yes!"—must always be uttered. We are here, friends, sipping tea. Together. In Alaska.

I pulled out a ten-dollar bill. *Da, da, da. I'll take the little book.*

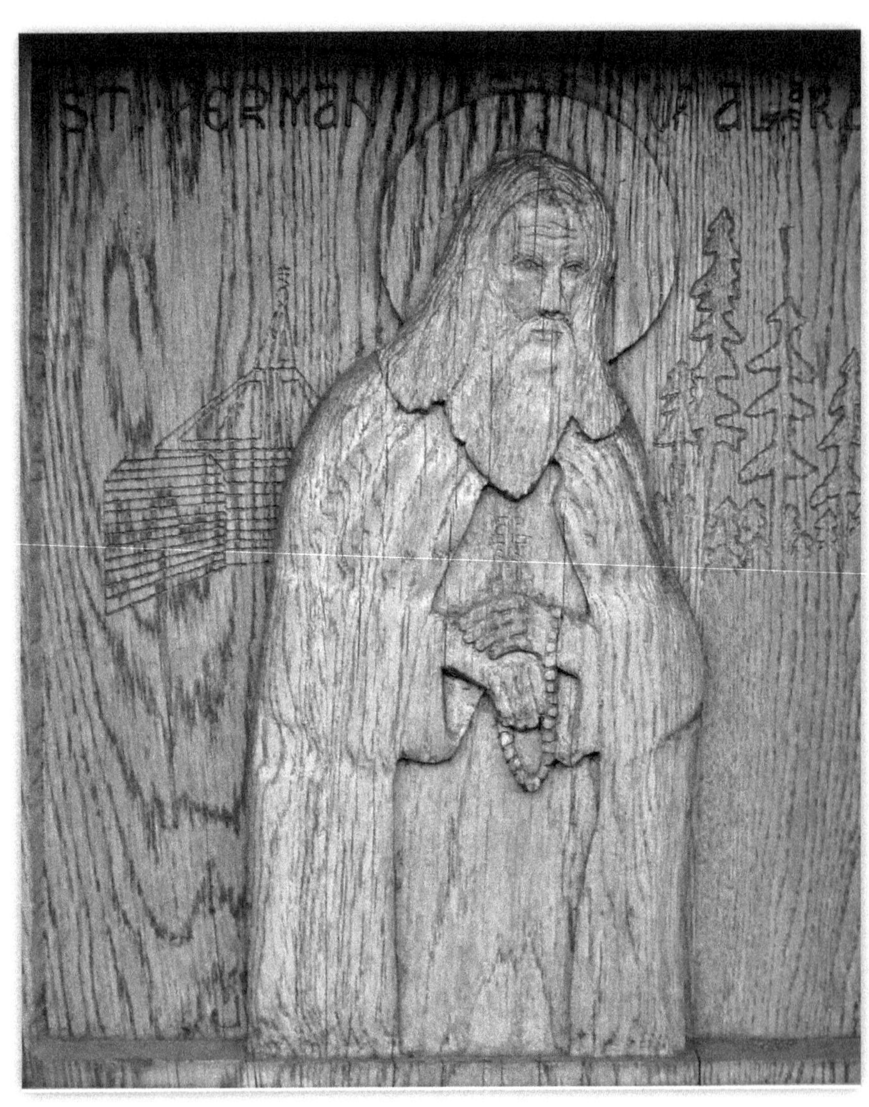

Saint Herman of Alaska, Denny Gill

Anaktuvuk Rose

KARLA LINN MERRIFIELD

In Anaktuvuk Pass, two cultures meet as Rose, verging on womanhood, steps into the dim midnight sun, Nikes on her feet, a grinning caribou-skin mask hiding the broad planes of her face.

"We are all related here," she says of these eight village families, her many cousins, many aunts.

In autumn, soon after the first herd passes through the valley in the granite shade of the Brooks Range, more caribou follow, trailing their kin's scent. Some will offer themselves to Anaktuvuk's hunters, and as many as five per family will be taken. "If an uncle is unlucky, we share," Rose says, but knows that all the grandmothers' freezers will be filled before the long winter.

"I don't eat it raw after the big kill like many do," she continues. "Some, we cut it in strips, dry it. Most goes as steaks or cutlets in our freezers or community meat cache. See, it got flooded this spring; it stinks. I like caribou stew. It's my favorite. Once, it was only flesh in broth with rice. Now, we add vegetables, like carrots and celery. We fish, too, a couple miles away, by foot or snowmachine. In our lake are arctic char, burbot, lots of whitefish. I like berries in fall, tundra cranberries mostly, sometimes blueberries. You can get hamburgers at the general store. I see McDonald's on satellite TV all the time."

When Rose removes the caribou-skin mask, one fringed with a ring of wolverine fur, wolf-gray eyes stare with no answer to my unasked question. A wisp of naturally blond hair laces her forehead, which is paler than this white woman's.

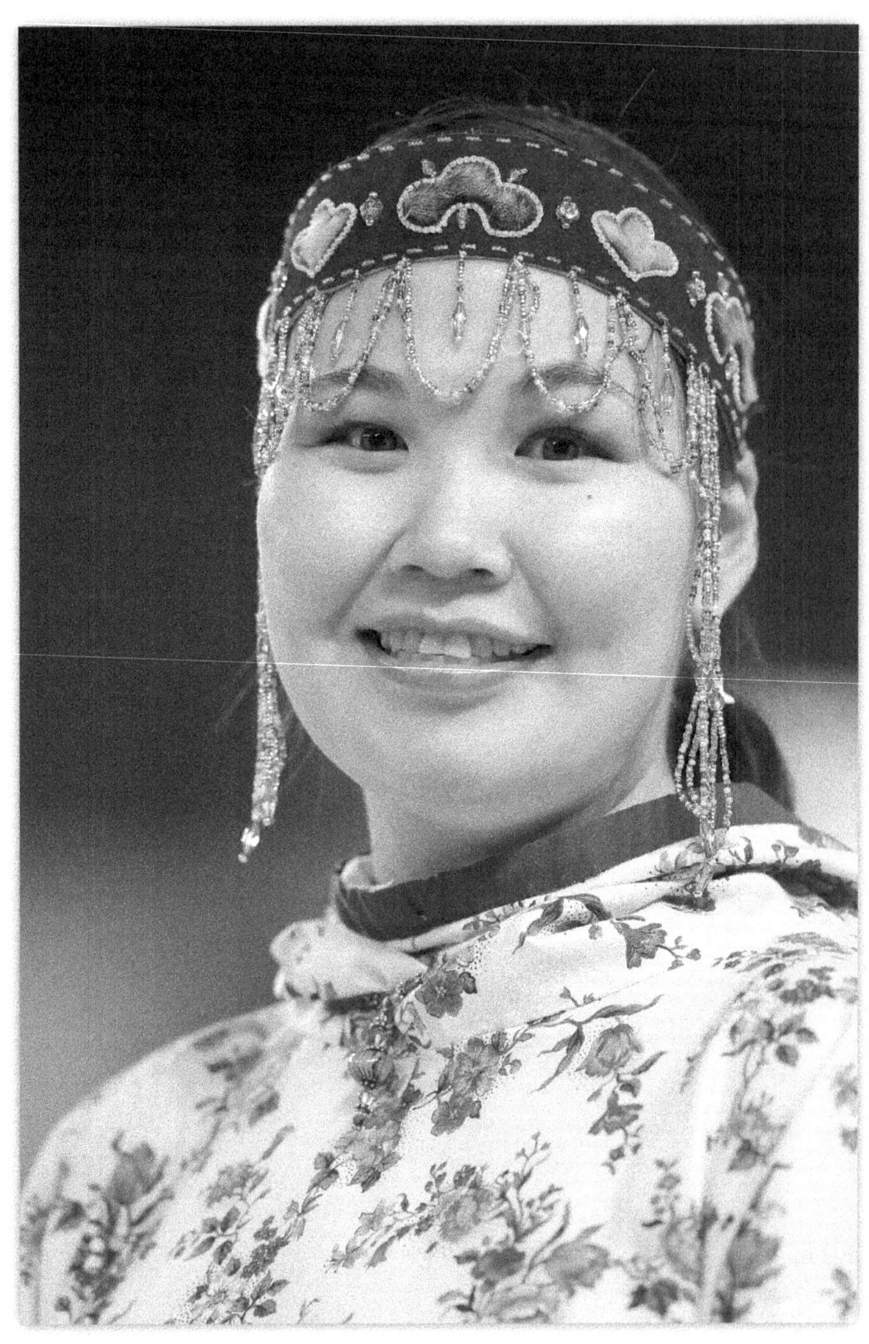

Karlene Waghiyi, Siberian Yupik, Patrick Endres

Eagles Every Day

ELIZABETH BRADFIELD

Local kids put on robes and masks we'd walked past in the museum. Materials (mountain goat hair, buttons, grizzly claws, eagle down) and Context (for potlatch, to welcome back the salmon, for the dance of peace).

Elders sang while the kids, in the range of attitude and attention found everywhere, danced. Wolf moved like the back-row guys in my eighth-grade math class: slumped, habituated. One boy danced Raven and *was* the bird. Nailed it—quick stop-start tilt of eye and beak, awkward and menaced hop, the sense of bright mind turned for a while toward you, making you strange. He must have been thirteen.

I could see the sheen of his basketball shorts, baggy and long, at the hem of his robe. And the back of his head under the mask: black, straight hair gelled to another sheen.

This at the end of a week among the bays and islands of the Inside Passage. Drip of cedar in rain. Killer whales mid-channel. Swaths of hill, bright green where the timber had been sold and taken. Gill net buoy lines. Eagles every day.

I grew up on Tok-A-Lou Avenue, below Mana Wana and Ton-A-Wanda, above the Puyallup's outflow. On clear days, the mountain they never renamed Tacoma pinned the horizon. There was a totem pole on the lawn of my junior high that none of us ever really looked at until Todd and Wade cut it down one night with a hand saw and left it toppled in the grass. It took the PTA months of bake sales and pledge drives to raise it again.

Everywhere, there were stylized logos with Salmon or Thunderbird, tow trucks rendered in form line design. Every year, we bought illegal fireworks from the reservation stands.

There was head-shaking about the casinos and the fishing, talk we'd lose our house to reclamation. I drew pages and pages of black and red shapes—ovoid, clean, and full of stories I didn't bother to learn.

We sat in the cedar room with a dirt floor and regulation fire doors that was new-built as showcase and home for what had never fully leached away. We watched and listened. The all-aboard time was 3 p.m. That boy's Raven—

We applauded. We had no dance to offer. We ate what they gave us: soapberries whipped with sugar to froth and handed out in paper cups with carved spoons.

The berries were sweet, sweet beyond reason, then strangely bitter. We filed out, saying *thank you, thank you.* Sincere. Someone, probably the purser, handed an envelope to the woman by the door. The kids milled out back in street clothes. We walked down to the boat.

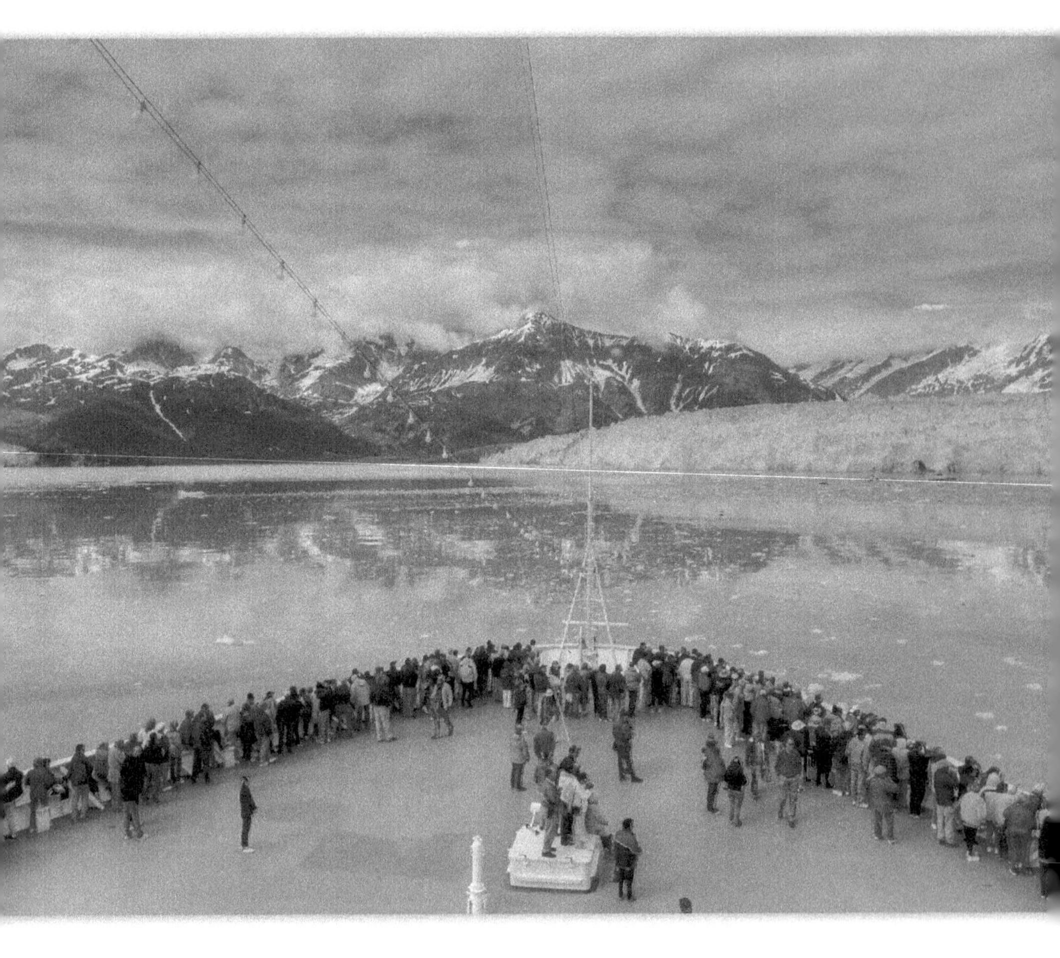

Ship, Glacier, People, Mark McElroy

Those Who Saw This Coming

DON REARDEN

This village doesn't belong here. Nothing belongs here. The tundra and the plywood-box houses seem to agree. The hungry ground slowly swallows the wooden blocks propping up the homes. Everything is sinking. The Arctic isn't supposed to melt like this.

No solid ground exists here. Nothing is stable or reliable, except the ringing of the church bell on Sunday, the hungry yapping of sled dogs at feeding time, and the innocent screams of kids playing in the mud or snow out in front of the school. Slick boardwalks stretch from one end of the village to the other. The children race their bikes down the narrow wooden runways knowing that if a tire gets caught in a gap between the boards, or if they stop too suddenly, they will slide off the walkway and become mired waist-deep in the cold thick mud.

Across the river, a cemetery filled with listing white crosses waits. Beneath the crosses, the black earth threatens to rupture and expose the bones of those who saw this coming. In the evenings a raven sits on one of the white wooden markers and watches the people of the village scurry about. Behind that raven a fiery orange sun melts down into the horizon, and the tundra stretches flat forever.

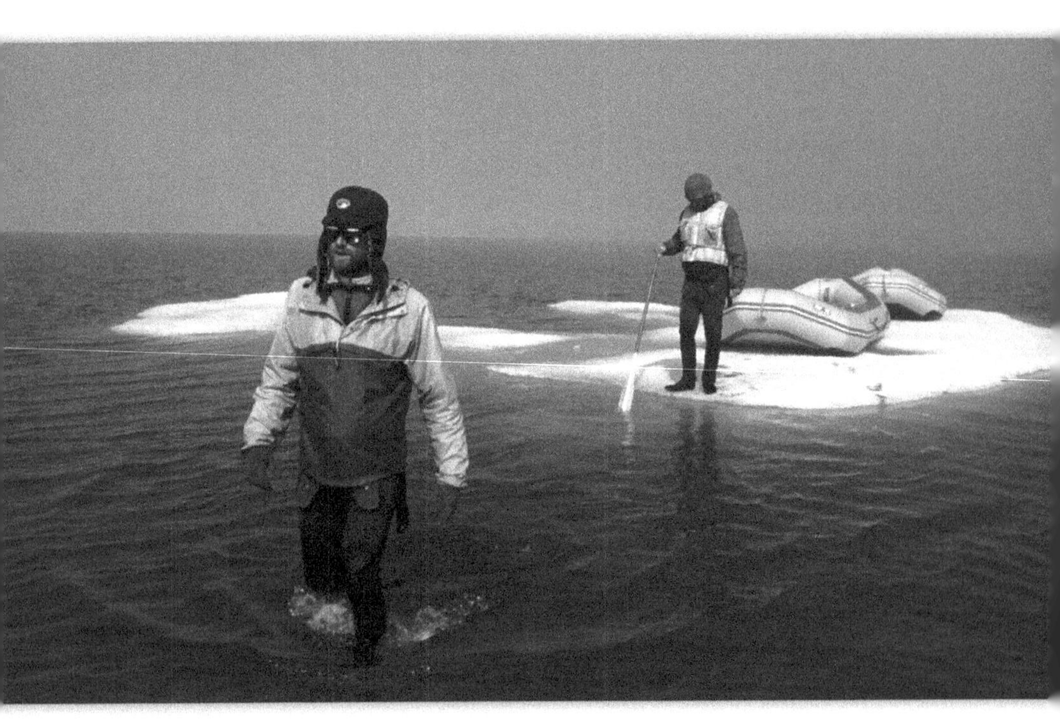

Ocean Walk, Arctic Wild Collection

Anchorage, 2110

EVAN BUXBAUM

I studied my worn Anchorage map. Most of Hillside had been picked clean, but I'd paid fifty bucks for a tip about some diamonds in a Mountain View safe, and I hoped I hadn't wasted my money. The treasures of a lost city, hidden thirty meters below sea level.

The buzz of Billy's approaching outboard dragged me out of bed. Like mine, his house on Hiland had become oceanfront, his weekend fishing boat his only transportation.

We headed west, sunlight playing on the inlet's chop. I rolled a cigarette.

My stash was dwindling, and my source had joined an apocalyptic cult. The whole damn country was an apocalyptic cult now, but tobacco was still a crime. I had to laugh.

It all had happened so suddenly, Shishmaref first, then the other coastal villages. In under a month, the currents changed and the world was under water. Still we drove our cars, and dug for oil, and argued over pot and tobacco, deaf Noahs in a melting world.

I thought about Becky. Just twenty-two, she'd never have given me a second look, but these were different times, and a treasure diver with his own scuba rig was a pretty good catch.

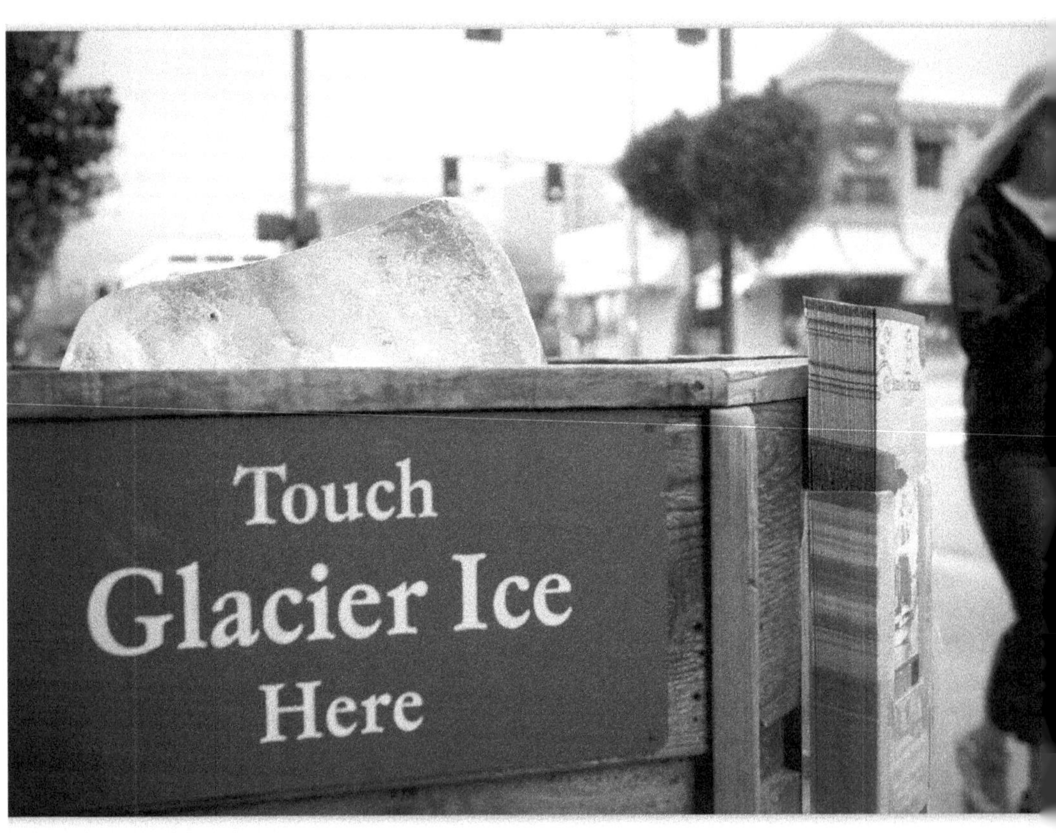

Tourist Street, Stephen Nigl

XtraTuf

CHRISTINE BYL

The foreman for my new trails job in Cordova had some tips. Buy the heavy Helly Hansens, not the lightweights, and leave the Gore-Tex at home. Dipped rubber gloves, or lined elbow-length ones, skip the leathers. And don't get off the ferry without XtraTufs, he said.

New to Anchorage six months earlier, I had heard someone refer to her "Tufs," and I thought then it was a joke, her childlike name for rubber boots. Of course, it was no joke. XtraTuf is a brand, Tufs their affectionate nickname, and good luck wearing another boot in Alaska and holding up your head. Tufs are the choice for commercial fishermen and cannery row, biologists and dip-netters, day hikes and trail work. Tufs are so ubiquitous in coastal towns that the foyer of a house during a potluck is piled with them. People use magic marker to label the vanilla-colored stripe around the top, ensuring they'll go home in the right pair. With a tight-fitted calf and tapered toe, Tufs are far superior to the boots of childhood puddle walks, those with the handles at the top and a fit like a bucket. You'd rather your Tufs didn't go home with someone else.

Tufs aren't perfect. A heavy object dropped on the flimsy toe hurts, and running a chain saw in wet weather, they're sketchy, steel toe or not. Ten miles on a trail in Tufs will leave you footsore, and a tussock walk courts a sprained ankle. The neoprene lining quickly stinks of mold and fish guts and gull shit and feet. But, in places like Cordova where it rains for days, weeks on end, in places where other footwear disintegrates in months, Tufs hold up. Feet stay warm and damp instead of cold and soaked. Small victories.

I have worked trails on the Sound, in the Interior, and in Southcentral, and in seven years, have worn through only two pairs of Tufs, the old ones now cut into low-top slip-ons for drier chores. In recent years, I have seen chic Anchorage girls headed to Koot's in shiny new Tufs, sashaying in workboots recast as fashion. They're trying to own a place, I know, trying to stake the local claim, just as I was, getting off the ferry in my first pair. But the girls have missed the point. What makes Tufs sexy is where they've been, and what they bear to prove it—the fish stink, the mud, the moose dung mashed in the tread. Few of us are local, and those who are know best: none of us own anywhere. All we—or our boots—can say is where we've been.

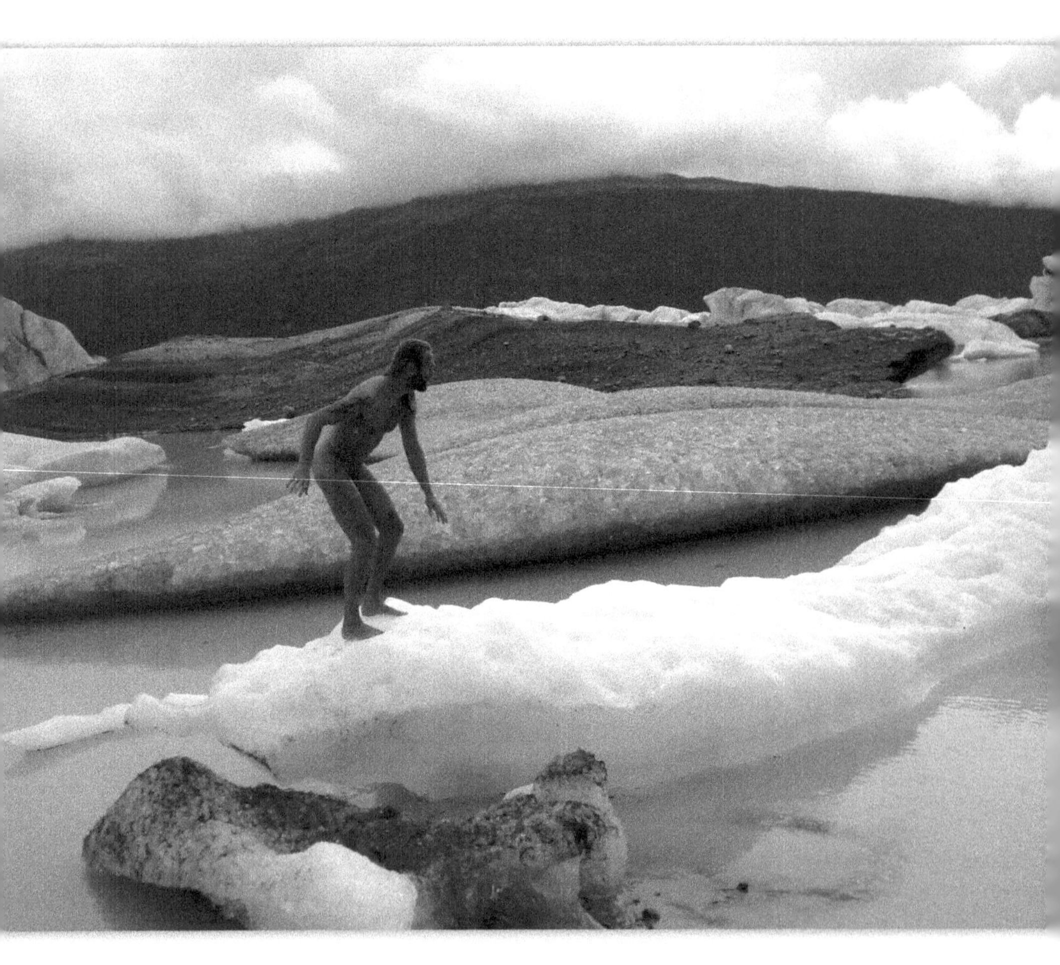

Ice Surfing, Melissa Guy

Biking Cool

MICHAEL ENGELHARD

Each fall I compile a to-do list for winterizing my bike, hoping to get around to these things before first flurries make tinkering outside undesirable. *Buy studded tires. Apply low-temperature chain grease. Attach pogies* (mittenlike shells) *to handlebars. Add reflectors....* Needless to say, each fall I step outside my cabin some morning to find snow piled on the seat of my still-unmodified ride.

This is no place for tight spandex outfits; heavy wool Army pants—baggy enough for two pairs of long underwear—will keep vital parts functioning. Footwear consists of knee-high mukluks. A down parka, beaver-skin hat, and fleece mittens complete the outfit. Because of the cushioning garments, body protection is unnecessary, unsightly, if not impossible. Helmets don't fit over Soviet-style fur hats, and the only chance for abrasions is doing a facedown on salted roads. A full beard or facemask does come in handy on breezy days. (I take off the mask when entering banks or convenience stores.)

The greatest challenge is staying upright. I've learned to avoid rash braking and steering maneuvers on "black ice" and perfected the paratrooper's shoulder roll. Steering one-handed between buried sidewalks and bully trucks while flipping off drivers also demands fine motor skills.

There's glass from broken whiskey bottles. (As stores have specials on six-packs of hard liquor, business is brisk.) Moose cross at unpredictable intervals, and—in the dark—may mistake bikers for rivals or possible mates.

Though there is little topographic relief around town, considerable weight loss and aerobic workouts can be expected. This is mostly due to snowdrifts on the road and excessive sweating inside of bulky clothing.

But let's not ignore those nuggets of beauty by the roadside. Snow dervishes spinning on blacktop. Gamboling ravens. Mock suns, from ice crystals quivering in the air. On days when I'm too chicken to face traffic I shortcut through the woods behind campus, bisecting moose tracks, tree shadows, and spokes of sunlight.

I'm not that exceptional—Fairbanks hums with cold-weather biking activity. There's the French expatriate, an accomplished classical violinist, who hauls bags of dog food on a trailer for the huskies that share his backwoods home. There's Bob, who wears felt Viking helmets and wraps birch bark around his bike frame, which appears cobbled together from saplings. Another guy pulls an enclosed trailer with a clear plastic window, at forty below. (Is he carrying live babies in there?)

With our snotsicles and waxy cheeks, our breaths' plumes and hulking silhouettes, we may look like members of Scott's last expedition. But an inner flame fuels us, some deep-down awareness: what is *sport* for some is *transport* for others. Regardless of trends, we are biking cool.

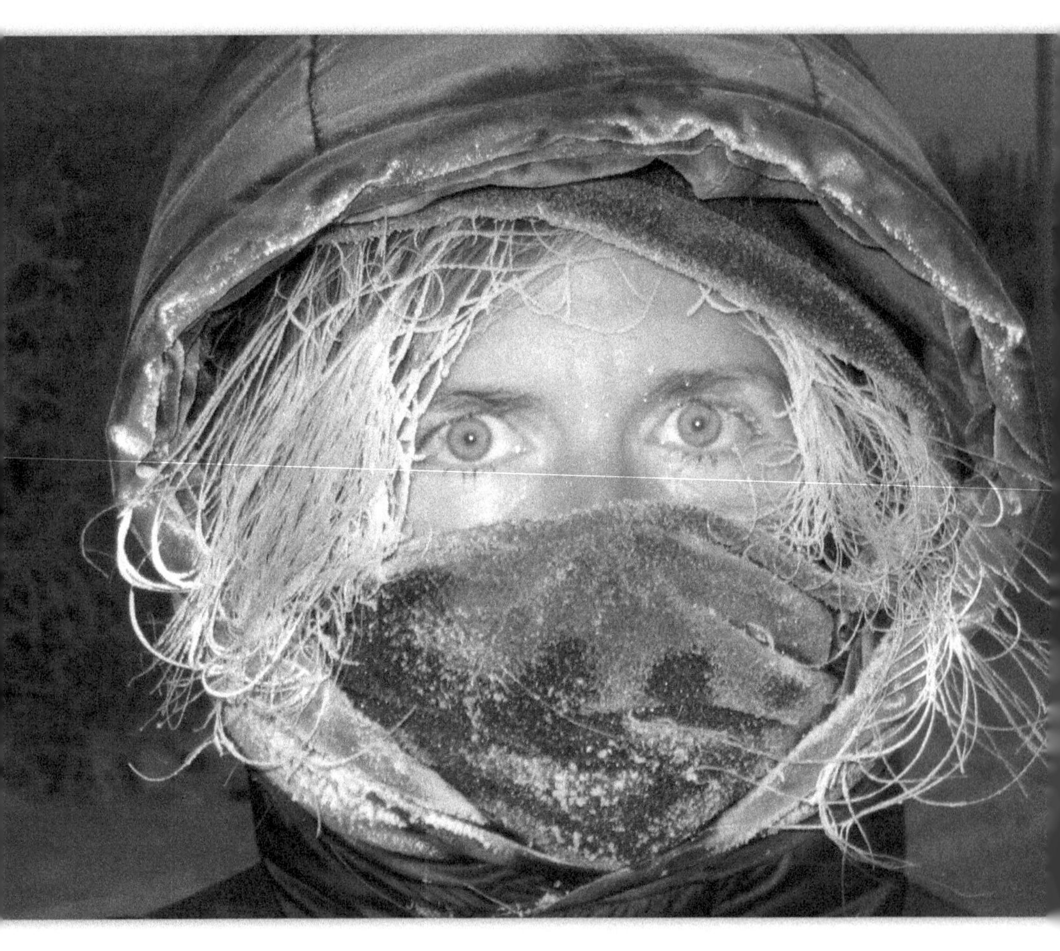

Frosty, Michael Engelhard

The Bra Brawl

MAREI BENTON

One weekend last fall, JC Penney had an unbelievable bra sale—it was buy one at regular price and receive a second bra free. All brands included, no limit, sale Friday through Sunday only.

I arrived early on Friday morning, an hour after they opened. I was not there for the bra sale; I was there for an amazing, concurrent deal on Lock & Lock plastic ware.

Standing in line, Lock & Locks in hand, I witnessed the showdown. The combatants made a lopsided circle—a clerk at the checkout desk, two women in line ahead of me, another two standing off to the right.

"I just don't understand. The sale started today. The store has only been open for one hour. How could you have possibly sold every bra in the store?" one of the women in line asked the salesclerk.

"We had an unusual morning," the salesclerk replied.

"What exactly does that mean?" grumbled the first woman's friend, as I absentmindedly admired the way she'd rolled her jeans over her XtraTuf boots.

The clerk explained, "Well, apparently, a couple of women in Fairbanks heard about the sale and began taking orders from all their friends and family and coworkers in Fairbanks—'cuz there is no JC Penney in Fairbanks. After these women had a couple hundred bras all paid for, they rented a van and drove down here for the weekend. They were waiting at the door when we opened today … and they just bought everything."

The two women in line in front of me clearly had not counted on a bra-crazed delegacy from Fairbanks to show up, unannounced, uninvited, and buy up every cheap bra in Anchorage. The first woman turned to her friend and snootily stated, "Well, it figures. I suppose there's nothing better to do in Fairbanks. This was probably a big weekend for them, to get out of that dump."

The two women who had been previously politely standing off to the side interrupted at that statement. "Excuse us, but we are those women from Fairbanks. And this town is the dump, not Fairbanks."

The tension soared between the two sets of women, as they stood there, frozen, waiting to see who would back down first. Frightened, I made eye contact with the clerk, put my Lock & Locks down, and slowly backed away. (A great deal on plastic containers is one thing—being caught in a fistfight between these women would have been another.) As I left the aisle, I heard the clerk announce with an enormous deal of cheer that she had coupons for an extra ten percent off of bedding … if anyone wanted one.

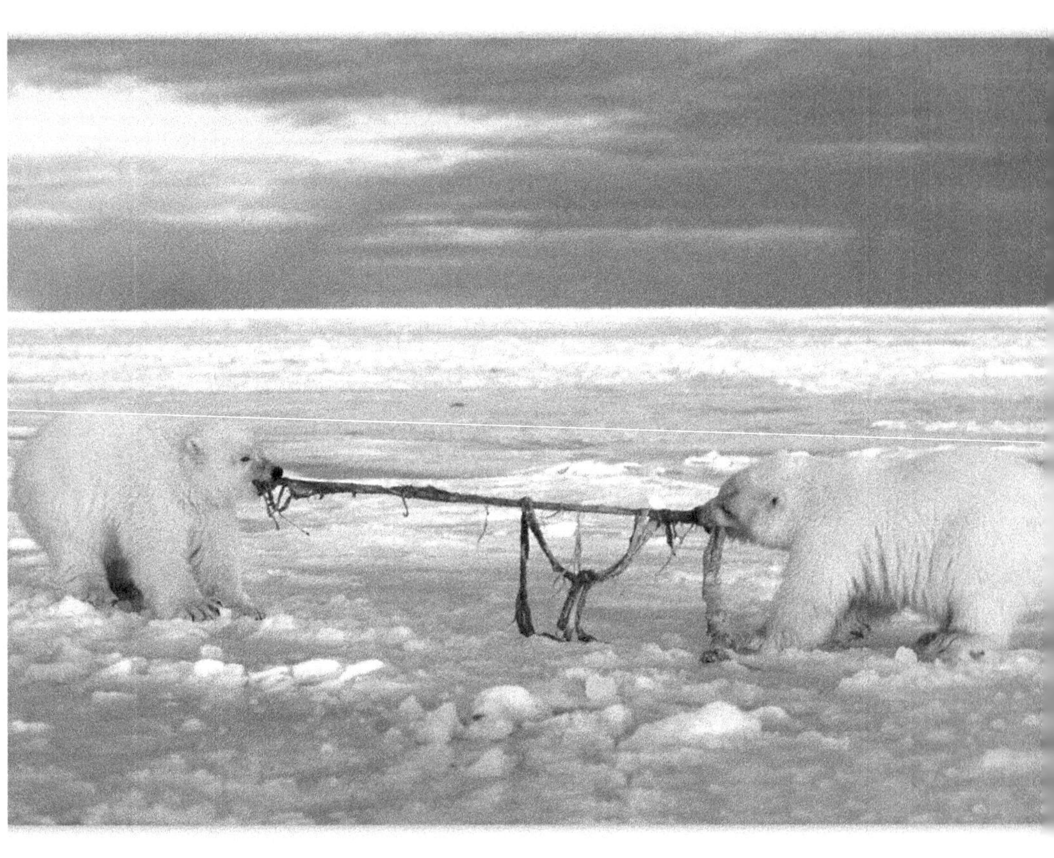

Sibling Rivalry, Steven Kazlowski

Just a BB Gun

LOUISE FREEMAN

My mistake was showing up at the Alaska Airlines ticket counter at the Fairbanks International Airport with a BB gun in a duffle bag.

"You can't check in a gun with your regular baggage," the ticket agent barked. "It has to be in a gun case and checked in through security at TSA."

"It's just a BB gun."

"Any kind of gun has to be in a gun case with a lock."

"I don't have a gun case. It was a gift."

"Well then you have to buy one from TSA or surrender the gun."

"How much is a gun case?"

She quickly looked up the price on her computer.

"Ninety dollars."

"That's three times what the BB gun cost!"

"You either buy one or you don't fly with it. Those are the regulations." She looked at me suspiciously, something suddenly occurring to her. "It's not loaded is it?"

"Yes, actually, it is." I jiggled the bag so she could hear the BBs rattle.

"Oh my God! A loaded gun." She picked up the telephone and called TSA. "We've got a loaded gun here. I need someone over here. Now."

Within seconds two TSA agents were at my side.

"Step this way, please," the taller of the two said as they escorted me behind the counter and into a back room. They stopped at a table with a wastebasket next to it and then moved away from me.

"Unload the gun and put the ammo in the trash," instructed the shorter one.

I pulled out the BB gun that Sam had put into my hands so lovingly just the day before, never dreaming it was going to cause a problem. Now I might miss my flight. Turning the gun over, I shook it until the BBs sprayed out, ricocheting around in the empty metal trash can, sounding like, well, like buckshot.

I wasn't about to surrender the gun. It was a gift from Sam. I bought the damn case. It was enormous, and strapped inside, the little Red Ryder BB gun looked like a kid's violin in a cello case. My flight was leaving in less than twenty minutes and I still had to check the gun case at the TSA security counter. I stood self-consciously in line with several burly men, all carrying rifle cases. The guy behind me, decked out in clothes fit for a safari, looked at my brand-new case and said, "d'ya get anything?"

"Excuse me?"

"Did you get anything? Caribou?"

I just said, with what I hoped was a knowing look, "Nope, not this time. You?"

He shrugged sympathetically and shook his head.

I made my flight with four minutes to spare.

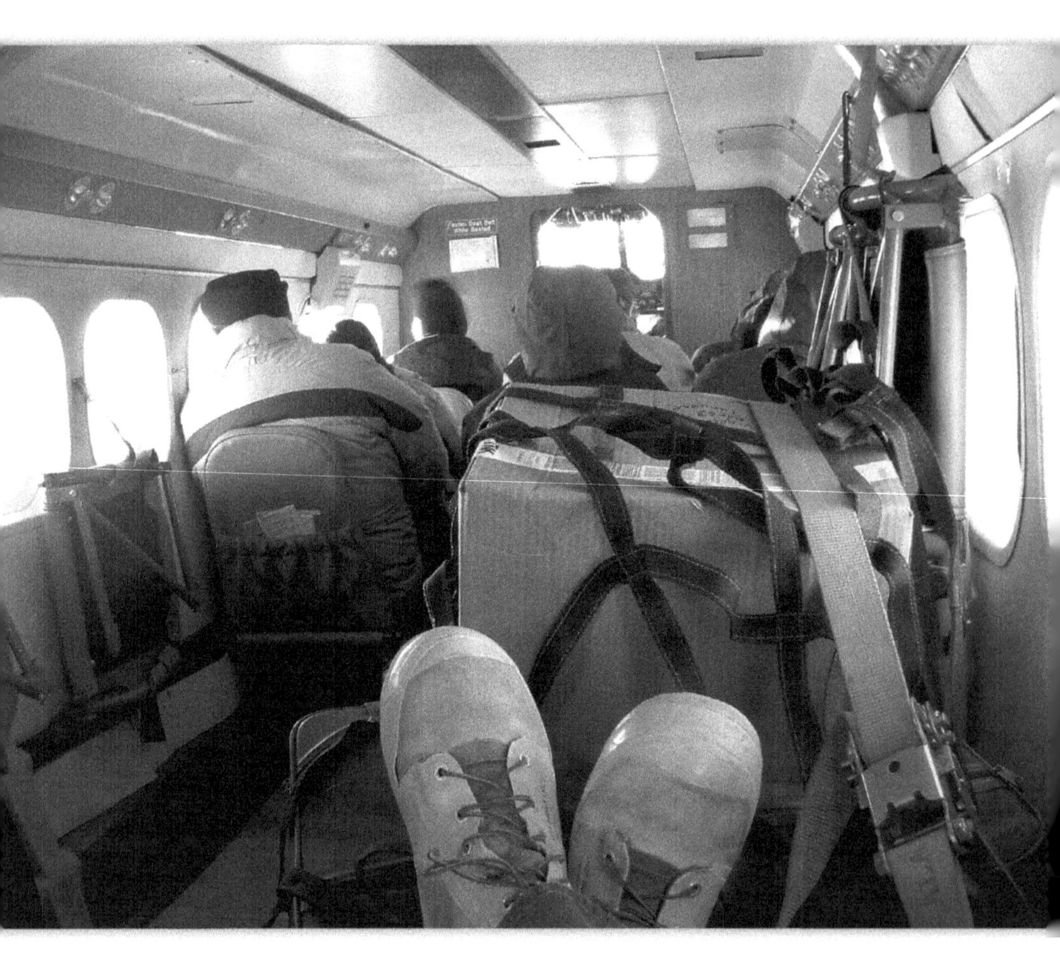

Bush Flight, Robert Drozda

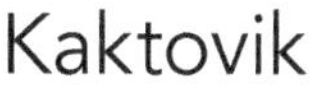

Kaktovik

BRUCE RETTIG

Our plane slices a fog bank and turbulence slams us against the sides of the cabin. I pull my seatbelt tighter. My co-worker, Squirrelly, points to the cockpit. The copilot's knees are shaking. Squirrelly pulls a knife from his pack, a Buck Folding Hunter. It's clicked open.

If we go down I'm slitting my throat before we hit the ground, he says.

I rub my eyes and tell him that he's going to feel pretty damn stupid if we somehow happen to land safely.

Last fall the boats and barges had ripped free of their moorings during an arctic blast and drifted two hundred miles east, toward Canada. A makeshift crew rounded them up like a devil after lost souls then ditched them on Barter Island before the sea froze solid. They wait for our crews and the spring thaw to release them.

We descend to an unseen airfield. I pull a tin of Skoal from the pocket of my Carhartts and jam a wad behind my lower lip. The last thing I told my girlfriend before I left for the summer was that we'd be together again—soon. She only smiled. Most of me left that day.

Squirrelly wipes the blade with his denim shirt and says it's a damn good thing we smoked that fatty before taking off.

The pilots crane their necks and wipe the windshield, but there's only flat whiteness. I try to convince myself it's probably best not to look anyway. Close your eyes and think of something else ... anything else. Maybe I'll go to grad school when I get back home.

Holy shit, Squirrelly shouts.

I open my eyes to see a crane boom less than fifty feet from the nose of the plane. The engines scream as the pilot throttles up and we arc to the left. Air whistles through the crane's stanchions when we skim past. The copilot has lost pigmentation.

Drifts of sand and ice speed underneath us until a faint light appears, a beacon signaling the end of a runway. The pilot takes a breath then zeros in. Squirrelly closes the knife. He says the flight's a piece of cake and he's had worse trips. No big deal.

The plane skips twice on the gravel before settling down. As we bounce across the washboard surface, the Eskimo village of Kaktovik comes into view. Polar bear skins hang from the porches of a couple of government-built houses, and behind a Quonset hut lies the jawbone of a whale. Beyond Kaktovik, a road leads to the boats.

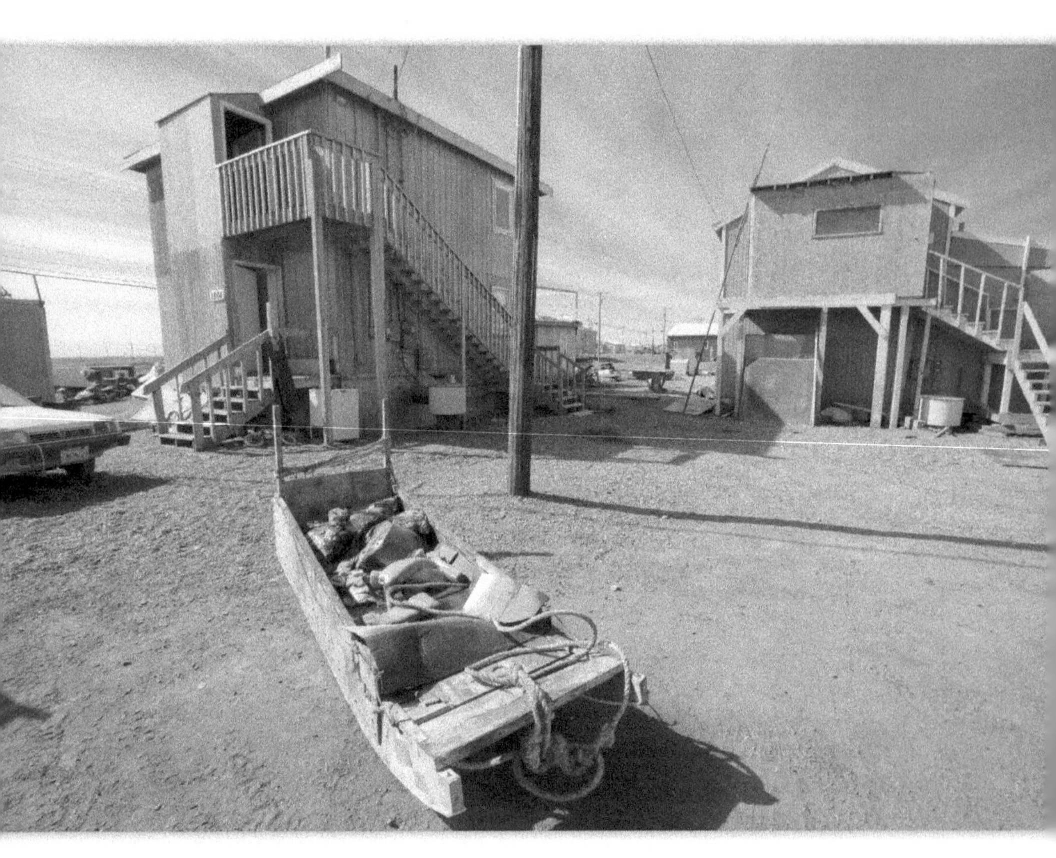

Meat Sled—Barrow, Patrick Endres

Fog

LESLIE LEYLAND FIELDS

It was three weeks before my due date with my fourth child. I flew from fishcamp into Kodiak for a checkup and was trying to fly back. The flights had been cancelled for the entire day, because fog, the solid definitive kind, had sent airline employees home. The next day, I drove out to the airport again, the day wrapped in a different kind of fog, the ambiguous kind that prompts weather holds rather than cancellations. At 8:30 a.m., we were on weather hold again. This time, compelled by hope, I waited at the terminal instead of going straight home—maybe the fog would lift.

Three hours later, the pilot appeared and faced the five travelers determined to get to the other side of the island. "We'll give it a try," he said with a casual wave. "We'll go up and take a look. We may turn around in five minutes. We'll just see." We were locals, we understood. No commitment, no promise of anything: maybe. Maybe we would get all the way through to Larsen Bay. Maybe we'd get as far as Port Bailey and then have to turn back. Maybe we'd fly the shoreline for an hour longer. Maybe—anything. We had to think it, all of us, anyone who flies regularly in Alaska, and especially on Kodiak. You do not have to live here long before someone you know, or at least know of, dies in a plane crash.

We made it that day, in a single try. It was not our normal route. The fog pressed us low to the ground; the clouds, like veils, alternately revealed and concealed the usual passes. But the pilot nosed his way through, rising, dodging, until, finally, the village emerged through a rent in the sky. As we circled to land, I could see three tiny figures in rain gear near the gravel runway, faces to the sky. A *maybe* flight that ended in *yes*. Not the kind of yes that exults to a high five—this, a yes that you breathe, a prayer.

Two weeks later, a flight on the same route ended *no*. It was foggy again. The pilot successfully maneuvered his three passengers across the island's treacherous interior. Five miles from the airport, through the last pass, where on a clear day you could see the runway, a wingtip hit the ground. Someone planted four crosses there, on a burnt piece of earth just two hundred feet from the road. No one who lives here asks, *why was the plane so low?*

Winter Fog—Creamer's Field, Robert Drozda

Parcel Pickup

GEORGE GUTHRIDGE

On my worst day of teaching on St. Lawrence Island in the Bering Sea, I arrived at school to learn that there were two boxes waiting for me on the tarmac. My hydraulic weight set had arrived! I headed back into the blizzard.

To my relief, the boxes still sat on the runway. I balanced the larger one across my snowmachine and put the smaller, heavier one on top. That left just enough room to squeeze in my knees. By leaning over the boxes, I could drive home.

When I tried to turn the machine, the smaller box slid forward, smashing my thumb. I pulled away in pain. The box hit the throttle—the machine leapt forward and bucked me off.

I ran after a snowmachine driven by two boxes; sparks flew whenever it hit an ice-free spot of tarmac.

A plane droned through the snowy gloom, its lights like the eyes of a predator.

I dove off the runway. The plane kept coming, on collision course with my snowmachine.

I already saw the headline: barrage of dumbbells wipes out arctic aircraft!

But for once, luck seemed to be on my side.

The snowmachine hit a bump and headed toward the icy sea. I knew the boxes would fall off and the machine would stop when it hit the snow berm alongside the runway.

The machine hit the berm—

The boxes, teetering crazily, did not fall.

I barely noticed the plane's screeching brakes and revving engine upon touchdown.

My snowmachine was headed toward the ocean.

Finally, as if God had wearied of His jest, the boxes tipped off. The snowmachine stopped ten feet from open water.

I walked to the school's maintenance shed for a seal hook. From the ocean's edge, I crawled onto the ice as far as I dared, and, after several throws, caught the hook on a runner. Hand-over-hand, I pulled the snowmachine ashore.

Then I did a truly stupid thing.

Fearing witnesses to my predicament, I quickly looped one end of the seal hook rope around the snowmachine and snugged the other around my waist. I inched up to my boxes on all fours, ice cracking underneath. After dragging them to firm ground, I collapsed.

My heart pounded—I was alive, and nobody had seen me.

"You okay?" The pilot's face entered my field of vision. "I sent the school custodian for the school sled. He'll be right back."

When I arrived home, the padlock was frozen. I broke into my own house.

Inside, I ripped open my treasure boxes.

The weight set—a wall-mounted one—turned out to be six feet six.

My wall was six feet four.

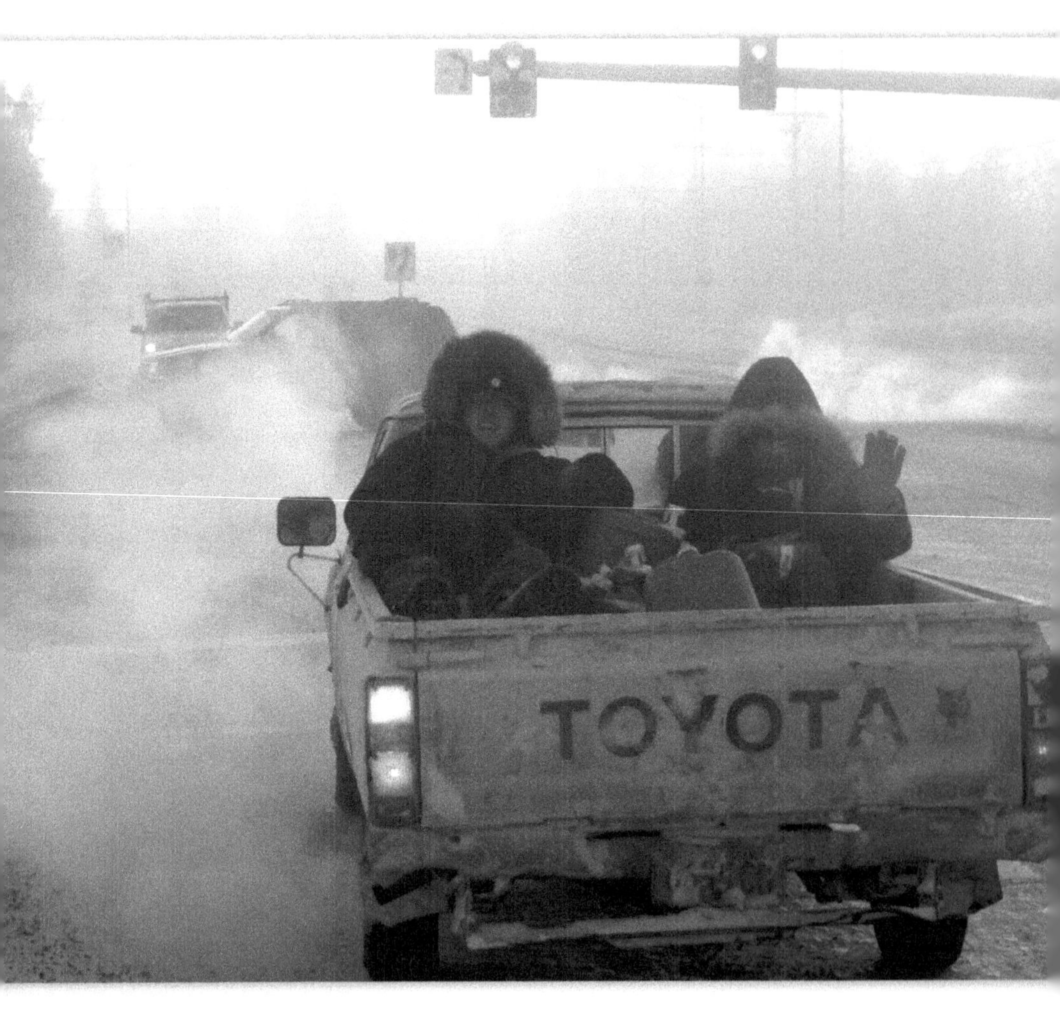

Cruising at Forty-two Below, Robert Drozda

Half-House

JULIE WILLIAMS

The road to home is mud, either frozen or thawed, and sometimes flooded. A half-mile slog from the pavement to what is known as Yurtville, considered swamp, but what we could afford. We catch our drinking water in buckets, have a battery bank and a generator. By a small act of God and the telephone lady, there is a primitive phone line, our internet connection, which runs across wet moss for half a mile. It's spliced into an old hookup on the wall of an abandoned house, two stories made from particleboard. A local named Bob built it when he was seventeen, then lived there with his family. For some reason I have never asked, they moved just across town but didn't take *any* of their belongings with them. It looks like a tornado hit only the house: old kids' clothes, naked dolls, dilapidated wet furniture, and the occasional small appliance strewn around the yard. In the kitchen window, there is a neat row of coffee cups hanging from the sill, untouched, perfect. The house stands, electricity on. Occasionally, Bob ventures in to retrieve moose meat he keeps in his freezer that hums downstairs.

One day, I ran into him. "Hey, I sold part of my house to a friend. Don't worry, they aren't taking the half with your phone line." Bob owed this guy, and apparently, it was equivalent to half his house.

A month later, I got out of bed and heard a chain saw. I walked down the trail and sure enough—two guys hung off the roof, sawing the house in half, right down the middle. They clung precariously to its peak, chain saws running. They waved.

Most of the buildings in this Alaska bush town have been moved from their original spots, but this was a first. At the end of the day, there it was, in two pieces—the carnage of its previous life on display—a white-trash model home with the back off so you could peer in. The chain-saw guys shoveled all the old moldy stuff from the half they bought into the half that was staying.

Later that week, they dragged their share down the trail with heavy equipment. Huge muddy ruts replaced the vegetation. A frantic search for the phone line showed it hanging in alder branches but still intact. I followed the trail of debris. On a newly cleared lot sat half the house with blue tarps stapled to the open end, and a claw-foot bathtub, upside down, as a step.

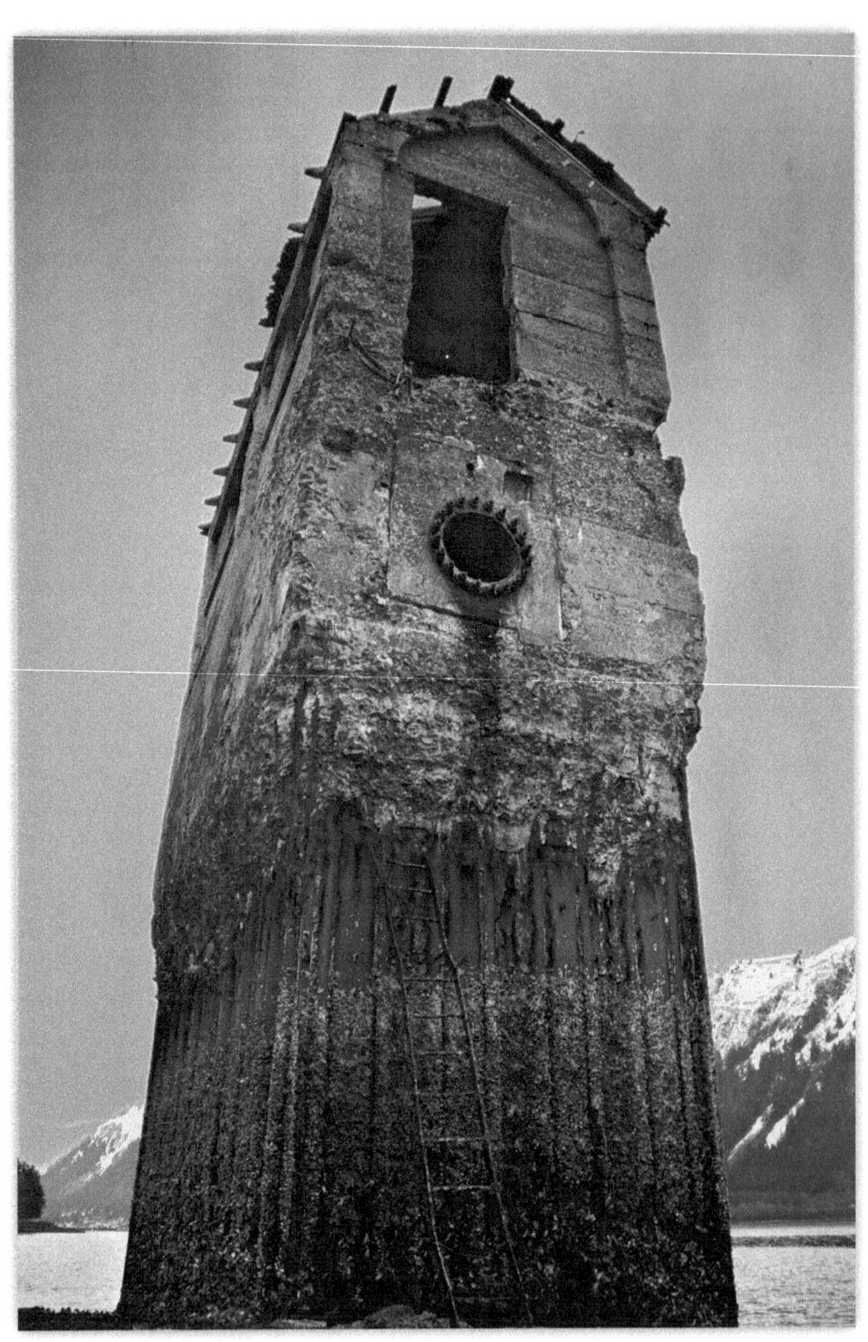

Sandy Beach Pumphouse, Kelli Burkinshaw

Apostle of End Times

LESLEY THOMAS

He had to be careful when he brought up these ideas, never forgetting the award-winning author he sat next to on the small plane coming back from the conference. They were in the south above the peninsula, and he tested the waters.

"Lotsa' devastation from those beetles, eh?" he said nonchalantly, leaning over as if to see better the waves of dying trees below. You could practically hear the billions of jaws munching through the cambium.

"Yes." She glanced out the porthole then peered at her notes. The shamanic pendant on her bosom and her librarian's glasses signaled that she was not afraid of big scary ideas, not a denier.

"Yeah, half of Siberia is burning up this summer—as if the permafrost needed that—but over there, trees die from caterpillars!" His voice rose like at those economic development meetings, which were considered socialist but weren't. The corporate net dragged in fishermen like him. Crabs lost their shells from acidification. Jellyfish and monstrous squid were replacing salmon. You learned this from science magazines, not from whacko conspiracy bloggers. Alaska was fucked. They all were.

"Caterpillars ..." mused the author, and jotted down something. He knew she went to fishcamp and so might not be repelled by his attire—he wore a Carhartt, and it was stifling, and now he saw that the sleeves were bloodstained, but in the narrow seat he couldn't squirm to get it off, because she might take it the wrong way. He took it to the next level.

"Yep, where I'm from they brought in twenty windmills; they could've supplied the town with electricity, but they broke, and no one can fix 'em. There they stand. I think a fellow poet would find that pretty symbolic."

"Symbolic of what?"

"Of how we're not going to go easily into that dark night."

Her look was blank. "The coming collapse?" he prompted, and her eyes sharpened, abruptly hostile. No, she was no Alaskan but a city slicker, a transplant. "Peak oil?" he hinted contemptuously.

She reared back from him like the words stung, like he was going to kidnap her to be his mate in the end times, like he'd said "Have you taken the Lord as your savior?" or "cunt." She turned her head to stare out the window and, at the airport, rushed into the bathroom where he couldn't follow.

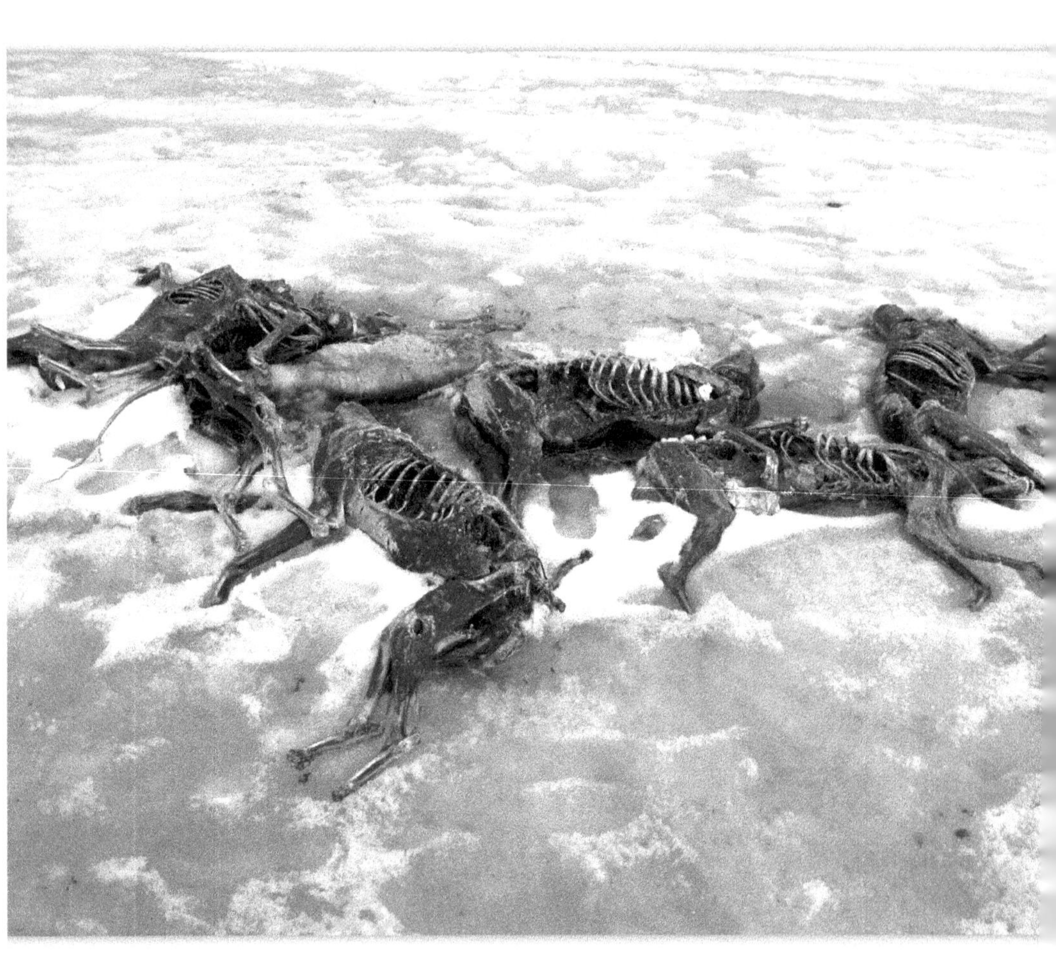

Wolves on the Kuskokwim, Tom Jamgochian

Escape from Planet Alaska

VIVIAN FAITH PRESCOTT

In the dusk, Lisa climbed out of an orange van and trudged up the trail to her former house on the hill to kidnap her children. Last night, their spaceship *Starlighter* failed to arrive. The "Family of Aurora Dea" figured they must have misinterpreted the data they had channeled from their god, Father. Now, new data revealed the *Starlighter* was going to land in Oregon.

As usual, Wrangell Island folks left their doors unlocked. Lisa roused her four children while her ex-husband slept. The Family told Lisa her children were spiritually asleep; it was her job to wake them, to raise them in the Family. She carried her toddler son across the yard toward the salmonberry bushes. Her three young girls, Katie, Becca, and Rachel, followed.

Katie's feet slipped inside her rubber boots. She stopped. "Momma, where are we going?" she asked.

"We're going to Oregon," Lisa said, grabbing Katie's hand.

"Why?" Katie asked.

"Well, we get to ride on a spaceship," Lisa explained.

"Is Daddy coming?"

"No hon, Daddy's asleep and he won't wake up."

"Why?" Katie asked again. Her final "why" went unanswered.

Halfway back down the trail, Lisa looked out toward Woronkofski Island's silhouette, wondering about the lights often seen zipping over the treetops. These sightings were common in Wrangell lore. Local fishermen often saw them, her grandfather had seen them, Lisa had seen them. She convinced herself that the lights proved the existence of alien spaceships; and that the *Starlighter* would soon rescue the Family, displaced gods and goddesses, and transport them back to their planet. Lisa imagined her planet like the utopias in *Worlds of Tomorrow* magazine.

Inside the van, Lisa's new lover, John, was smoking a joint and listening to the radio blare Count Five's "Psychotic Reaction." The children climbed into the back of the windowless van. They held hands and sat among oil and black mold. Rusty tools clanked at their feet.

John and Lisa drove to the airplane pullout. Soon, the Grumman Goose would be landing on Zimovia Strait and crawling up the ramp. The Goose was now the only way off the island—other than hitching a ride on a troller—to Ketchikan in order to take another plane to Oregon. But Alaska's gravity was already folding in on Lisa; sensing a kidnapping attempt, the airline agent refused to sell her the tickets.

Near the event horizon, Lisa stood outside the small airline shack with her four children, not realizing that the lights flickering above the island would never reach her. The flash of insight would eventually come, but light cannot escape a black hole and neither could she—for the next twenty years—the alien goddess from the universe called Home.

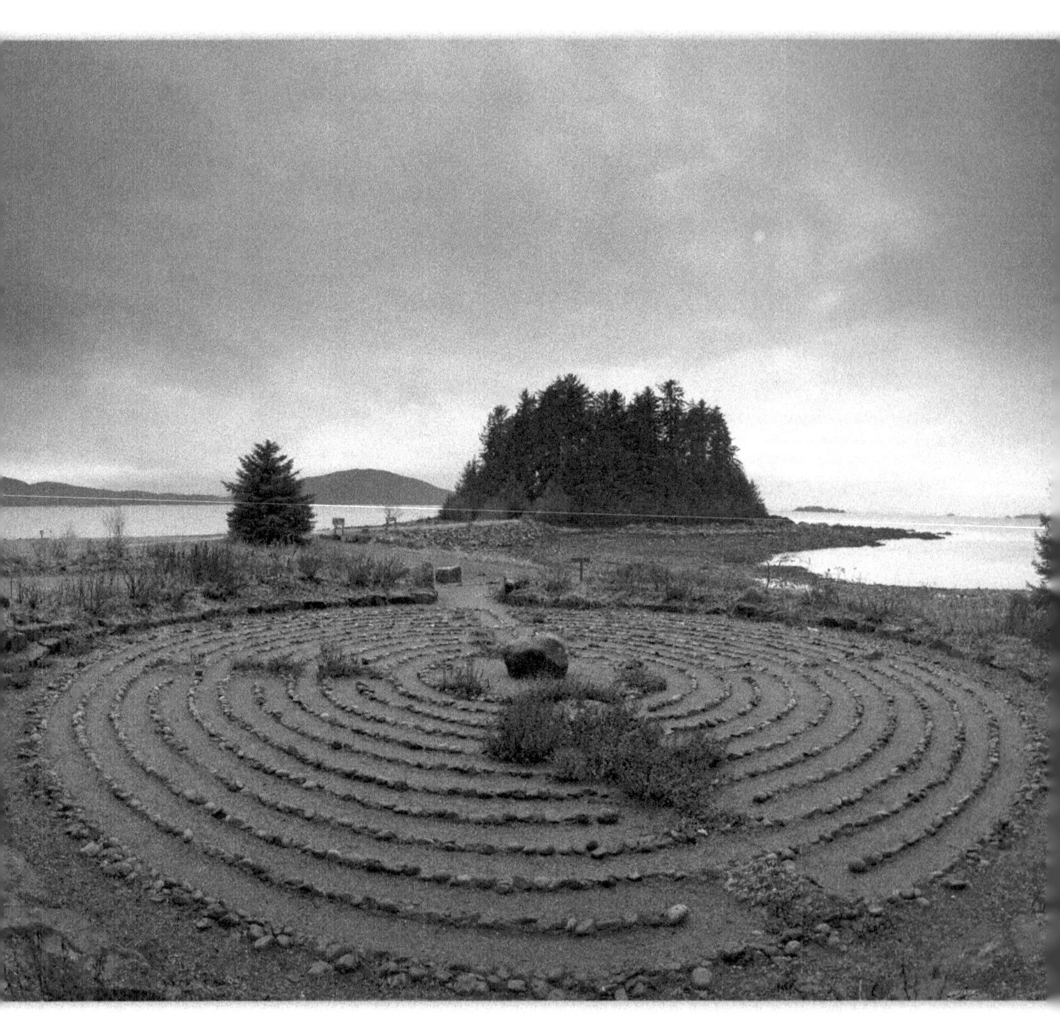

Faith, Laurent Dick

About Ravens

BRUCE ORTON

Raven shouted in a wooden voice as he/she? scooped my lunchbox off a mossy stump. I put down the saw, staring through mist beading my face as Raven circled once with the prize, stroking damp air with benighted wings. The pint steel thermos within didn't slow Raven a bit.

The sun broke through clouds. Rainbows danced in obsidian plumage. Raven laughed from the throat, dropping the box in a gully full of devil's club and distance, to burst its seams, spilling sandwiches and peanut butter cups across damp logs.

I swore at the sky. More laughter echoed from the trees around me like branches breaking in the wind. It was a long day ahead without food, and the truck wouldn't pick me up till six.

The guy here before me lost his lunch to Raven. He started banging with a .44 at the big black birds, sending other loggers diving for cover. Raven laughed. The guy never got one. He lost his job.

It definitely was a laugh from the dark spruce above Tyonek as I climbed down the gully for my looted lunchbox.

The next day, duct taped, I put it under a log.

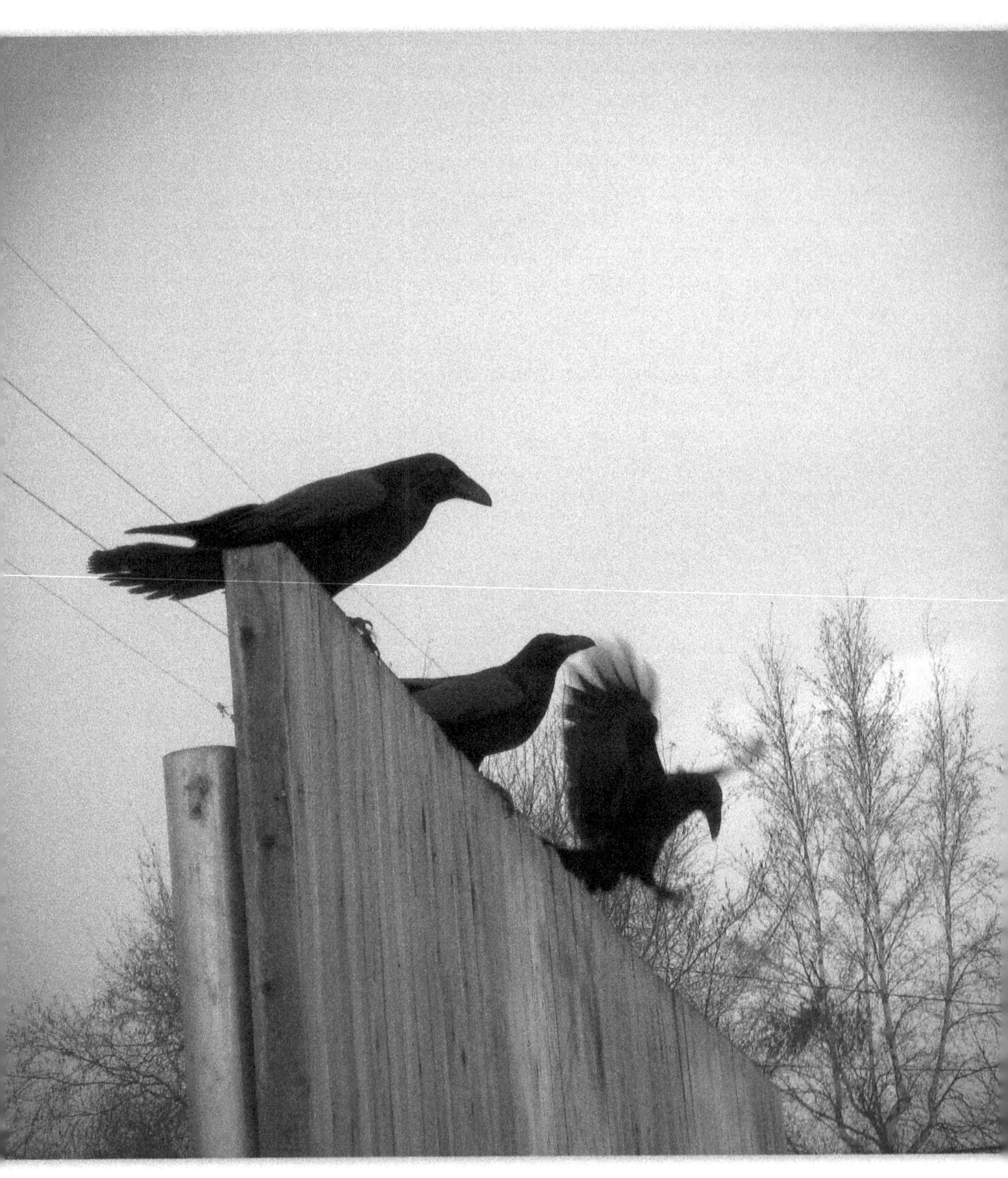

Raven's Roost, Stephen Nigl

M-E-W Gulls

DOUGLASS BOURNE

I assume they are husband and wife, retired and beyond romantic gestures. They walk close to each other but don't hold hands. The man's hat tells the number of his local VFW.

"What are you looking at?" she asks.

"There are a couple of chicks down there that just hatched. Take a look," I say, gesturing toward my spotting scope.

The man scans the gravel bar of the river below us. She puts an eye to the scope.

"What kind of chicks are they?" she asks.

"Mew gulls," I say. Then spell, "M-E-W."

"You mean these seagulls," the man says.

"Mew gulls," I say again. "There's no bird actually called a seagull." Then I shift slightly to speak more directly to her. I tell her about the gull's wintering range, their late nesting because of an extended winter in Denali this year, and how they should have hatched a few weeks ago.

"They are pretty little birds," she says, her voice a bit askew from squinting and stooping in a position to see. "Their feet are so big."

"Aren't they though," I say. "They might not be mature enough to migrate south before winter arrives. They probably won't be able to fly through the Alaska Range. They will die."

She steps away.

"You can take a look if you want," I tell the man.

"No," he says. "I've seen seagulls before."

I shift and stare directly into his eyes, only he doesn't face me. He looks downstream where the river bends behind light green vegetation and enters a narrow canyon. I can feel him trying not to look at me. I want to ask him why he resists using their actual name, the name I must have used four or five times during the conversation with his wife.

"Come on, honey," she says. He looks to the ground, and then steps around me to follow her.

"Flying rats," he says.

I imagine grabbing him by the collar, saying some vulgar words, and then flipping him off the bridge. The adult gulls would protect the hatchlings by whacking his head, pecking his eyes. I would jump off the bridge and hold him down, not allow him to run. The gulls would continue to thump him but avoid me. "Say it right," I would tell him.

He would resist, grunt, and struggle.

"Just say it." More mew gulls would join in the attack. The area below the bridge would look like a storm of circulating white, like a down pillow dispersing into the air. "Just say it."

One gull would slash his nose. Another would yank on an ear. "Mew gull," he would finally say. "*Mew gull.*"

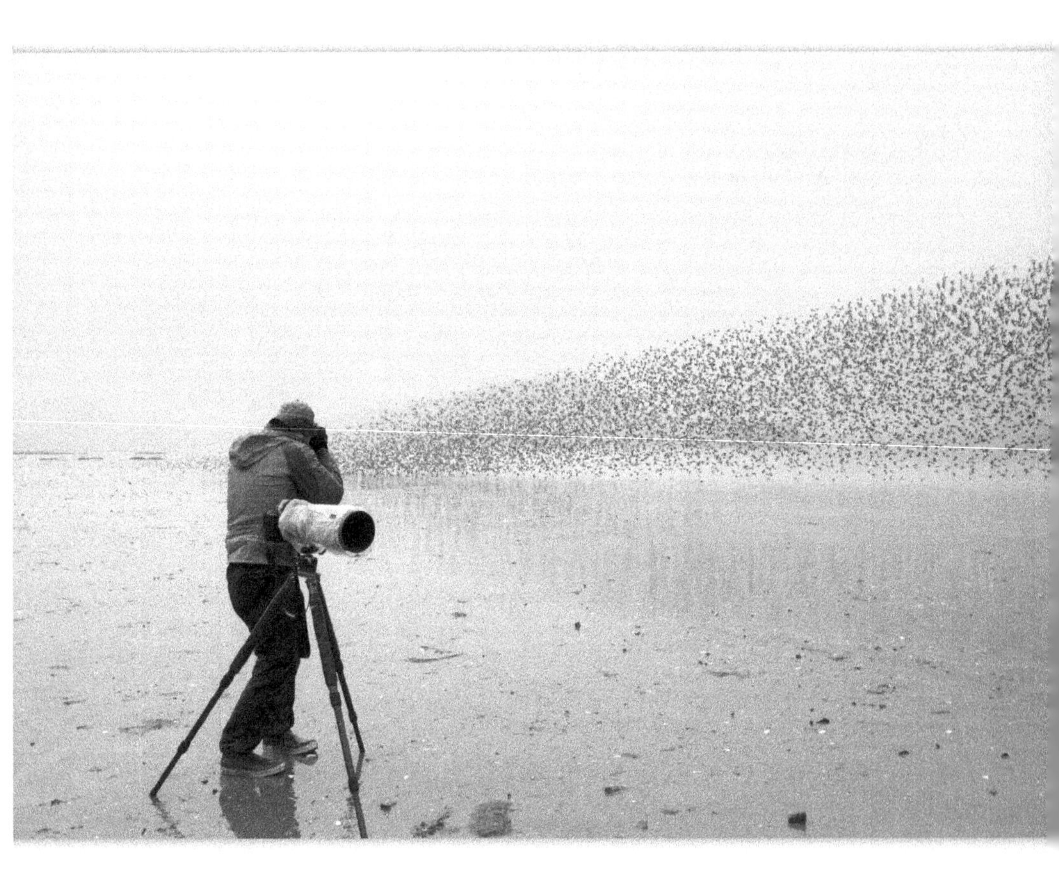

Swarmed, Patrick Endres

A Cliffside Whale

NAOMI JUDD

I tie into the rope and pull my hair back. Warm rock under my fingertips is enough to keep me smiling for days in rainy Juneau, Alaska. The break in weather will not stay so we've clambered down the steep narrow path through spiny devil's club and Sitka spruce to where the briny water laps at the base of gray igneous rock. It's not more than a rope length, but it's ours alone for the afternoon. I stand on a jumble of barnacled boulders, looking up to see if Tim is anchored thirty feet above, his colorful climbing gear and heavy camera dangling across his chest.

He yells to come on up and my heart knocks from inside as a fist on a door. I navigate the first few difficult holds, separate myself from the rocks below by twenty feet and come to a precious foothold two inches deep. I relax into the rock, rub my palms one at a time on my pant leg and smile up at my partner. He's got his camera out. While I'm reaching for the next nub of rock far above, an enormous exhalation sprays forth from the water below and behind me. I nearly fall but my foothold is like a little horizontal oasis in a vast vertical world. I cling to the rock while whipping my head around to see the head of a humpback whale, gigantic and gray-blue, lunging up from the water.

I feel like I am floating next to the cliff; my mind disconnects but my fingers pinch the sharp hold until they're white. I hear Tim's camera shutter clicking wildly. We both shout expletives that begin with "holy," and I quickly glance back toward the rock to better position myself, my braid whipping around my neck.

The enormous shiny body of the whale lunges again and then, as playful as a dog, it rolls over, waving an eight-foot-long flipper. I feel wind pushed by the spray of its breath. It turns slowly, dancing, curls of blue water unfurling around it. The white underside of a flipper dips back into the water, and then its fluke briefly pops up. As if waving hello, it looks at us up on the cliff from its side. With a large black eye gazing at our cliff-clinging forms, it appears to be just as curious as we are about its nautical life.

My shoulders burn from hanging on to the rock, but the Chilkat Range across the channel is catching pink and yellow rays of setting sun on its six-thousand-foot peaks, and a thirty-five-ton animal is playing a stone's throw away. I have forgotten things like pain.

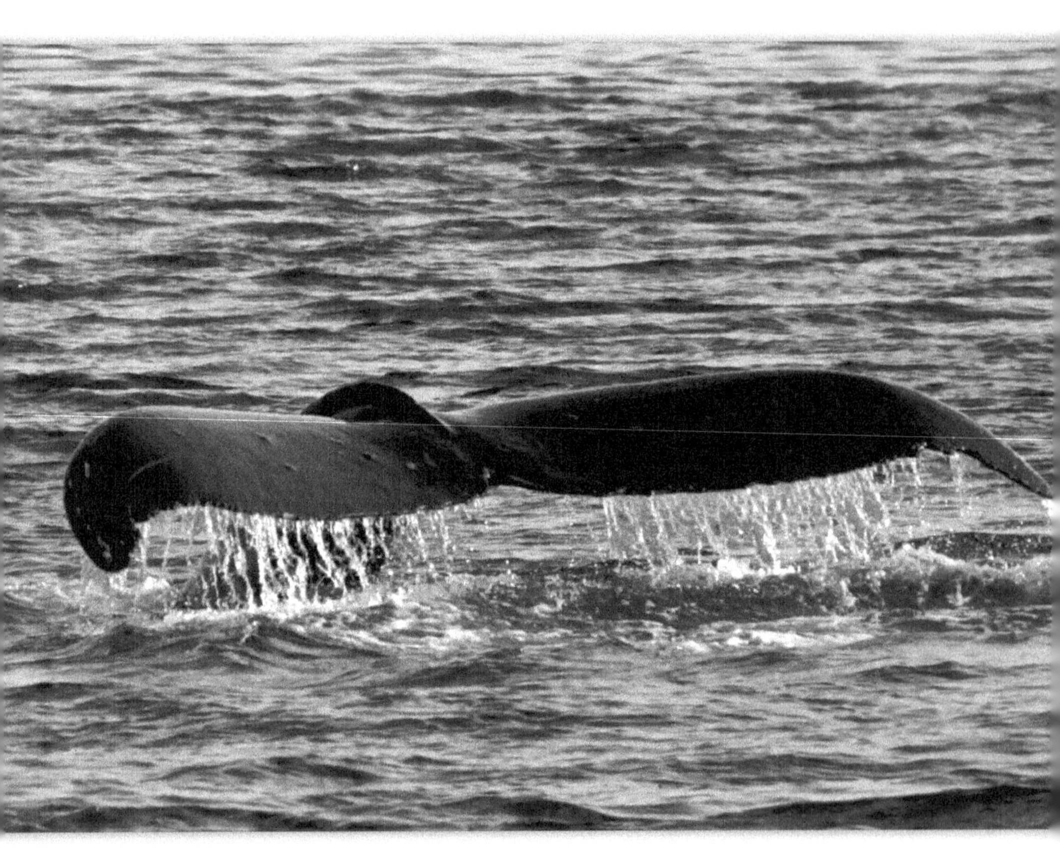

Sounding, Kelli Burkinshaw

Moose Legs

NITA NETTLETON

Without music for the trip to town, a shopping list in my head kept growing and shrinking as I thought of things I couldn't afford. Why didn't I at least get a radio in my pickup? The bench seat was comfortable enough. And I did have a good heater. I was always grateful for that, but perhaps even more so as I approached Willow on the Parks Highway.

It's always about ten degrees colder in Willow than anywhere around it. This causes hoarfrost and ice and on that particular evening also created fog. As I dipped into a ghostly drainage, my headlights, suddenly ineffective, caught swarms of glitter. I let off the gas. It's hard not to get lost in the glitter. "Focus on what's behind and under the glitter," my brother always said.

There is a collective nightmare in these parts about "trees" in the road. By the time headlight beams outline moose legs it's usually too late to avoid them. Locals get a little twitchy driving in the dark watching for the legs. Suddenly, in the glitter in the hollow near Willow, I saw legs. A massive shot of adrenaline wiped out my shopping list.

Maybe it's a good thing that time slows when your gut turns and your nerves scream in overdrive. It allows you to appreciate just how much trouble you're in. When I'd let off the gas, I could feel the tires losing traction. Braking would have been pointless and likely sent me off the road. As the first set of legs shot past the driver's side window and more took shape directly ahead, I faced the terrifying prospect of a moose in my lap. Fortunately, I was alone, so no one else to worry about—and I'd had a wonderful life so far. On the downside, . . .

At the last moment, survival instincts convinced me—what the hell—to brake anyway. I tapped the pedal, and immediately the back of the truck swung around. I steered to counter. Continuing sideways in the glitter, I thought, *what brilliance, I'll hit the moose with the rear of the truck instead of with my face!*

The moment passed and I regained control. The fog thinned and cleared. I topped the hill, pulled over, and stopped. With my headlights out of its eyes, the moose must have felt a survival impulse of his or her own and jumped. Getting out on shaky legs, I walked to the back and all the way around the truck. Stars as distinct as the throbbing of my heart sequined the snowscape and the fog layer I'd pierced. I decided to buy a truck stereo in town.

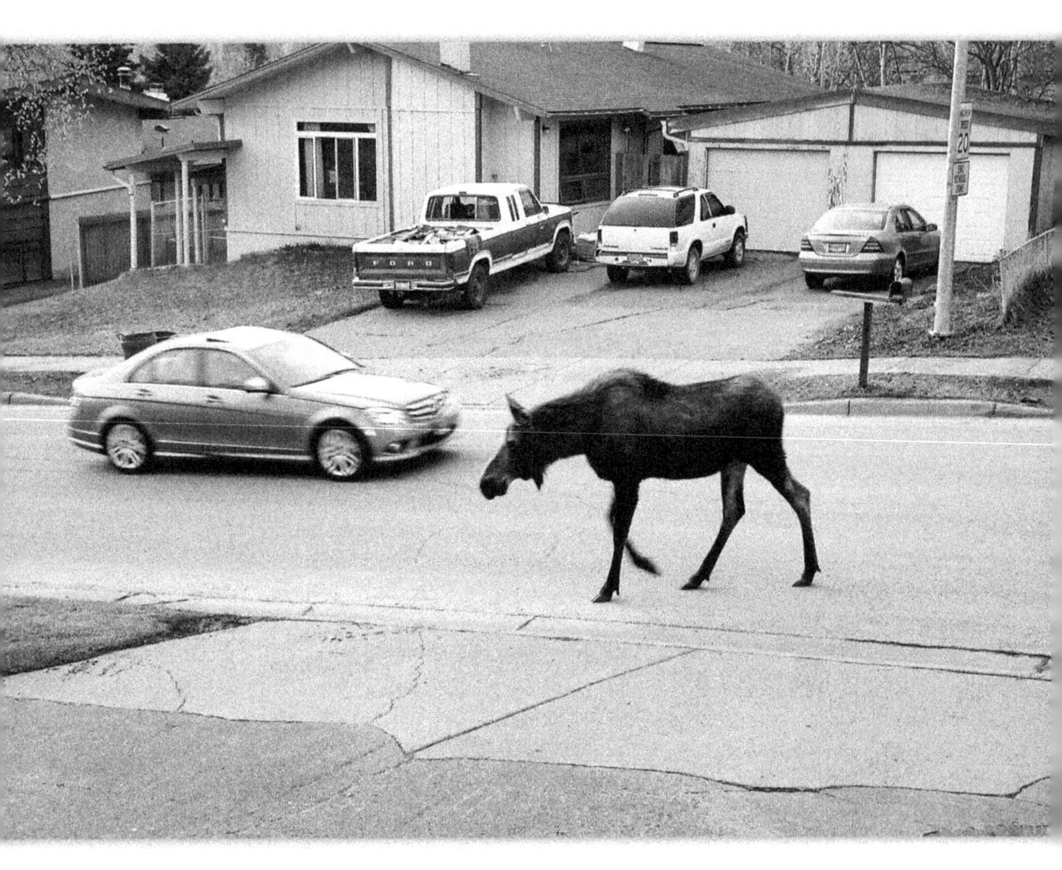

Northern Exposure, Stephen Nigl

Anima Mundi

LESLEY THOMAS

The visitor to the Arctic learned that the prevalent fear there was the fear of being eaten. The fear had grown as the population of the Animal had grown. This, though so few humans were eaten, and mostly after they had already become carrion. The visitor's mother—still living up north and in keeping with the circumpolar ethos—whispered of the "Big Animal," just in case one was listening from afar with supernatural acuity and terrible pride, because even calling it by its name would be disrespectful enough for the speaker to be punished. At her fishcamp, the Animal left tracks every night outside the outhouse, peering in the little window. Then on to the smokehouse, where recently, perhaps to humble her or because of the shockingly low runs of salmon and lack of blueberries, it had torn out the maggot-raven screen and taken the only fish.

The human mother would not admit her uneasiness but would sneakily tinkle into a chamber pot rather than go out. She had met the Animal mother the previous fall. It reared up, dark, huge, "like Grendel's mother," and looked through the cabin window, making eye contact but with little empathy. The human mother, who had read Beowulf and camped safely for forty years, suddenly felt the frailty of the wooden door, propping a shotgun near where she sat to write poems.

The fear came and went. At times, outings with heavy artillery felt foolish, even neurotic, as if she were a soldier clambering up a slope with a hundred-pound load. At other times, the stories of maulings got to her, as did the piles of scat and scattered ungulate vertebrae, or having to thrash through thick, tall alders. Then, too, there was the knowledge that THEY were starving.

The giant wolf-dog was useless; he cowered behind humans if he smelled an Animal, and never barked. The visitor, who had grown up there, once surprised a huge one at the summit of a barren hill near camp and felt certain that she would soon be just a spinal column. Often the shotgun, the Mace, the bells, and pebbles rattling in her berry picker, and singing and whooping, felt right. But this clamor of a monkey troop drove away all of life except bugs, diminishing the landscape's anima mundi.

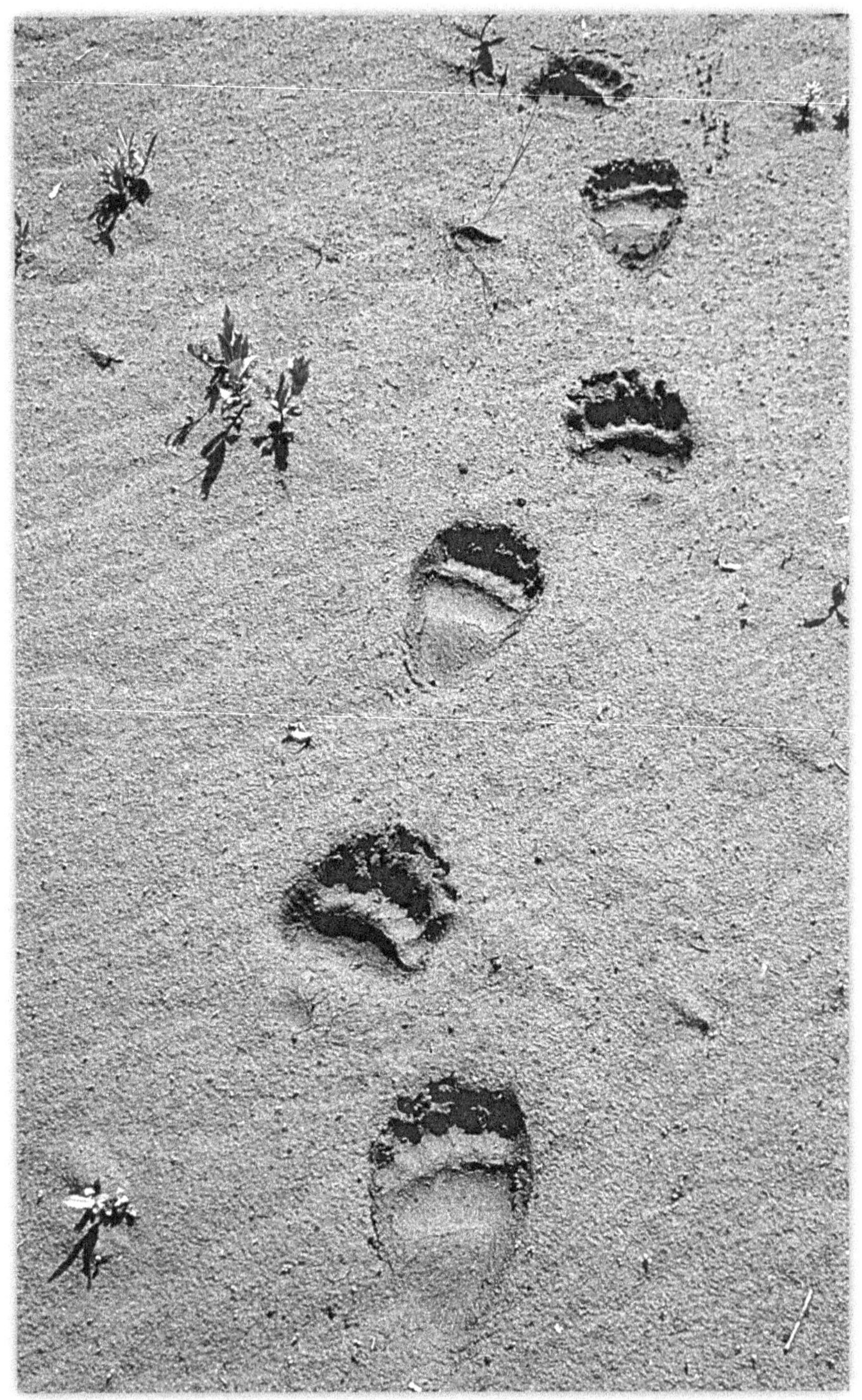

Tracks, Christa Sadler

Kuiu Dreamtime

DANIEL LEE HENRY

The alarm clock flashes 3:21 a.m. as I sit up. Kelly slides halfway out of his sleeping bag, JJ's eyes snap open. Coastal murk paints the nylon tent walls summer-solstice gray.

"The dream—" I start.

Eyes widen, heads nod.

"The raven—" I continue.

"Come on," blurts Kelly. "That's too much!"

JJ: "There's a message here."

A few details later, the meaning of our shared dream clicks.

Twelve days into a three-week kayak outing in Southeast Alaska, we are deep in the belly of Tebenkof Bay, a wilderness bite out of Kuiu Island's open west coast that encloses a hundred or more islands. Two-thirds the size of San Francisco Bay, Tebenkof's intricate shoreline is walled by spruce trees whose crowns hide twenty stories above, in sopping sky. Black bears and whales intersect our route daily; wolves serenade us each night.

We rounded a promontory yesterday to encounter the only other humans of the trip—a PhD anthro student and two field assistants cooking dinner on a beach. Herb was cataloguing evidence of the Kuiu *kwaan*, which once numbered two thousand residents tucked in all corners of the bay. After mugs of rum-and-coffee, the map came out. Here, the ruins of a palisaded fort. Here, fish traps. Here and here, totem poles a hundred, two hundred years old.

"I shouldn't show you this," Herb said. "It's very sensitive. If you go to any of these places, don't touch. Especially here." His stubby forefinger tapped a crease. "Shaman's grave. Old totem pole on the island's north end—forget I told you."

An hour's paddle delivered us to the two-acre island. Nearly invisible in blueberry bushes, a killer whale dorsal fin rose atop a fallen, weathered pole on the island's northern point. In moments, we landed on the south-end sand spit, a perfect tent site.

Most islands here are a boggy tangle; this one wasn't. Spruce sentries ringed the periphery, hiding an open interior. Dead center: the grave box. Above, a sullen sky-eye wept. Like expectant disciples, we sat cross-legged. Unable to focus, I tried scribbling sense into the moment, but words looked trite. I set the journal aside, closed my eyes, and listened.

I was the last to drift back to camp, last in the tent and asleep.

Crouched near the grave box, I peer into the sky. Atop a tall spruce, a raven meets my gaze. It swoops in a long dive toward me, spreading its wings until I am smothered by darkness.

That's when we wake up.

Without words we break camp and slide our boats into an outgoing tide. I turn for a last glimpse—a fog bank filters through trees. From a branch, Raven watches.

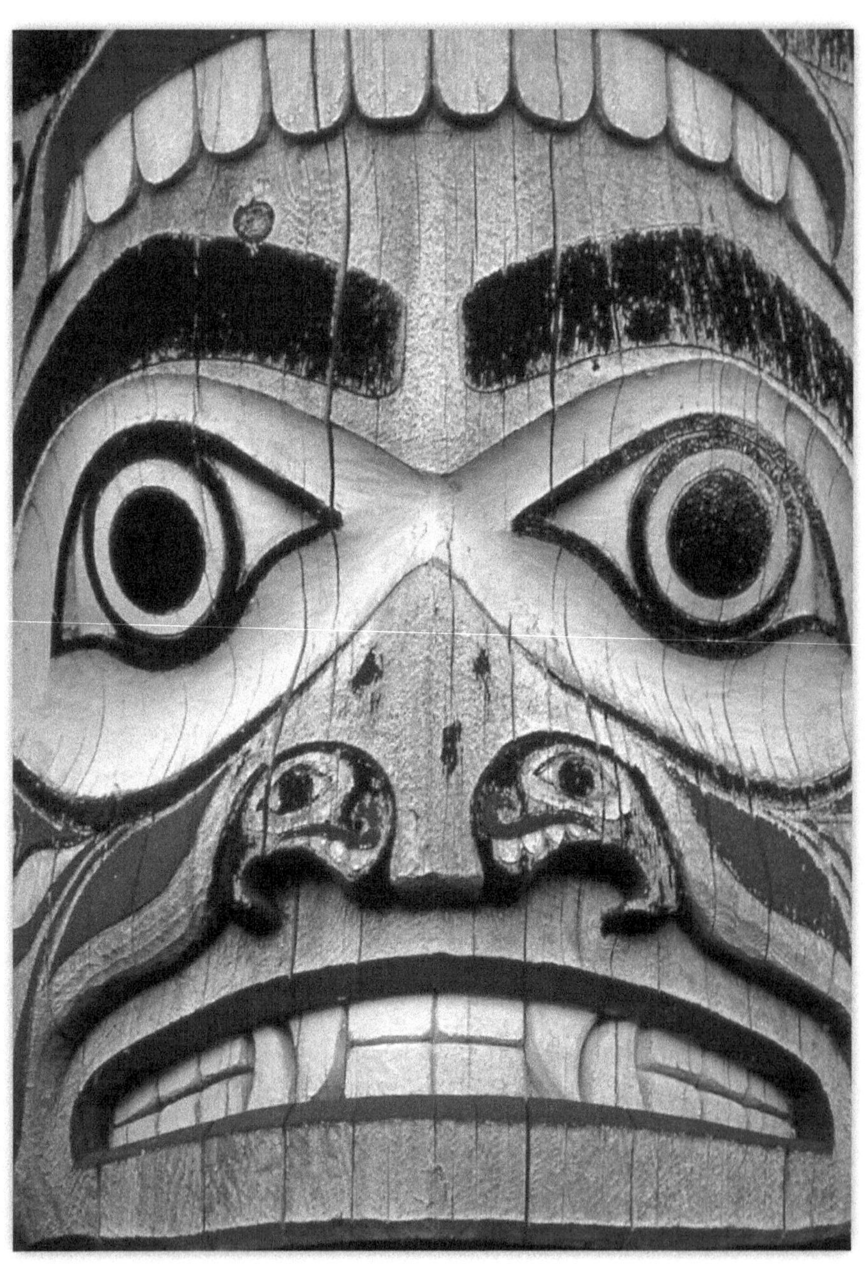

Tlingit Totem Pole—Saxman Village, Karl Agre

Ghost Story

TANYO RAVICZ

The two-seater cleared the yellow birch trees along the Yukon and landed. I had come to investigate complaints that a gold miner was ferrying sections of a disassembled dredge across Conway Creek. But I also had personal business in Conway.

There are really two Conways—the white mining settlement, and the Indian village, but neither Conway has use for the government, and I was relieved when my exchange with the miner went smoothly, though my biologist credentials and state-issued camera probably didn't stop him from hauling his equipment across the salmon stream after I left.

I headed for the cemetery. The wind had raised thousands of dancing points on the broad, swiftly moving surface of the muddy Yukon.

When I found Norman's grave, I dug the bottle from my bag and toasted him. Six summers he had been my best friend on the fire crew. It now seemed that a vast melancholy had hung over Norman's life. Yet he had lived with a light heart. There was no end to his pranks, obscenities, and ghost stories. He loved his Seagram's, he drank himself under; but despite the booze, scars, and sickness, Norman swore by life: he was happy.

I glanced at his grave, looking for answers, and what I saw confused me. The bottle leaned where I'd put it, but the shot glass was empty.

There was a laugh from behind the berm. A girl peeped across the willows at me.

"Keeping an old promise," I explained.

"It won't hurt Norman no more." Her voice was clipped and cheerful.

"You're the one sent moose for the funeral potlatch," she said. "How come you never came to the village?"

"Don't know. Another whiskey?"

"I don't drink."

"Go on."

"You thought—?" She smiled, watching me refill the shot glass. "Norman tricked you."

"I don't believe it."

She shrugged and continued picking rosehips along the berm. I watched the red, frost-softened fruits pass through her fingers into the basket. She never left my sight, I swear, but when I turned to Norman's grave again, the shot glass was empty.

I ran back, groped the earth, sliced the air with my hands, searching for strings or buried gadgets. My crawling across Norman's grave amused her. The white man wanted proof.

Yellow birch leaves fluttered in the sky. I straightened, breathing deeply of September. The river vibrated underfoot, a mighty, invisible presence. On paper the land is a rat's nest of disputed jurisdictions. Above the rat's nest, though, you respond with your very soul.

That night, haunting the cemetery in a dream, I was tripped and knocked to the earth. The bottle was torn from my grasp. I heard the faintest echo of her laughter.

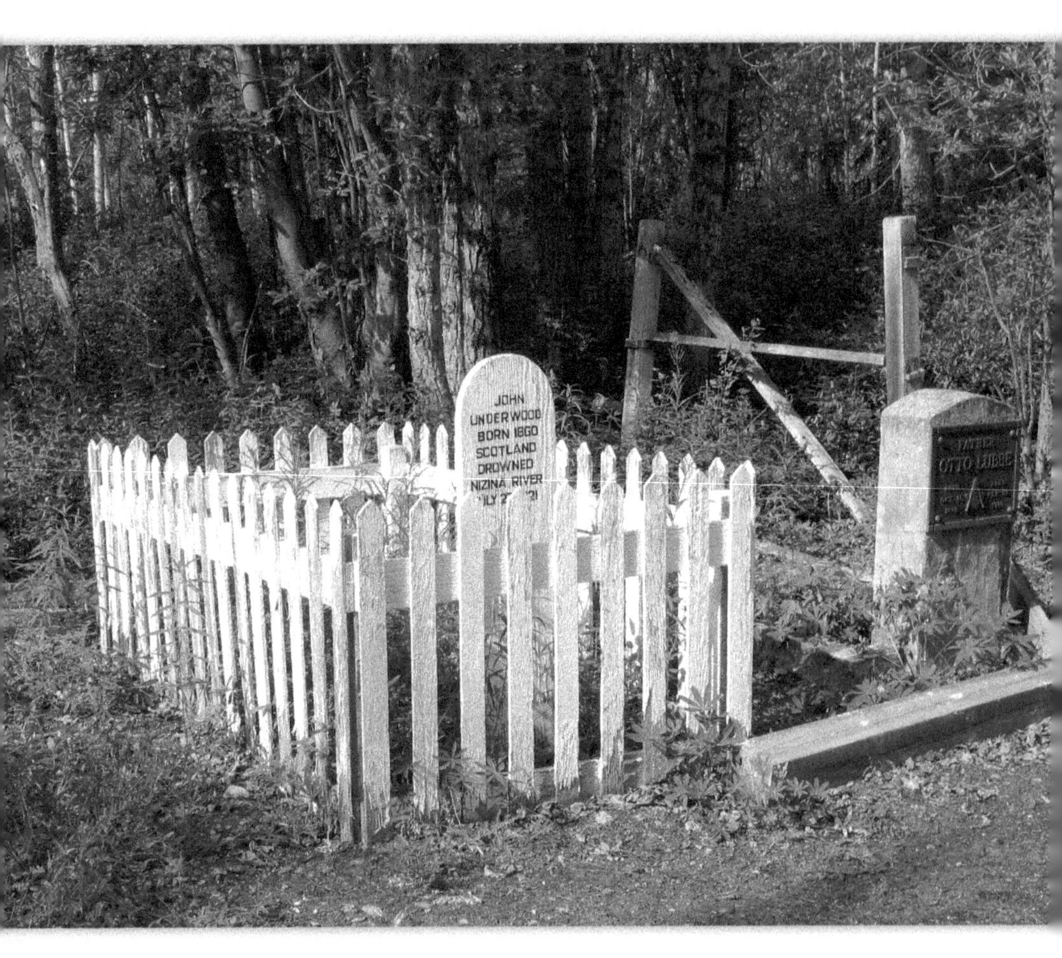

Born 1860, Scotland, Drowned Nizina River, 1921, Greg Fensterman

A Boat Named Coffin

VIVIAN FAITH PRESCOTT

William Binkley pressed his foot on Game Warden McKephin's chest, sinking him deep into Yellowstone's Heart Lake. Blood spurted from the hole in McKephin's belly. Binkley didn't hear the curse rising up in the last bubble from the man's lungs, but he would always remember the smell of geyser sulfur—*For you and your children, water is the enemy. The curses of the perishing are upon you.*

Binkley slammed his fist on the counter of Diehl's Dry Goods. "Goddam Diehl," he said, flipping back his jacket to show his holstered .45 Savage, "when the cows arrive on the barge, I'll pay for 'em then."

The *Los Angeles Examiner* lay beneath the counter with Binkley's wanted poster on page seven. Mr. Diehl thought of bringing it to the *Wrangell Sentinel,* but no one had messed with William Binkley since he'd sauntered off the steamship with Eva and four kids. They'd bought a place on Shustak Point and talked about farming up the Stikine River.

Binkley's son, nine-year-old Albert, warmed his hands by the woodstove in the corner. Binkley tugged the kid up. "Get your ass out there and load up the *Coffin.*" When Wrangell old-timers heard what the Binkley kids named their skiff, they shook their heads. It was young Al's idea. It came to him in a dream smelling of blood and sulfur.

Now, they loaded up the cart, rolling it down the boardwalk to the beach where the *Coffin* bobbed against the rocks. Binkley sat in the skiff while the kid rowed toward the Point. "Faster," Binkley bellowed, "the tide's catching us."

Binkley stuck a pinch of tobacco in his mouth. He thought about how Wrangell was the perfect hideout. After all, Soapy Smith used to hole up here. In fact, Binkley chuckled to himself, Wrangell was so rough-and-tumble that a few years back, Wyatt Earp left town because the place was wilder than Tombstone.

The wind and rain picked up as they rowed the *Coffin* from the harbor. The boat pitched and a wave rolled inside, wetting their feet. "Steer into the waves," Binkley yelled.

"But, Pa," Al said, "the waves are coming from everywhere."

Binkley spit out his tobacco. He tasted blood. *Sonofabitch. Must have bit the inside of my cheek,* he thought. The swells slapped the boat. The smell of sulfur mixed with salt spray. "Damn this tub," he grumbled.

Behind him, an arm reached up from the water and pulled down the stern. The sea poured into the *Coffin.*

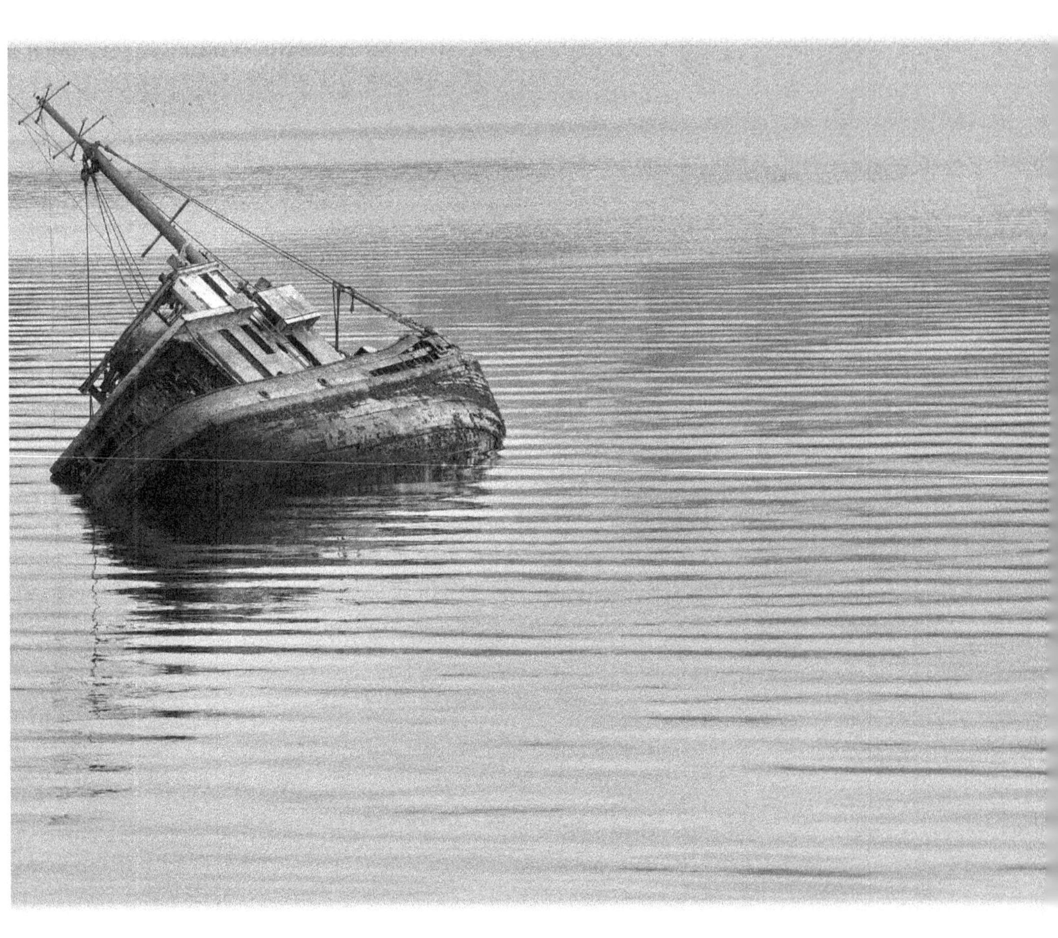

The Annette, Gil Aegerter

Contributors

Gil Aegerter was born and raised in Ketchikan. He worked at newspapers across the country and is now a senior editor at msnbc.com. He lives in Brier, Washington, with his wife and two teenagers.

Karl Agre is a retired research physician with an interest in photography dating back to the 1950s. Originally from Brooklyn, this lighthouse buff and passionate world traveler now lives in Illinois.

Angela Busch Alston is a social studies teacher in an Inupiaq village twenty miles south of the Arctic Circle, where her husband teaches third grade. An amateur photographer, she has a penchant for kids' portraits.

Rosemary Austin is the author of *Mountain Bike Anchorage*. She and her husband Jon Kunesh live in Anchorage with their cat.

Scott Banks grew up playing hockey in Anchorage and still haunts rinks in search of a good game of shinny. He's been published in *American Heritage Magazine, Alaska, Alaska Geographic,* and a number of national newspapers.

Miriam Beck is an aspiring writer who lives near downtown Anchorage. She has two grown sons, a husband, and a dog. A childhood spent in Fort Yukon in the sixties nourishes her writing.

Marei Benton, a self-proclaimed city girl, has lived in Anchorage for three years. Her goal is to visit Wrangell-St. Elias National Park—if she ever manages to stick with one major and graduate from college.

Celeste Borchardt is a "recovering" mother, a former registered nurse who married a bush pilot, and lived for thirteen years in the Arctic before moving to Anchorage. Lately, she has found precious time to write.

Douglass Bourne's essays and poetry have appeared in *The LBJ: Avian Life, Literary Arts,* in *Tusculum Review,* and in *Pank*. Currently, he is researching a book on wolves and finishing a manuscript, *Denali in Summer.*

Elizabeth Bradfield is the author of two poetry collections, *Approaching Ice* and *Interpretive Work,* and founder of Broadsided Press. She designs websites and works as a naturalist aboard small boats in Southeast Alaska and elsewhere.

Kelli Burkinshaw has a deep love for the Intermountain West, where she spent her first forty years. After photographing Southeast Alaska's beauty, influenced by the breathing tides, she now calls Juneau home.

Bob Butcher has lived in Anchorage for the past thirty-six years. A retired Anchorage police detective, Bob's interest in photography began at age fifteen. His favorite subjects include Alaska's landscapes, wildlife, birds, and aircraft.

Evan Buxbaum is a pediatrician and writer who lives with his family on Orcas Island, off the coast of Washington State, on an idyllic farm more than three hundred feet above sea level.

Christine Byl lives in Healy, Alaska, where she spends her time on trail work, writing, and mountain adventures. Her pieces are excerpted from a nonfiction manuscript, *Dirt Work: An Education on the Ground.*

Mary Cook came to Alaska for a summer job and stayed for fifteen years. She's worked as a boat cook, lodge chef, barista, and ground crew for an air taxi, but secretly, she's a writer.

Anne Coray is the author of the poetry collections *Bone Strings* and *Soon the Wind,* coauthor of *Lake Clark National Park and Preserve,* and coeditor of *Crosscurrents North: Alaskans on the Environment.*

Lynn DeFilippo lives in Fairbanks, where she teaches seventh-grade English. She loves to travel, spend time outdoors, and eat wild meat harvested by her husband. Originally from the East Coast, she now considers Alaska her home.

Traveling widely as an expedition guide, park ranger, and freewheeling nomad, **Doug Demarest** makes images of wild landscapes and people who venture to experience them. He lives in Alaska and Minnesota.

Laurent Dick is the author of *Yukon Quest, Climb Denali,* and *Antarctica.* He explored the frozen continent in the footsteps of a historical expedition and now lives in Juneau with his partner Greta and their son Florian.

Robert Drozda lives in Fairbanks, Alaska, with his long-time partner and their seventeen or so Alaska Husky sled dogs.

Deidre Elliott lived half her life where it snows all winter. After moves to the Sonoran Desert and the second-largest city in Mexico, she now teaches creative writing in the mountains of western North Carolina.

Fairbanks-based professional photographer **Patrick Endres** has trekked Alaska's vast spaces for more than twenty years, capturing images that reveal the state's diverse and rugged beauty. His work has been widely published.

Michael Engelhard lives in Alaska, working as a wilderness guide in the Arctic. He has contributed to numerous magazines and anthologies. His most recent book—*Wild Moments*—is a collection of writers' encounters with northern wildlife.

Matthew Evans lives in Anchorage and flies for a major airline. When he's not roasting coffee, he spends his off-days exploring the wilds of Alaska and trying to refine his discoveries into prose.

Greg Fensterman is the owner and a senior guide of Trek Alaska, a backpacking outfit in McCarthy. He has written a guidebook, *Hiking Alaska's Wrangell-St. Elias National Park,* and pioneered many routes in that park.

Leslie Leyland Fields is the author of six books and numerous magazine articles. She lives in Kodiak, where she fishes commercially for salmon. She also teaches creative nonfiction in Seattle Pacific University's MFA program.

Louise Freeman's memoir, *Standing Up to the Rock,* won the Idaho Book Award and the Pacific Northwest Booksellers Award. Her work has appeared in the *Christian Science Monitor, Alaska,* and other publications.

Mike Freeman left Alaska after living for ten years in Yakutat. Another Alaska essay can be found online in *The King's English*. He is currently writing a book about canoeing the Hudson River for the SUNY Press.

John Frisch is a retired engineer with a longtime interest in nature and travel photography. Whether at home in the Kansas tallgrass prairie or on the road, he enjoys discovering nature's everyday wonders.

Adrian Gall lives in Fairbanks, Alaska, and enjoys documenting wily critters, epic landscapes, and human elements wherever her job as a wildlife biologist takes her.

Denny Gill is a sixty-two-year-old retiree of the United States Air Force. He's been an Alaska resident since 1992. Husband and father of one daughter, he loves life and photographing his home state.

Sierra Golden was born in Ketchikan, and though she no longer lives there, continues to fish in Southeast Alaska during the summer. She graduated from Gonzaga University. Her work has been published in *Reflection*.

In 1994, **Rebecca Goodrich** left California's glitter for the houseboat *Brigadoon* in Unalaska. Now Alaska Writers Guild Marketing chair in Anchorage, she writes, edits, and consults regarding books and manuscripts, and promotes books and authors.

George Guthridge has published five novels and was cowinner of the Bram Stoker Award for best horror novel. His Siberian-Yupik students became the only team of Native Americans ever to win national championships in academics.

Melissa Guy is an artist, graphic designer, and nursing student with a passion for hiking, berry picking, and natural yarns. She currently lives in Arizona but hopes to return to Alaska soon.

The seven years **Julie Hammonds** spent in Southeast Alaska left their mark on her imagination, as these stories show. She now lives in Arizona, where she writes for a wildlife magazine.

Karla Hayward has lived in Southeast Alaska for fifteen years and always carries a camera. Her husband works at sea for a month at a time, so photography gives her an excuse to get out and explore.

Chris Heaton is an aviation photographer from Modesto, California, who enjoys capturing interesting moments wherever his travels take him.

Daniel Lee Henry's book *Dancing at Deer Rock* chronicles five hundred years of land use conflict and peacemaking in Chilkat Country. Henry lives with his wife and son on a roadless shore near Haines, Alaska.

Kathy Ingallinera has been a resident of Sitka for thirteen years. When she is not taking care of her rescued dogs, working with injured raptors, or writing, she stays busy as a Family Nurse Practitioner.

Eowyn Ivey was raised in Alaska and continues to live a largely subsistence lifestyle there with her husband and two daughters. She works at Fireside Books, an independent bookstore in Palmer.

Tom V. Jamgochian is a recreational photographer living in Fairbanks, Alaska.

John Jensen, born in Juneau in 1935, was raised in Douglas. He has published books on spirituality, social change, and education, and helped write his father's life story, *One Thing After Another: Adventures in Alaska.*

Naomi Judd is a freelance writer, interpretive guide (having led hiking and glacier tours in Juneau), and student. She is currently earning an MFA in Creative Writing from Eastern Washington University.

Steve Kahn is a lifelong Alaskan. His essay collection, *The Hard Way Home: Alaska Stories of Adventure, Friendship, and the Hunt,* is forthcoming from the University of Nebraska Press.

Nabil Kashyap summers in McCarthy, guiding in Wrangell-St. Elias National Park. Otherwise he teaches, in Montana, or more recently, in India. His work has appeared in *Versal* and the *Seneca Review.*

Steven Kazlowski is a Seattle-based photographer with a special interest in polar bears. His work has appeared in *Audubon, National Wildlife, Sierra,* and *TIME* magazine, and his book *The Last Polar Bear* won critical acclaim.

Alan Kesselheim lives in Bozeman, Montana, and is the author of nine books and hundreds of magazine articles. His contribution comes from a family canoe trip on the Yukon River.

Peggy King is a self-taught photographer living in north Georgia. Working mainly in black and white, she strives to capture the often hidden beauty of her everyday surroundings.

Sandra Kleven's writing has appeared in *Alaska Quarterly Review, Oklahoma Review,* and *Topic Magazine (NYC).* She has also written *The Right Touch: A Read-Aloud Story to Help Prevent Child Sexual Abuse.*

Carolyn Kremers lives in Fairbanks and recently returned from a year in Ulan Ude, Russia, as a U.S. Fulbright Scholar. Her books include *Place of the Pretend People* and the anthology *The Alaska Reader.*

Jeff Manes is an amateur photographer and web developer. He lives in Anchorage with his wife, Shawna, and their two pets, Butters and Bailey. They enjoy traveling, cooking, and spending time with friends and family.

Mark McElroy, author of *The Absolute Beginner's Guide to Tarot* and *Lucid Dreaming for Beginners,* lives in Atlanta, Georgia, where he works as a consultant.

A Pushcart Prize nominee and Everglades National Park Artist-in-Residence, **Karla Linn Merrifield** is widely published with four books to her credit, including *Godwit: Poems of Canada,* which won the Andrew Eiseman Writers Award for Poetry.

Nita Nettleton carries half a century of Alaska in her head and compares all other places, sounds, smells, and tastes to it. Somehow, that works for her. Besides essays and novels, she likes flash fiction.

Stephen Nigl is a published professional photographer specializing in commercial news and art photography. His work is periodically exhibited in Anchorage, Alaska, and has appeared recently in *Alaska* magazine.

James O'Rear photographs anything in front of his lens but is especially fond of things with wings: hummingbirds to jumbo jets. He currently resides with his wife in Arizona, pining for the homestead in Alaska.

Bruce Orton has been writing since age twelve. He studied at San Francisco State and the University of Oregon. His three novels are set in 1899, 1906, and 1919, in Alaska, the Yukon, and the West.

Scott Page learned photography with a Brownie camera as a kid. When not working as an environmental scientist at the University of Nevada, he enjoys activities that feed his photography addiction—birding, hiking, and backcountry travel.

Jeremy Pataky earned an MFA in Creative Writing at the University of Montana. His work has appeared in *Black Warrior Review*, the *Northern Review*, the *Southeast Review*, *Anchorage Press*, and elsewhere. He lives in McCarthy and Anchorage.

Ron Perkins of Gold King, Alaska, lives with his wife, Trish, and two daughters in the same Alaska Range he so stunningly photographs. His most recent showing was at the New Horizons Gallery in Fairbanks.

Vivian Faith Prescott was born and raised in Wrangell and lives in Sitka, both in Alaska. Married with four children, she is Sáami and Suomalainen, among other heritages. Her children are Ravens of the T'akdeintaan clan.

Tanyo Ravicz's most recent book is *Alaskans: Stories*. He lived in Alaska for many years, in Fairbanks and Kodiak. Currently based in California, he's writing a novel about an Alaska homesteading family.

Cyrus Read is an engineer and geophysicist with the Alaska Volcano Observatory. He lives in Girdwood, Alaska.

Don Rearden grew up on the tundra of Southwestern Alaska. He is a produced screenwriter and published poet, and his debut novel, *The Raven's Gift*, will be published by Penguin Canada in 2010.

Bruce Rettig has worked on tugboats, barges, and icebreakers. He is one of the founding members of Tahoe Writers Works and publisher of its literary publication, *EDGE*. Many of his short stories have been published.

Mattox Roesch's novel, *Sometimes We're Always Real Same-Same*, was published by Unbridled Books in 2009. His stories have appeared in various magazines, including the *Sun*. He and his wife and daughter live in Unalakleet.

Christa Sadler has worked in Alaska since 1990 as a naturalist and river guide. She spent a winter in Haines as a newspaper reporter and, except for the bobsled course in her driveway, loved it.

Keith Schuessler, a nomadic commercial carpenter, travels where the work takes him. A few years ago, mentally stagnated by work, he decided he needed a hobby. So he picked up a camera.

Katey Schultz's fiction and nonfiction have been published in *Perigee*, *Writers' Dojo*, *Cadillac Cicatrix*, *Silk Road*, and elsewhere. Her art essays appear regularly in national magazines. She also edits for *Main Street Rag* and *Memoir*.

Jeremy Edward Shiok is a poet, writer, and editor from Anchorage. In 2003 he received his MFA from the University of Alaska Anchorage, where he teaches in the undergraduate creative writing and literary arts program.

David Stevenson has been the book review editor of the *American Alpine Journal* for many years. He directs the low-residency MFA program at the University of Alaska Anchorage.

Kathleen Tarr lives in Anchorage, where she teaches creative writing at the University of Alaska. Her work has appeared in *Creative Nonfiction*, *Alaska Airlines Magazine*, and the *Anchorage Press*.

Brandon Thibodeaux is a photographer based in Dallas, Texas, who creates portraits in the documentary tradition. In addition to his assignment work and creative commissions, he continues to explore life in the American south.

Colorado photojournalist **JT Thomas** has spent nearly twenty years exploring Alaska's Wrangell Mountains and getting to know the communities of McCarthy and Kennicott. Most often he is traversing the Americas covering environmental and cultural issues.

Lesley Thomas grew up in Southeast Alaska, the Bering Strait region, and Fairbanks. She now lives in Seattle. Her multicultural family remains in the Arctic, the setting of her novel *Flight of the Goose*.

Tara Wheatland is a former resident of Anchorage and currently lives in San Francisco.

Mark Arvid White has had his poems, stories, articles, and reviews published in numerous venues at home, online, and abroad. He is the current Alaska Region Coordinator for the Haiku Society of America.

Erin Wilcox has been published in *Text: Journal of Writing and Writing Courses*, *Veil: A Journal of Darker Musings*, and the *Freelancer*. Her creative writing has aired on radio programs like Alaska Public Radio's *AK Radio*.

Julie Williams has been living and working in Alaska since 1987. She's been a park ranger, kayaking guide, massage therapist, retreat coordinator, and artist. She lives off the grid, in a yurt in Gustavus.

Kaitlin Wilson was born and raised in Fairbanks, Alaska. Her primary interest in photography is people, because of their predictability and unpredictability. Wilson is currently working on a BFA in photography at Columbia College, Chicago.

Dennis Witmer moved from Pennsylvania to Kotzebue and in 1991 to Fairbanks. Over the past decade, his work has been included in over sixty exhibits, including twenty one-person shows and numerous invited and juried shows.

www.ingramcontent.com/pod-product-compliance
Lightning Source LLC
Chambersburg PA
CBHW061124100726
47911CB00013B/672
* 9 7 8 1 6 0 2 2 3 0 9 3 4 *